The Destiny of
Fu Manchu

The Destiny of
Fu Manchu

by
William Patrick Maynard

A Black Coat Press Book

In memory of Arthur Henry Ward and Dr. Robert E. Briney.

This book is dedicated to my loving wife, Steffanie and to our family: Steven, Michelle, Alexandra, Michael and Annie.

Visit our website at www.blackcoatpress.com

ISBN 978-1-61227-088-3. First Printing April 2012. Published by Black Coat Press, an imprint of Hollywood Comics.com, LLC, P.O. Box 17270, Encino, CA 91416. All rights reserved.

Acknowledgements

Thank you to Anita Fore and Jeremy Crow, administrators of the Sax Rohmer Literary Estate, for granting me permission to bring these classic characters back to life once more. Thank you also to my publisher and editor, Jean-Marc Lofficier, for his willingness to publish my recreation of times past. I am also grateful to three talented artists for their generous contributions: Christine Clavel, Mike Vosburg, and Michael McQuary. Thank you to Will Murray for agreeing to provide the Foreword to this book—Will has much to answer for, and it was an honor to meet him. Special thanks are due to the late Cay Van Ash and especially to Rick Lai; their scholarship and speculation were a source of inspiration for the story arc that developed as I set about filling in the gaps in Rohmer's chronology.

I am grateful to the following for their support and encouragement: James Bojaciuk, Christopher Paul Carey, David Colton, Randy Cone, C. S. E. Cooney, Michael Cornet, Ric Croxton, Bill Cunningham, Win Scott Eckert, Ron Fortier, Damon Goldstein, Ralph Grasso, Tommy Hancock, Michael Hudson, Ed Hulse, Maxim Jakubowski, Dr. Lawrence Knapp, Andy Lane, Andrew Latimer, Brian Lindsey, Mirek Lipinski, Mark Maddox, Miguel Martins, Don Murphy, Adrian Nebbett, Don O'Malley, John O'Neill, Charles Edward Pogue, Charles Prepolec, Mark Redfield, Joshua Reynolds, Deuce Richardson, Jayaprakash Satyamurthy, Frank Schildiner, Jason Simos, Eric Stedman, David Stenhouse, Bill Thom, Robert Tinnell, Maria Towers, Julien Vedrenne, and Christopher Yates.

Very personal thanks to Dr. Joseph Krajekian and Dr. William Waters for borrowed time.

W.P.M.

Foreword

Dr. Fu Manchu, the brilliant criminal mastermind, first appeared in "The Zayat Kiss," an engaging mixture of British detective fiction and supernatural horror that graced the pages of *The Story-Teller* in October 1912 to instant acclaim. The honorable, but deadly Chinese doctor personified, transcended, and (arguably) went a long way toward rehabilitating the racist stereotype of the "Yellow Peril " that followed in the wake of the Boxer Uprising—the international conflict that ushered in the 20th century.

Arthur Ward, under the *nom de plume* of Sax Rohmer, would author a total of thirteen bestselling novels featuring the character from 1913 to 1959, as well as a posthumous collection of short fiction.

Rohmer, a prolific author, playwright, songwriter, poet, comedy sketch writer, biographer, occultist, and amateur Egyptologist was never able to escape the shadow of Fu Manchu as far as the public was concerned. The character became the subject of dozens of films, radio series, television series, newspaper strips, and comic books.

Rohmer's long-time assistant, Cay Van Ash (who co-authored the only book-length biography of Rohmer with the late author's widow) carried on the tradition by penning two further Fu Manchu thrillers in the 1980s. A third manuscript was left incomplete when Van Ash passed away in 1994 and is now believed lost.

My first effort, *The Terror of Fu Manchu*, marked the first authorized appearance of the Devil Doctor in over twenty years. *The Destiny of Fu Manchu* has the honor of being published in the same year that we mark the centennial of this timeless character's first appearance.

Shortly before his death, Rohmer stated that, while he would one day be forgotten, Dr. Fu Manchu would live forever.

The original Fu Manchu stories are being reprinted by Titan Books for a new generation of readers to savor. As classic Rohmer and new period Fu Manchu thrillers from Black Coat Press find their place on bookshelves, can it be very long before the Devil Doctor finds his way to the 21st century?

Readers would do well to recall the stylish ending of the 1960s film series when Sir Christopher Lee's voice would ring out in movie theatres with Fu Manchu's ominous threat that "the world shall hear from me again."

W.P.M.

PROLOGUE:
THE WRATH OF KHUFU

"Who's there?"

Silence answered my question. Yet, unless I was very much mistaken, there was someone lurking about just outside my door. An old fear gripped my heart as I found myself reaching into the top drawer of my desk for my Browning.

The weight of the gun reassured me and, cautiously, I moved from behind the desk and crossed to the doorway. I threw the heavy wooden door open wide, but there was nothing outside but the cool night air of Cairo to greet me. I stopped and listened for a moment, but there was no one there. A flash of lightning lit up the sky momentarily, but there was no rumble of thunder following in its wake.

Feeling foolish, I shut and bolted the door and returned to my chair. I replaced the pistol in my desk drawer and had just resumed pouring over my papers when, once more, I was disturbed, this time by a queer cooing sound issuing from just outside the door as if a nightjar had settled there.

"What the Devil?" I muttered irritably as I rose once more and crossed the room. I threw back the heavy bolt, but as I gripped the door handle, an electrical charge passed through my hand. No cry escaped my lips. I was paralyzed where I stood until, all at once, the handle twisted in my hand as the door was pushed open. I fell to the floor, gasping in pain. My mind turned to my pistol that lay safely tucked away in my desk drawer. Barely did I have time to register the severity of the electrical shock I had received when I beheld three cowled figures dressed in black robes standing in the doorway, staring down at my prostrate form. Crimson bandanas were tied about their heads.

Dacoits!

The word flashed through my head as I was lifted easily and thrown over the shoulder of one of the hulking forms, while another slipped a woolen sack about my head and secured it tight just under my chin. I was aware of a sharp blow to the back of my head and then the blackness gave way to nothingness as all sense of time and space fled my mind like water down a drain.

My dreams were strange juxtapositions of the recent past. I saw anew Kara and Greba depart aboard an ocean liner bound for Corfu with Greba's fiancé at her side. Greba had served as my nurse for almost as long as Kara and I had been married—soon to be 24 years.

Greba's fiancé was an archaeologist called Simos. She was eager to begin life anew with her husband. My practice was thriving and did not afford me the luxury of a two-week vacation with Kara, but I insisted she should not pass up the opportunity to enjoy Corfu herself after attending Greba's wedding.

I had fallen in love with Kara during those terrible years when Dr. Fu Manchu had waged his war of terror on Britain. Happily, that was all in the past. I rarely saw Nayland Smith these days.

Despite our friendship, I did not miss the life of excitement and danger that he followed. He had made the hunt and capture of Fu Manchu his life's work. I understood the reason for this. I knew the emptiness he felt compelled to fill with his all-consuming obsession to end Fu Manchu's menace. He lived a charmed life for having survived so many deaths. He lived a cursed life for never knowing a moment's peace. His was a lonely road, but it was the path he chose to walk.

What of Kara after all this time? She was still a beautiful woman. Few would guess she was nearly the same age as me. In the dark of night in our bed, I was regularly amazed by the youthful ardor of her lovemaking that had not lessened in the intervening years. Still, there was more to a marriage than mere physical pleasure. Kara was haunted by memories that my love for her could never erase. It is hard for the Western world to accept as fact that slavery still exists in this day and age, but it is a way of life in the East. I tried for many years to eradicate the pain and hurt that weighed so heavily upon her. In time, I came to accept the limits of her love.

Time...something about time...I tried to focus on the jumble of my memories. Working alongside the great Sherlock Holmes in Wales when Smith had been abducted by Fu Manchu...the tragedy Kara and I shared over the loss of our daughter...my time at Nayland Smith's side coming to an end after the Great War...over a decade had passed before I found myself fighting the Si-Fan again, now under the control of the Mandarin Ki-Ming and Fah lo Suee, the daughter of Fu Manchu, and then once more under the direction of her terrible father, now restored through his miraculous *elixir vitae* to the vitality of a man nearly my own age...I re-lived the heartbreak and joy of finding our baby, Fleurette, alive and grown to womanhood...our family reunited at last...heartened by Fu Manchu's solemn vow to harm us no further. Peace at last...nothing but peace and time.

I blinked.

The darkness had not ceased, but sound had returned to me and, with it, some semblance of reality. I heard the low hum of an automobile engine and felt the roughness of the road beneath its tires. I was being driven somewhere. A rank smell and a sense of wetness overcame me. My head was still covered in the woolen sack, but I appeared to be otherwise unharmed.

After what seemed an eternity, the vehicle jerked to a halt. I heard the creek of the doors and then the sound of the trunk being opened. My senses were alive to the sounds and smells of the night. Rough hands grasped my arms and legs and I was carried out of the vehicle and dragged for some distance from it. I offered no resistance as I listened to the change in the crunching beneath my captors' feet. The crunching gave way to near-silent steps. The night sounds and smells had disappeared; we were now indoors. A cold chill enveloped me as the temperature dropped significantly from the outdoors.

Presently, my captors reached a halt and placed me on the cold ground. I lay still for a few moments, not daring to move my arms or legs. I sensed a face near mine. I could feel warm breath against my cheek. The woolen sack was untied and torn from my head.

I coughed and rubbed my eyes until I grew accustomed to the torchlight. I was in a cave. No, not just a cave...I had been here before! I blinked and looked around the iridescent limestone walls and red granite floor. It was the lower chamber of the Great Pyramid of Giza!

The three dacoits stood at my side. Presently, a towering figure cloaked in crimson entered the chamber. To my great surprise, I saw from his bare arms and legs that he was a white man. His face was covered in a heavy metal helmet, free of any markings save for a single eye slit. He stood staring down at me, his arms folded in arrogance.

"Welcome, Dr. Petrie."

His voice boomed about the chamber.

I lowered my head to help drown out the sound.

"I do not come here by choice."

I spat the words in defiance.

The masked figure threw back his head and laughed.

"You are mistaken. It is your actions that have brought you before me tonight. It is your actions that demand the attention of the Si-Fan."

Testing my strength and the patience of my captors, I struggled to my feet. I felt weak and exposed. Setting my jaw, I stared up at that horrible blank-faced mask.

"You should know that Dr. Fu Manchu has given his word that no harm is to befall me or any member of my family."

A low chuckle escaped from the mask and sent a chill down my spine.

"And you should know that Fu Manchu has no authority over me. The Si-Fan is mine to command, for I am Khunum-Khufu of old. You have stolen what was rightfully mine. You stole the Seal of Solomon."

My mind reeled at the madman's words. There was no point denying that I knew of what he spoke, but it had been so many years...

"I do not have it any longer. I cast it into the Nile years ago. Only evil and destruction can come of it."

A single muscular arm reached out and grasped me by the collar and lifted me effortlessly from the ground.

"As a medical man, surely you are aware of how many bones are contained in the human hand. You realize, of course, that if I crush even half of those bones, your career is finished?"

I said nothing. I fought to control my racing heart as I stared into the eye slit of the metal helmet.

"You also realize how easy it would be for me to take those who matter most to you and make them like me?"

His fingers released me and I fell roughly to the ground.

Winded, I looked up as he grasped the sides of his helmet between his hands.

"Stare with wonder upon my visage and remember the words I have spoken."

He lifted the helmet off of his head. I gasped in surprise.

"No! It can't be! It *is* you!"

Holding the helmet in one hand, he pointed at me with the other while I watched that hideous deformed countenance contort in rage.

"On your knees, Pagan! Come and worship your god."

The dacoits lifted me from the ground and forced me to kneel before him. My arms were pinned behind my back while another grabbed me by the hair and forced me forward. A wave of revulsion overwhelmed me at the dawning realization of the humiliating act being forced upon me. I clenched my teeth and howled with fury at the Heavens while mocking laughter filled my ears.

1. ONE NIGHT IN CORFU

My taxi pulled up outside the bistro just as night had begun to settle over the Mediterranean. I gave my name to the waiter and told him the party that was expecting me. He led me through the labyrinth of winding tables until I spotted Spiridon seated at a table with two beautiful women.

"Mr. Michael Knox."

The waiter bowed slightly as he announced my arrival.

"Michael!"

Spiridon was positively ebullient this evening. He half-stood in his seat and his handshake turned into an awkward bear hug as he threw his arms about me, chuckling.

"Ladies, I would like you to meet the finest archaeologist in all of the British Isles...a man I would go so far as to call perhaps the second finest archaeologist in the whole wide world...Professor Michael Knox."

The two women laughed politely at Spiridon's vanity. Evidently, my colleague had started drinking early this evening.

"Kara Petrie."

The strikingly beautiful woman I had the good fortune to sit next to extended her hand. I took it and kissed it. Dark eyes highlighted a face of a smooth olive complexion. It was impossible to guess her precise heritage from her features or her accent. I felt a pang of disappointment as my gaze fell upon her wedding ring. I took in her eyes with a sweeping glance and saw they promised nothing in return. I feared the night was to prove as disappointing as I had expected.

I turned to the equally pretty woman seated opposite her.

"And you must be..."

"Mrs. Spiridon Simos!" My friend beamed.

The beautiful woman glanced at him for a moment; I felt sure I detected a slight annoyance in her look.

"Miss Greba Eltham," she said as she extended her hand to me, "...for a few more hours at least."

I kissed her hand and told her how nice it was to finally meet the woman who had managed to take Spiridon's mind off our excavation. I was aware that this was to be her second marriage, her first husband having passed away a few years ago. I found it somehow distasteful that she had chosen to revert to her maiden name.

I settled into my seat next to the charming Mrs. Petrie.

"Spiridon was just telling us that you will be leading the dig in Luxor while he and Greba are enjoying their honeymoon in the Ionian Islands," she said. "Do you really think that you may have uncovered another Theban Necropolis?"

I exchanged a quick glance with Spiridon.

"Steady on, old boy," he said. "I didn't disclose any sensitive information."

I smiled politely and turned my attention back to Kara. I knew very well that the University would have been beside themselves had they known Spiridon had said even that much. Athens' relations with Cairo at the moment were strained at best without his dropping hints about our project to the wife of a distinguished Cairo physician...particularly considering that she and her husband were old friends with the foremost Egyptologist alive today, a man who would sell his very soul to have possessed the knowledge Spiridon had stumbled upon through sheer good fortune.

"Are you married, Professor Knox?"

I noticed that her voice held a delightful musical lilt.

"Heavens, no," I chuckled. "I have enough sense to know better than that."

There was a pregnant pause and I was immediately conscious of my blunder. My mind raced to think of something pithy to say to amuse the women and salvage the moment.

"Perhaps you've not met the right woman then."

Her eyes smoldered as she spoke. I pictured losing myself in them as she disappeared beneath me.

"Oh, there's no shortage of right women. That's just the problem. Women are not so different from the entrées on this menu. You might fancy one dish more than any of the others tonight, but what about tomorrow? Imagine having to choose just the same entree to enjoy every night for the rest of your life. That's my argument against monogamy. It is in violation of basic human nature and all known laws of logic and yet men willingly defy their nature and logic time and again."

I had made this argument many times before. If my delivery was just right, I would have salvaged the evening and possibly more if the stars were with me. I continued after what I hoped sounded convincingly like a reflective pause.

"Still, most men and women in this world are happy to do just that, you three included and all blessings to you for it. As for myself, I'm afraid I love women too much to

17

limit myself to just one...although I'm always willing to be proven wrong. Maybe one day I'll find that one special girl who makes me want to defy logic and deny my own stubborn nature, but until then, I'll keep right on choosing the tastiest morsel at hand every time."

I opened my menu and reached forward and squeezed Kara's hand where it rested on the seat next to mine, confident that we were out of Spiridon and Greba's line of vision. At worst, she would be offended by my boldness, but would say nothing of the matter so as not to embarrass the happy couple across from us. At best...I hadn't time to finish that particularly pleasant thought when her voice cut through the air like a knife.

"In the meantime, you conduct yourself like a frightened little boy fleeing from commitment lest you be forced to grow up. You must dread the many nights you spend alone, Professor Knox."

I felt my face redden as Spiridon snorted in amusement and Greba laughed out loud at Kara's churlish rebuke.

"Happily, there are not many of them, Mrs. Petrie," I snapped.

She smiled, seemingly pleased with herself.

"Yet the inevitable nights of solitude must ring with the hollowness of failure as you sadly realize that with each passing year, the number of lonely nights is doomed to grow until one day you find yourself having crossed the..."

She wriggled her fingers in irritation, trying to think of the phrase in English.

"He will find himself having crossed the Rubicon," my friend interjected, "the dread point of no return."

Yes, thank you for that, Spiridon, I thought as the three of them chuckled at my expense.

"Forgive us for teasing you so, Professor Knox," Kara patted my hand like a mother would a petulant child, "but it is only fair play for us dreary old married people to return the favor."

"Nonsense," Spiridon roared to the obvious irritation of the couple at the next table. "I've been telling Michael the same thing for years. He never listens, but one day, I'll have the pleasure of telling him..."

"I told you so!" Greba joined in with her fiancé and the three of them cackled gleefully.

I couldn't believe I was pissing away my evening while these boors ribbed me with all the subtlety of a church bell at evensong. Why did Spiridon have to ask me to be his Best Man in the first place, and why was I fool enough to accept?

The waiter took our orders for dinner. Barely aware of the passage of time, I sat and drank and hardly touched my *pastitsada* when the waiter brought it while the three of them chatted aimlessly. A dreadfully long hour crept by interminably. Our plates had just been cleared when my beautiful, if dull, dining companion stifled a yawn and rose from her seat.

"I think I had best turn in for the night. I'm exhausted from our voyage and tomorrow will be a very busy day for us all. If you will forgive me, I think I will grab a taxi back to the hotel. I would like to get a good night's sleep before it is very late."

I forced myself to smile when, in truth, I was irritated with Spiridon for not delaying his wedding date until after we had completed the dig. His decision had placed an undue burden upon my shoulders. I would be hard-pressed to drive the team to finish the excavation on schedule while he was off gallivanting in the islands with his bride. I would then have to swallow my pride yet

19

again and let Corfu's favorite son take the lion's share of the praise from the University once we returned to Athens.

I watched Kara as she rose and said good night to us. She made a point of avoiding making eye contact with me. Such a beautiful woman and such a shame, I thought, as I watched her hips lightly sway as she made her way to the exit. Another fifteen minutes dragged painfully by with more trite conversation until Spiridon finally managed to rouse himself.

"Yes, why don't we turn in for the night?"

He casually stretched an arm around Greba's shoulder.

"Spiridon, no, we will do things properly. One more night apart and then...no more waiting."

He started to argue, but she covered his mouth with the tips of her fingers and then leaned forward to kiss him.

God, what did she see in that drunken sod apart from his looks, his charm, his wealth, his reputation?

The taxi ride back to the hotel was diverting enough. I kept my eyes off my sickeningly affectionate companions and on the narrow cobblestone streets that our driver skillfully navigated. The view of the promenade along the Bay of Garitsa was breathtaking as we left the Liston, the name given to the esplanade with its many bistros and restaurants, behind.

We must have made quite an unlikely trio as we stepped into the lobby of the Theotokis Hotel. Their gaiety quickly vanished when Kara rushed to greet us upon our entry. Her face had drained of its wonderful color. A look of dread marred her perfect features.

"What is it, Kara? What has happened?" Greba gasped.

I grabbed Kara's elbow to steady her as she started to swoon.

"I received a telegram. It's Dr. Petrie...he's disappeared. There was no sign of forced entry, but he wouldn't just go off in the middle of the night. I'm sorry, both of you, truly I am, but I have to return to Cairo as soon as possible."

"Good Lord," I murmured, "some local trouble of some sort, what?"

Greba shook her head and reached out a hand to hold Kara.

"No, darling, I absolutely forbid it. If you return to Cairo now, you will be placing yourself in worse danger. You know very well what this is likely all about. It is a small miracle that you are with us at all. You must wire Sir Denis. He will know how best to handle the situation."

A look of pained indecision swept across that beautiful ashen face before she sighed resignedly. "I suppose you're right, Greba. It is the only sensible course of action under the circumstances."

Great Scott, I thought to myself, *what sort of mess has Spiridon dragged us into now?* The dire urgency of the matter had certainly sobered him up. I felt bad for him. There was precious little he could say or do under the circumstances. He must have felt a right ineffective clod for having to swallow his pride and sit back while his bride-to-be took charge of some frightfully dangerous situation that we never should have been involved with in the first place. This sort of business didn't suit us. We were respectable academics...professionals, not brash muckrakers like that stubborn old fool...

"Sir Lionel Barton!"

I started as Spiridon spoke up unexpectedly. The two women turned to stare at him. A wide grin had spread across Spiridon's face.

"Forgive me, dearest, but I believe you were speaking of Sir Denis Nayland Smith just now, correct? I met Sir Denis once. He was with Sir Lionel Barton. Extraordinary men, the both of them...why, if I possess even half of their boundless energy when I am their age, I'll..."

Greba smiled patronizingly at her fiancé as she interrupted him mid-sentence. "Fortunately you don't, or I'll never have a moment's peace on our honeymoon. Now, why don't you and Michael have a drink at the bar while I talk over things with Kara?"

She leaned forward to kiss him passionlessly on the lips. "Until tomorrow, my love."

He stopped her with a firm, but gentle grip on her left elbow.

"And then...no more waiting?"

Strangely, Greba looked at me and blushed slightly before returning her gaze to Spiridon. "No more waiting. Pleasant dreams, lover."

I watched my friend stare after her as the two women approached the front desk. I couldn't help but wonder at the apparent look of sadness on Spiridon's face.

"Having second thoughts, old cock?"

A look of genuine terror crossed his countenance at my suggestion after we settled down at a corner of the bar away from the other tourists.

"What? God, no! Why should you even suggest such a thing?"

I shrugged and smiled. "Natural instinct of a committed bachelor, I suppose."

I drank down most of my rum in a single gulp and swirled what was left of the alcohol around the nearly drained glass, watching it intently before placing it next to its empty siblings on the bar. I had consumed too much and eaten too little over the past few hours, and the effects were beginning to make themselves known to my nearly empty stomach.

"I never liked Sir Lionel."

Spiridon looked up from the pocket watch he was fumbling with as if distracted by my declaration.

"Oh, why is that? Not professional jealousy, I trust."

I shook my head. "Nothing of the sort. You know me better than that, Spiridon. The man may have singlehand-edly dominated the field of Egyptology for far more years than I care to remember, but he's also a certifiable loony."

Spiridon laughed. "I suppose he can be a bit eccentric."

I shook my head, feeling decidedly cross and resolved to speak my mind. "It's not a matter of being eccentric as much as the fact that he is out and out dangerous. You've seen him when he gets going. There's no stopping him. He treads on the toes of diplomats, peers, and potentates. One of these days, someone will give that fat, bloated bastard the right proper thrashing that he so richly deserves."

Spiridon glanced around to make sure no one had overheard me. I was uncomfortably aware that I was angry and speaking louder than was advisable, but at that particular moment, I found that I didn't care. I was going to have my say and that was all there was to the matter.

Spiridon lowered his voice as he replied. "Steady on, old boy. No need to cause a scene. You ought not to go about saying such things. No good ever comes of such talk."

I finished what was left of my rum and banged the glass on the counter to signal to the bartender that I desired another.

"Oh rubbish, Spiridon! I know what I'm saying and I have every right to be resentful. Sir Lionel Barton conducts himself as if he's playing a perpetual game of Red Indians and why? Because of his terribly influential friend from British Intelligence that everyone finds so impressive. Sir bloody Denis Nayland Smith."

Spiridon palmed my glass and waved the bartender away. "That's quite enough for you for one night, chap. You need a good night's sleep. You'll feel better in the morning. Come on, off you go."

I let him lead me away toward the lobby where I still needed to pick up my key at the front desk. As we passed by the tables on our way out of the bar, I noted a swarthy-looking man wearing a fez and dark glasses who was smiling in evident amusement at my condition. I had had quite enough of being laughed at for one night, so I stopped to give him hell, but before I could utter a word of invective, Spiridon led me away as if I were an errant schoolboy.

Somehow, it all seemed right at the time. Before morning, I would have cause to regret the looseness of my tongue.

2. AN UNEXPECTED VISITOR

My eyes opened. I felt wide awake as I lay on my bed. I was still fully dressed. I hadn't extinguished the lights, nor had I bothered to climb under the sheets. I felt hot and stared at the ceiling fan as it began another creaking revolution.

God, what a city, I thought. How long had I been in Greece now? Too long was the only answer that mattered. I needed a drink.

I pulled myself up off the bed and waited for the room to cease imitating the ceiling fan. No, I didn't need another drink at the moment, but there was something I could use.

I stumbled over to the sink and peered at myself in the mirror. I pulled the comb from my back pocket and held it under the faucet until it was soaked and then set about taming my unruly hair.

Feeling confident once more, I quietly opened my door and stepped out into the corridor. I had made a point of finding where the rest of the wedding party were staying when I had checked in at the front desk a couple hours earlier. Kara Petrie's room was at the end of the hall.

Kara Petrie with those gorgeous eyes. Kara Petrie with her smooth velvet skin burning to be touched. Kara Petrie with the fool of a husband who stayed behind in Cairo and let her walk into my life.

I rehearsed the line I would deliver when she answered her door. I stopped suddenly and blinked. How

25

much had I drunk tonight? For a split second, I thought I saw a blur of a figure at the end of the hall entering her flat. It couldn't be.

As I reached the end of the hallway, I stopped and smelled the cologne hanging in the air. I'll be damned, it was Spiridon! That old devil! Still, three offered greater possibilities than two. I, at least, was an old hand at this particular game, although I felt certain my friend had never tried anything so adventurous. Greba would spell the end of carefree flings for him once they were married. Better he make his last night of freedom as memorable as possible. He certainly couldn't have picked a better play-mate. Now it was just a question of whether he was willing to share.

I rapped gently on the door.

There was no answer as was to be expected.

I knocked lightly again and stole a glance back down the corridor to make sure that no one was about.

"Kara, it's me," I hissed at the door, smelling the alcohol on my breath. "I know you're not alone. Let me in. I must see you right away."

I scarcely breathed as the sound of furtive footsteps moved quickly to the door. The key in the lock turned and the door opened. I found myself staring into Spiridon's grim-faced countenance. Any thought of a witty quip disappeared as I noted the gun in his hand. He motioned with it for me to enter and then stepped aside.

The door was quickly shut and locked behind me. I turned slowly.

"Spiridon, what is this all about, I was only..."

"Shut up," he snapped. "Take a look around you. Tell me, what do you see?"

I did as I was told and glanced round the room quickly.

"Packing...suitcases...Kara is going home to her husband after all, I imagine."

Spiridon smiled faintly. I could never recall having seen my old friend behave in this fashion before.

"And where is Mrs. Petrie now?" he asked.

So it was Mrs. Petrie again, was it? I shrugged and attempted a knowing grin.

"One would suppose the bedroom."

"One would be wrong."

I had had just about enough of this for one night.

"Now, see here, Spiridon, stop pointing that damned thing at me. It's liable to go off. If Kara's gone and left already, why would she leave her baggage behind? Surely, she would have taken them with her when she checked out."

"For an intelligent man, you can be awfully dim, Michael," he said, shaking his head, sadly.

"Thank you. Since we've established that I wasn't top of my class at Christ College, would it be too much to ask for some sort of explanation as to what is going on around here?"

Spiridon sighed and gestured for me to sit at the little table in the small kitchen area of the flat. He sat across from me in the opposite chair and, setting the gun down next to him, pulled his fingers through his hair and sighed.

"Where to begin?" he said.

"The beginning would be the logical place."

He shook his head as if he were genuinely mystified as how best to explain his actions.

"Things are not what they seem, Michael. What I learned regarding the High Priests of Thebes was not a question of good fortune as much as it was a matter of opportunity."

Good Lord, I thought as I rubbed my forehead in exasperation, *this was not the night that I had envisioned at all.*

"I made my choice to act and now I must pay the cost. You had your opportunity as well, and you made your choice to join me, albeit in ignorance of some of the facts. However, your blundering down here to satiate your overactive libido was your choice alone and you must accept the regrettable consequences of that decision."

He had caught my attention again. This conversation was taking on a distinctly menacing tone.

"What sort of consequences?" I asked warily.

His hand reached toward the gun in front of him.

"You mean to kill me?" I asked.

He nodded. "If I have to, yes."

I pushed my chair back a few inches, sizing up my chances to act.

"You're making my decision easier, Michael. You really don't want to do that."

I relaxed. There was no point getting shot if there was a chance to avoid it.

"That's better. Now stand up and walk over to the closet behind you."

I did as I was told.

"Don't forget this gun is trained on you."

"Spiridon, you may believe me when I say that the gun in your hand is of the utmost importance to me at this particular moment."

I stopped at the closet door.

"Now open it and get inside. All the way in the back with your nose against the wall. If you even think about turning around, you are a dead man. Do I make myself clear?"

I thought better of responding. I did as he asked. I opened the door and stepped into the closet and placed my nose against the back wall. I shut my eyes and waited for the fatal bullet. It seemed unavoidable. I had no idea what the Devil had happened to Spiridon, but there was no denying he was quite serious.

The door clicked shut, but no other sound followed. I turned slowly to look behind me. I could see Spiridon staring at me through the grated paneling of the door.

"Now, be smart, Michael, and keep quiet, and you may just live through this. I have no wish to kill you, but I will not hesitate to do so if forced."

I stepped forward to the grated paneling so that only a few thin pieces of wood separated our faces from one another.

"Why, Spiridon?"

Cold, hard eyes stared back into mine.

"That would not be an example of your being smart and keeping quiet, Michael. I shan't warn you a second time."

I stepped back almost involuntarily. He stared at me a moment more and then turned away; he crossed to the suitcases and began shutting each of the bags.

I heard the sound of a key turning in the lock. Spiridon froze and looked up nervously toward the door. I heard the hinges creak as the door opened and then quick-ly shut again. Someone had locked it just now from the inside. I could not see the new arrival, but I heard him speak.

"Where is the woman?" the new arrival asked in a thick Greek accent.

Spiridon's features were frozen for a blink of an eye; then, he beamed and turned on the charm.

"My dear Neapolis, why so suspicious, my friend? Have faith in Simos. All is well. The Petrie woman is already in a taxi cab on her way to the safe house. I am almost finished with her bags. I will personally see to it that they are delivered to the driver when he returns. My lovely fiancée will understand that Mrs. Petrie has rushed to her husband's side and will regrettably be unable to attend our wedding. All is proceeding according to plan. Have no fear."

The man called Neapolis stepped forward and I recognized the swarthy man with the fez and dark glasses that I nearly had an incident with in the hotel bar earlier in the evening. I felt a cold chill as I recognized the fact that boring, pompous Spiridon Simos was not the man that I had judged him to be.

Neapolis pushed a stubby forefinger into Spiridon's chest, visibly moving him backwards several inches.

"Let us understand one another, my friend. The Si-Fan does not accept failure. That smooth tongue of yours will be of little use when it is no longer connected to your mouth. Do not fool yourself into thinking you have an ally in Our Lady. She will discard you without a second thought once you cease to prove useful to her."

Spiridon chuckled, but I knew him well enough to recognize the nervousness he sought to conceal.

"Keeping my tongue intact is critical to my usefulness to Our Lady of the Si-Fan."

Neapolis slapped him roughly across the face. Spiridon's fingers curled into a fist for a second or two before the fire went out of his eyes; he gingerly rubbed his cheek with his hand instead.

"Do not be crass," Neapolis snapped. "Our Lady's eyes and ears are everywhere. Were she to learn of your insolence, your own mother would not recognize your corpse. Finish packing and come and get me at once as soon as the driver has left with the bags."

"As you wish," Spiridon nodded.

Neapolis turned and stepped out of view. I heard the key turn in the lock and the door shut once again. The door was locked from the outside this time, and Spiridon quickly resumed packing as if he had completely forgotten about me. I debated whether I should clear my throat to attract his attention. Presently, he finished with the bags and approached the grated paneling to face me once more.

His eyes looked hard and his face was haggard as he spoke. "You see, my friend, there is much more to life than chasing after every shapely pair of legs that cross your path. The opportunity is there if one does not fear to take it. The cost is sometimes high. The risk is sometimes considerable, but the reward...can be beyond imagination."

I hesitated a moment until I was certain he had nothing more to say.

"What is to become of me?"

"What indeed?" Spiridon smiled. "The choice is entirely yours, Michael, as before. You may choose to forget about this incident. Attend my wedding, return to the dig in Luxor, and live to a ripe old age never appreciating just how generous I have been to let you live. Alternatively, you may choose to be...indiscreet...and if so, it shall cost you your life. No policeman, no weapon, can help you avoid your fate. You will die. This is fact. It would be best to decide the path you choose now and save me the bother. Shall I release you or must I do something unpleasant?"

I forced myself to laugh, painfully aware of how badly I was perspiring.

"You may release me, of course. You know that I am, above all else, a reasonable man and a man who loves living. I am not inquisitive...at least not overly so...nor am I a hero. I wish to live, Spiridon, I wish to live to love another day...and another, and another. Whatever business of yours is just that—business of yours. I have no part in it. My interest in the Petrie woman was purely physical. She is of no concern to me. Women are like taxi cabs. There are plenty to be had, and the best rides are the fast ones, just as I have always said, yes?"

My laughter sounded hollow and forced, but Spiridon smiled and, for the first time in too long a while, I felt I might live to put this encounter behind me.

"You are a coward, Michael."

I felt the color drain from my face as his smile abruptly faded.

"You are a singularly shallow man. Perhaps more so than any other I have ever known. That is why you will live to survive this unfortunate lapse of judgment of yours. "

I laughed until tears streaked my face as Spiridon unlatched the closet door. My death sentence had been commuted. I had my freedom and it was bought only with silence. Being branded a coward was a small price to pay for living. Cowards were survivors, and I preferred being branded a coward than being remembered as a courageous martyr.

I was still shaking when I reached my room and my heart finally stopped racing. I vaguely recalled Spiridon slapping me on the back as he opened Kara's door for me. Words passed his lips, but I did not hear them. I was conscious only of my misery and my fear. I lay on my bed wide awake and stared at the slowly revolving ceiling fan, and thought how truly wretched I was.

3. PAYING THE COST

I awoke to the sound of panic outside my door. I sat up in bed fearing that I had cried aloud, but the commotion had nothing to do with me. I reached the door in less than half a dozen steps and threw it open. There was a crowd filling the hall, murmuring worriedly.

"What's happened? What's wrong?" I asked in both Greek and English.

A middle-aged man jerked his head in the opposite direction. Speaking with an American accent, he said: "There's been a murder...one of the guests down the hall. The police haven't arrived yet."

Oh, God! Kara was dead and I was partly to blame.

I pushed my way through the crowd when, suddenly, it occurred to me that the center of activity was not the end of the corridor, but a room at the middle. I fought my way to the doorway and peered inside. What I saw nearly caused me to faint.

Spiridon lay on the floor, covered in blood. Past the initial shock of that sight, I noted a peculiar jagged metal wheel lodged in the centre of his forehead. The wheel was splattered with blood. The wound had opened winding dark red rivulets along his nose and down both cheeks that collected in a pool of blood on the carpet.

A second jagged metal wheel was lodged in his throat. His shirt was soaked red with blood from his neck down, well past his chest. He lay perfectly still with glassy eyes staring at the ceiling. His knees were bent slightly. I realized his death must have come quickly, and hopefully painlessly. His assassin must have stood in the same spot as me as I looked down upon his corpse.

"It is a *shuriken*."

I recalled the accent, but did not recollect where I had heard the voice before. I turned and was startled to see Neapolis standing at my side, watching my reaction carefully.

"I'm sorry?"

My voice sounded like a hollow echo. I was aware how badly I was shaking. I could feel the sweat collecting at my brow.

He would know. He would be a fool not to know that I recognized him for what he was.

"I said...it is a *shuriken*." He smiled and bared his sharp little teeth. "It is a traditional weapon of Japanese assassins or thieves. Your friend," he pointed down at Spiridon's corpse, "he was robbed, yes?"

"How...how did you know he was my friend?"

Somehow, despite everything, my subconscious was working rapidly to save my life. I had to allay his initial suspicions about me. He must think I was only distraught to find Spiridon dead. I was frightened of everyone, not only of him.

Neapolis smiled a second time, conjuring nothing less than the image of a devil let loose upon the world to lead the unwary down to the fiery pits of Hell.

"You forget. I was at the bar with you last night. You had a little too much to drink, no? Your friend, he took you up to bed and then came down again. He was still drinking when I went to bed," he smacked his chest emphatically while slowly shaking his head mournfully. "It is sad. One cannot be too careful these days."

My heart began to calm again. He believed me. I had done it. I recalled Spiridon's warning about the police and weapons being useless against the people he was mixed up with. I had done it. I had convinced Neapolis that I was not a threat.

"He was to be married today," I said.

I briefly saw Neapolis nod sadly upon hearing my statement, but my mind was elsewhere. I was searching the crowd for Greba. My God, she would be a hysterical wreck when she found out about Spiridon.

An old Greek woman on my right leaned close and asked in a loud whisper: "What is that in his head and in his throat, do you suppose?"

Distracted, I barely turned and responded: "It is a Japanese weapon of some sort. What did you call it, Neapolis?"

I could have strangled myself where I stood. I had spoken his name when we had never been introduced.

My head jerked to the left and I saw that leering smile on the Greek's face widen.

"It is...a *shuriken*," he said, leaning close so the old woman would hear him, but his eyes never left mine.

There was nothing for it now. I was found. I had given myself away. I was a fool. I was as dead as poor Spiridon lying there before me in his own blood. No amount of composure would change anything. Those dull, black eyes drilled into mine and declared that I was one already doomed.

I turned and fled as best I could. Pushing and shoving my way, I shouldered through the crowd. It seemed like an eternity before I heard the panicked cries of "Stop him! Stop that man!"

I was sure the cries were meant for the Greek. He was doubtless dogging my steps, ready to hurl one of those exotic Japanese weapons through the back of my skull. Fear blinded my reason and I did not understand that, in turning to run, I had branded myself Spiridon's killer in the eyes of the crowd assembled outside his room.

I felt a sense of elation as I made it to the bottom of the stairs. The front desk barely registered. The front doors were my only goal. I hit the door and stumbled down the steps, drunkenly taking in large gulps of fresh morning air and practically collapsing with joy upon reaching the pavement.

I did not stop to wait for my pursuers to reach me, or for the police to arrive. I ran on. People fell out of my way on the narrow cobblestone path as I pushed past storefronts, stalls, and sidewalk cafés. Eyes, both angry and frightened, peered at my face. There was no telling how many would report having seen me once word of Spiridon's murder reached the newspapers. I had a few brief hours, at best, to get out of Corfu before my face was on a wanted poster at every port, railway station, and airfield in Greece.

My right hand patted my front pants pocket. I was reassured to feel my wallet still in place. Normally, I kept it in my back pocket, but I did not feel safe from the pickpockets in Corfu, and I had taken to placing it in my front pocket where it would be less likely to be removed without my knowing it.

I had more than enough money to get out of the country, even if I had to buy my way out. The money belonged to the University and was to finance the completion of the dig, but that wouldn't matter. I would never see Luxor again if I didn't make it off Corfu soon. I would hang for Spiridon's murder, and that was preferable to the fate awaiting me if I were caught by his killer or his associates.

I jumped into a waiting taxi and barked at the driver that I wanted to take the ferry to Igoumenitsa. From there, I could easily arrange passage to Athens, and from Athens, I could escape Greece. It was all within reach if only time were on my side.

I felt like a child again. My God, would I never be free of those nightmares? Once, decades ago, I had found myself, along with my sister and a neighborhood friend, in the wrong place at the wrong time. We had run afoul of some bloody foreigners and had nearly paid for it with our lives. My entire life had been shaped by that one incident...perhaps warped was the better word. My choice of career and my decision to never marry were in reaction to that unfortunate twist of fate. Now, here I was in my thirties, and I had blundered into the wrong place at the wrong time again, and another bloody foreigner was ready to kill me for it.

"Excuse me, sir?"

I tumbled out of my reverie and looked up expectantly into the eyes of the Greek taxi driver reflected in the rear view mirror in front of me. The man's accent was thick, but his English was very good.

"I realize it is a peculiar question, but is there any chance that someone might wish to follow you?"

"Follow me?"

I shouldn't have sounded surprised, but I felt dazed and confused by the question.

"Yes, sir, that black sedan has made an effort to keep behind us. That is no mean feat when one is navigating the *kantounia*, particularly for a foreign driver."

"How do you know the driver is a foreigner?"

The eyes in the mirror looked away from mine to glance at the car behind us. I had not, as yet, summoned the courage to turn and look behind me to see the sedan for myself.

"The driver is Oriental. The passenger looks like a Greek, but it is difficult to be sure. Anyone can disguise themselves with a pair of dark glasses and a fez."

Dark glasses and a fez! I spun round and saw Neapolis clearly in the passenger seat of the sedan behind us. He gestured wildly to the driver and the sedan sped closer to us as if it intended to ram us from behind.

"Lose them! Lose them!" I cried.

My driver accelerated, his eyes staring straight at the narrowing cobblestone road ahead.

"Do not worry, sir, we shall lose him easily once we reach the Spianada."

Of course, I thought to myself, *the town square by the old Venetian citadel!* The road divides into the upper and lower square. We could easily lose them in the confusion between the Ano Plateia and the Kato Plateia. It was, in all likelihood, the largest town square on the continent. I began to feel some hope of escaping my would-be assassin after all.

My confidence was premature as a pistol discharged and was rapidly followed by the sound of a bullet striking the taxi's side. Foolishly, I twisted my head to look out the back window and saw Neapolis clinging to the black sedan's running board with his right arm outstretched and a gun clearly visible in his hand.

"He means to kill me!" I shouted at the driver, waving my arms frantically.

The driver shook his head without looking back at me in the mirror.

"He means to shoot out our tires is what he means to do. Do you have a gun, my friend?"

I stared at him in bewilderment. "I am an archaeologist, not an adventurer. I am as likely to carry a gun as I am a bullwhip."

The driver leant forward and, with his left hand still gripping the wheel, opened the glove compartment with his right hand, and withdrew a pistol.

"Here," he said, turning slightly to pass the gun to me in the back seat.

"Watch it!" I yelled as the taxi slid to the right and collided with a vendor's fruit stand. The windshield was awash in pears, kumquats, olives, and pomegranates.

The taxi jerked back onto the street as the driver somehow managed to increase his already considerable speed. Grasping the pistol tightly in my hand, I stole a glance behind me out the back window and was shocked to see the black sedan slowing down and then turning off the road away from us, but there was no sign of Neapolis.

He must have fallen off when we collided with the fruit stand!

My excitement quickly dissipated as a great weight thudded on the roof of the taxi. Before I had time to think, the hessian covering on the roof began to tear and a great rush of air entered the taxi along with a blinding ray of sunlight. I pointed my pistol at the opening and fired three times.

There was another thud as the weight flopped to one side. I hesitated, trying to determine whether I had struck him or not, and, in that moment, the hessian covering tore through and the figure of a man fell between the front and back seat.

Neapolis kicked his left leg straight out and knocked the pistol from my hand. It clattered on the floor in front of me. As I bent to reach for it, his leg shot out again and again. I fell back against my seat, grasping my bleeding nose.

The Greek hurled himself backward and fell into the seat next to me. His right hand held his stomach where his shirt was stained red.

"Where is this one going?" he asked the driver, gesturing with the gun in his left hand.

"The Contrafossa," the man replied. "He is taking the ferry to Igoumenitsa."

"I can answer my own questions. Thank you very much," I said, pinching my bleeding nose.

Neapolis looked at me and managed to smile despite his evident pain. He bared those sharp pointed teeth once more.

"You will tell me everything when I ask you," he turned back to the driver and gestured again with the gun. "You will take us to the Old Citadel. Our English friend wishes to see the observatory up close."

Oh, God. I was going to be murdered in public, in broad daylight, in clear view of scores of tourists. I was sitting there bleeding with a loaded gun at my feet and I could do nothing to stop my killer.

We were passing the Palaia Anaktora. I could smell the salt water from the Ionian Sea on the breeze coming through the torn hessian covering on the roof. I glanced past Neapolis and, out the window next to him, at the beautiful trees and flowers lining the palace gardens. The sound of a group of young men singing *cantades* caught my ear.

"They are singing of the Thaumaturgist," Neapolis stared at me as I spoke. I was as startled as he was to find I had the courage to speak. "The Miracle Worker...the

Patron Saint of Corfu and the Patron Saint of my friend who you murdered with your damnable *shurikens*."

The Greek stared at me and then laughed. "Do not tell me of my own people's history, Englishman. I am a Corfiote myself."

The taxi screeched to a halt. I glanced out the windscreen, but the Old Citadel was not yet in sight.

"I go no further," the driver said simply. "You will both please get out of my cab."

Neapolis grabbed his left shirt sleeve with his right hand and pulled the sleeve back revealing a tattoo of a Chinese ideograph.

"Do you see this? Do you know what it is?"

The driver turned to look at the tattoo and his face turned ashen.

"The Seven! Mother of God! I did not know. Spare me."

Neapolis pulled the sleeve back down and said: "You will proceed as directed to the Old Citadel."

The driver did as he was told.

It was not nearly long enough before we arrived at the foot of that mighty fortress with its Venetian architecture. I was so close to the marina. So close to escaping...

"You will get out of the taxi and open the back door," Neapolis instructed the driver. "There is a pistol at the Englishman's feet. You will carefully retrieve it and pass it to me with the barrel facing you. Do you understand?"

"Perfectly," the driver responded as he climbed out of the taxi.

He opened my door and avoided making eye contact with me. I could not blame the man. Surely, I would have behaved the same had our situations been reversed.

41

He bent over and reached between my legs for the pistol that lay at my feet. What happened next was a blur. I moved my legs toward the right to make room for the driver. There was a deafening blast and smoke and the smell of gunpowder, and then I saw Neapolis plastered against the rear passenger side of the cab with a gaping hole in his skull, wet with a glistening red stain growing larger by the second. The wound was a more prominent companion to the one on the side of his stomach, which had soaked through his shirt red. His features were frozen in a look of surprise that was nearly comical to behold.

The driver shoved the gun into my crotch.

"Give me your wallet. I want all of your money right now."

I couldn't believe this. After all I had been through, I was going to be robbed by a taxi driver, too?

I did as he directed and struggled to pull the wallet out of my front pocket. It bulged with bills. The taxi driver's eyes widened in surprise at his good fortune as he saw the amount of money I was carrying.

He looked at me expectantly after I handed over the wallet.

"That's all I have," I said, feeling rather daft and well aware I was lying, considering the additional money I had concealed in the band of the stocking I wore on my right foot.

He held the wallet out to me.

"I am no thief, my friend. Take enough to get your ferry off the island."

I didn't have to be told twice and reached for several bills.

"Not too much! Not too much! Don't be greedy!"

It was my money, I thought, but in point of fact, it wasn't. It was the University's money that I had now lost. Still, at least, he was honest for a crook.

"Now go. Do not stop for anyone. Do not trust anyone. The Si-Fan's tentacles are limitless. You must find a new identity once you have left Corfu; make a new life for yourself. It is the only way. Go!"

I didn't stop to thank him. I said nothing. After a final parting glance at Neapolis' corpse crushed against the side of the passenger door, I climbed out of the open door of the taxi. After a cursory glance to make sure the black sedan was no longer in sight, and that no one was close enough to pay me the slightest notice, I set off at a trot away from the cab.

In a short while, I had reached the marina and arranged for safe passage on the ferry to Igoumenitsa. I was emotionally and physically spent as I drifted in and out of a light slumber while the ferryman spoke of the mythical origins of Corfu. How the great god Poseidon had fallen under the spell of a bewitching young river nymph and had stolen her from her parents and brought her to this very island, which he called Corfu after her name. The modern Corfiotes are said to be the descendants of the offspring of Poseidon and his beloved river nymph.

I glanced up at the splendid range of mountains that ringed the coastline along the Ionian. Was it any wonder that its people created such glorious myths? How else could they hope to explain the unsurpassed beauty of their surroundings?

As the port of Igoumenitsa came into view, I heaved a sigh of relief. From here, it was a simple matter of taking a connection to Athens, a scant two hundred miles away where, if I had enough money left, I would board the Orient Express and soon be out of harm's way.

Spiridon had been correct; I had made my choice and had now paid my price. Now, I needed only hope that all accounts had been settled. At the time, I was foolish enough to think that I could be so fortunate.

4. ROMANCE ON THE ORIENT EXPRESS

As planned, I boarded the Arlberg line of the Orient Express at Athens. I had been to the cheapest barber I could find in the city and had my head shaved. I had declined to let him remove my two days' growth of stubble as I determined that the absence of hair and a newly acquired beard would change my appearance to the extent that anyone who had seen me in Corfu would no longer be certain that I was the same man. I had just enough left over to purchase false papers identifying me as Dr. Marvin Houghton. Happily, the black market in Athens was thriving and reliable, at least as far as the quality of their forgeries was concerned.

I regretted having thrown suspicion upon myself in fleeing the scene of Spiridon's murder, but I had little choice. Neapolis would have killed me. Indeed, he had nearly succeeded but for the cunning and quick gun hand of the taxi driver. Of course, I'm sure the man knew that Neapolis would have certainly killed him as well. He could scarcely afford witnesses.

My berth aboard the train was spacious and comfortable and, by the time I had finished my filet of beef with chateau potatoes and chocolate pudding, I was beginning to regain some of my old confidence. It was at that moment that I saw her standing there.

The door to my berth opened unexpectedly and there she stood, nervously clutching her bag. She was undoubtedly the most beautiful woman that I had ever seen. Jet black hair that curled delightfully around a perfectly sculpted face. Eyes that sparkled like emeralds and deliciously full red lips that obscured all but a glimpse of her perfect white teeth.

"Oh, excuse me," she spoke with a musical lilt that captivated me instantly. "I'm afraid that there was some mistake. This is supposed to be my berth."

I put down my spoon and dabbed at my mouth with my napkin. "I am afraid that you are the one who is mistaken, miss." I reached for the ticket in my breast pocket. "This is my berth. See?"

A delightful laugh slipped past her lips.

"I understand that perfectly well, sir. The mistake was not either of ours, but the Orient Express. It seems they sold this berth to two parties. I'm Helga Graumann. I was informed of what had happened when I boarded at Athens, and I've had the most dreadful time letting them try to find a place for me, so I just decided that enough was enough, and that if you seemed like a proper gentleman, you would certainly not object to helping out a lady in distress."

I stared at her stupidly for a moment before remembering my manners.

"Oh, excuse me," I said, struggling to remember my adopted guise. "My name is Houghton. Dr. Marvin Houghton. May I take your bag for you?"

She smiled sweetly and nodded somewhat nervously.

"How do you do, Dr. Houghton."

I took her bag and stowed it in the compartment above our seats.

"You don't have any bags, Dr. Houghton?"

I paused and hoped that my face did not betray my alarm, as I turned back to face her.

"No, not on this trip, happily."

She smiled slightly, but seemed ill at ease.

"It seems rather strange to find a doctor without a medical bag."

"Oh, that!" I laughed nervously, "I'm not that sort of doctor, you see. People are always making that mistake."

She nodded and looked expectantly at the empty seat. Realizing that I was forgetting my manners again, I half-rose from my seat and indicated the space opposite me.

"Please, sit down...Miss Graumann," I added her name almost as an afterthought. My manner had been too unsettling to expect her to suggest that I should call her by her first name. I would have to act quickly if I were to allay her suspicions.

"Thank you. What sort of doctor are you then?"

It was a natural question, but I found myself searching her eyes first before answering.

Do not say archaeologist, I repeated in my mind. *Do not say archaeologist.*

"A psychiatrist. I'm on my way to a conference...in Vienna. And you?"

She smiled, pleasantly.

"I am going home to Belgrade so we shan't be neighbors for very long, I'm afraid."

"What a shame."

She raised an eyebrow quizzically.

"I mean to say that it is most unfortunate that I will not be able to enjoy the company of so charming a young lady as you for longer."

"That is kind of you to say." She paused for a moment as if thinking. "You are very young for a psychiatrist."

I nodded and then struggled to think of an appropriate rejoinder.

47

"I have only just finished my schooling."

She laughed that wonderfully musical laugh. It reminded me of someone else, but I couldn't place who it was at the time.

"That explains a great deal. I am glad to meet you, Dr. Houghton and I, too, am sorry that we will not have longer to get to know one another better."

She glanced across the table at my dinner plate and I immediately felt self-conscious.

"Oh, forgive me. Have you eaten?"

She gave a charming smile and shook her head.

"No, but I am not hungry right now, thank you. Would you mind terribly much if I smoke, Doctor?"

"Not in the least," I said, returning her smile.

I watched with interest as her long thin fingers removed a purple cigarette case from her purse. She extracted a very small tan-colored cigarette from the case and fitted it into her holder. She struck a match and lit it. We chatted for a few minutes, but I cannot recall the subjects. As we spoke, the aroma from her cigarette wafted into my nostrils and I soon found myself fighting to stay awake. Before I knew what was happening, I had drifted into a deep slumber.

I dreamt that my beautiful traveling companion was by my side in the cramped sleeping quarters adjacent to me. We were huddled beneath the bed covers. She trembled slightly as a thunderous storm crashed outside. Rain pelted against the compartment's lone window pane.

"The storm is nothing to be frightened of, dearest."

She looked up at me as I spoke with those shining emerald eyes of hers. She smiled and reminded me of a child seeking comfort from night terrors.

"Tell me all there is to know about you, Michael," she cooed.

I did not question how she knew my real name. The smell of Jasmine in her hair and on her neck and the nearness of her warm, tender body were enough. I did not want to wake. I wanted this dream to never end.

"Both my parents are dead. I have only one sibling. A sister, three years my junior."

She shook her head slowly and made a clicking sound with her tongue against her teeth as a teacher might when correcting a particularly dense pupil.

"No, Michael. Tell me about the dig. Tell me about Luxor."

I shook my head, emphatically.

"Luxor is a secret. I can tell no one. The University would have my hide."

She rested a palm against my chest and, slowly, with fingers moving almost imperceptibly, let her hand wind its way down as far as her arm would stretch.

"There are to be no secrets between us, my love. You don't want to keep secrets from me, do you? You want me to have...everything."

I was in ecstasy. No woman had ever thrilled me with her touch as she did. I was helpless and I wanted her to take command of me...to have her way with me...to do anything...everything...so long as it pleased her.

Her lips touched mine lightly, like a summer breeze rather than a kiss. I was hungry for her, but she held me in check with but a single cupped hand.

"Tell me," she whispered, and the words seemed to amplify until it filled the entire compartment of our berth.

"The Priests of Thebes," I breathed. "Spiridon has found the secret burial chamber of the Priests of Thebes. It has been staring at us for nearly half a century, and yet no one has ever uncovered it."

"Where? Where is the burial chamber?"

49

"We haven't excavated it yet, but we're close. He found the location or...perhaps it was given to him. He's dead now, and I've lost the money we needed to finish the dig and return to Greece. They think that I killed him, but they're mistaken. It was Neapolis with his *shurikens*. Kara's husband is gone. They took Kara. Greba...poor Greba with her husband dead on her wedding day. She wired Sir Denis Nayland Smith. Sir Denis and Sir Lionel Barton. Sir Lionel will ruin everything if we let him. He'll take all the credit from Spiridon and me. We must stop him from ruining all of our hard work."

She released her hold and her arm snaked back up to my chest. Her fingers tingled as they stroked my chest hair. Her touch was oddly soothing and I felt my breathing relax.

"Don't worry about a thing, my pet. We will stop Sir Lionel and Sir Denis from ruining everything this time."

She leaned forward and kissed me, not gently, but with a stormy passion. My arms reached around her waist to press her body closer to mine when she suddenly bit down on my lip and cursed at me. She pushed herself away from me and then struck hard with the palms of her hands against both my shoulders, roughly forcing me on my back. She climbed astride me and, with a cruel smile, began to wrap her legs about mine. I closed my eyes and gave way to the passion of the moment. I was lost in her fiery body and, for the first time, knew the perfection I had been ardently seeking in vain for all these many years. I would do anything to keep her. I would do anything to make this moment last forever.

I awoke alone. Startled to find that I was still in my seat, I turned and saw that my bed was still made and that no bag was stowed above my compartment.

"What the Devil?"

I rose from my seat and pulled the door aside and staggered out into the corridor. I spied the conductor stumbling toward me from the opposite end of the train.

"See here! Where is Miss Graumann? The young woman who was sharing my berth. She gets off the train at Belgrade."

The uniformed old man puffed his cheeks out and sucked on his lower lip. An enormous white walrus moustache obscured much of his mouth.

"That's quite enough out of you, sir. You've been dreaming. There is no one on board the train by the name of Graumann. I would know, wouldn't I? We passed Belgrade not more than 20 minutes ago and you may believe me when I say that no one stepped out of your berth in all that time. When I passed by your door last, you were fast asleep in your chair. Now, please return to your berth. It won't be long before we reach Budapest, so just simmer down and read a book or take another nap."

He shook his head as he walked away from me. I was dumbstruck. That couldn't have been a dream and yet...I reached a hand up and gently felt my lip, but there was no bite mark upon it.

Good Lord, how could I have dreamt such a fabulous creature? It must have been the strain of all that I had been through since Corfu. It was enough to set anyone's nerves on end, but what a dream. What I would give for an actual waking hour with such a beauty.

5. DEATH RIDES THE RAILS

After a few minutes sitting alone in my berth, I resolved that I could not simply sit still and do nothing. I refused to accept that Helga Graumann was only a figment of my overwrought imagination. She was too perfect, too real to be only a dream. What if she had lied about Belgrade and was still on board? What if, like me, she had given a false name? My imagination was getting the better of me. I could not very well search every berth on the train for her, but I knew I would not rest any more this night, so I was better off putting my energy to good use.

I was on my way to the restaurant coach when I collided with a little girl emerging from the restroom. I apologized profusely and made certain that she was all right. She was a sweet little thing with her round brown face and heavily-lidded eyes and black hair gathered in a bun atop her head. I presumed she was Mexican or an Indian from the colonies.

"Are you certain that I didn't hurt you?" I asked, looking down into those baleful eyes.

She seemed somewhat dazed as she looked both up and down the corridor in some confusion.

"I...I don't remember which is the right way back to my compartment," she said.

She could not have been older than twelve and I was upset that I had disoriented her so that it caused her to lose her bearings.

"You're not travelling on this train alone, are you?"

"Oh, no," she shook her head. "My mother is with me, but she's sleeping."

"Well, we'll have to see if we can find the conductor to sort this out," I said, reassuringly. Regrettably, the man was nowhere to be found.

I kept her in front of me as we made our way in the direction opposite of which I had come as I was fairly certain there were no mother and young daughter in my car.

After several minutes of watching her scrutinize each door that we passed, and silently cursing the conductor for failing to turn up when I needed him most, the little girl at last found her berth.

"This is the one!" she cried.

She tugged on the door and I helped her push it open. As the door slid, I heard a voice cry, "Margarita!"

"Mother!" yelled the little waif and she eagerly ran into her mother's waiting arms.

I stood there, speechless, for before me in the berth sat Helga Graumann.

She stared at me with a look of genuine bemusement upon her face. Noticing her mother's silence, Margarita had turned back to the doorway where I stood and addressed her mother.

"That is the nice man who helped me find my way back to you...after he knocked me down!"

"What?" her mother gasped.

"She walked into me coming out of the restroom," I explained. "She wasn't watching where she was going. Speaking of which, didn't you tell me you were leaving the train at Belgrade?"

She shook her head and blinked in bewilderment.

"You have mistaken me for someone else, I am

53

afraid."

"Oh, no, you may be afraid all right, but I saw you and spoke with you earlier this evening."

"This evening?"

"Yes," I nodded my head with certainty. "You came into my berth. You claimed that your name was Helga Graumann and that the railway had inadvertently sold the same berth to the two of us."

I would have sworn that the look of astonishment upon her face was sincere, but I could not have been more certain that it was she who had haunted my dreams.

"You are mistaken. I have been right here with my daughter all day, apart from when we went to the dining car for supper."

"Then you must have a twin sister wandering around on this train, because I'm not very likely to forget a face as stunning as yours."

Her cheeks reddened involuntarily at my words while she frowned in irritation.

"I must insist that you leave my compartment at once or I shall be forced to call for help."

"Is this gentleman making a nuisance of himself, Madame?"

I turned to find the conductor with his white walrus moustache standing behind me in the open doorway.

"He was just leaving," she replied sternly.

"Let's go, you," the conductor stepped aside and motioned for me to move on.

"You don't understand...that's the woman I was asking you about."

"The one who left the train at Belgrade?" his voice betrayed the fact that he considered my claim to be dubious at best.

"Well, that's what she told me, but she obviously

lied."

"Do you know what I think, sir? I think you had best move along to your berth and if I so much as hear another peep out of you before Vienna, so help me God, I will have you thrown off this train while it is still moving."

Chastened, I made my way back to my berth feeling even more confused and frustrated than before. I was starting to doubt my sanity. Had I merely dreamt the entire episode after spying a beautiful woman?

I wasn't sure what nationality she was precisely...European, Egyptian, Chinese, or some intoxicating combination thereof, but she certainly wasn't Mexican or Red Indian like her daughter. I thought of that unique musical laugh of hers and it called to mind someone else, but who?

That was it! It was Kara! That peculiar laugh was very similar to Kara's. I felt a pang of remorse as I thought of that poor woman who had been spirited off by whatever criminal organization claimed Neapolis as a member. What of Greba? Poor Greba, having to learn that Spiridon was dead just hours before they were to wed. What hell must she be going through right now?

Briefly, I began to regret having fled in terror rather than standing my ground and trying to help the authorities clear things up. I was a coward, I readily admitted it. I was so terrified at the prospect of sharing Spiridon's fate that I had behaved irrationally and with abominable moral judgment. However, I had chosen my road and there was no turning back now.

"Meee...ster?"

I started in my seat and turned toward my door where a shadowy figure, notably short in stature, was just visible in silhouette. I rose and crossed to the door, sliding it back to reveal Margarita's beaming face looking up at me.

"I am very sorry to have caused you all of that trouble. You did seem like such a nice man."

I nodded and tried to hide my irritation.

"The nice man isn't troubled," I said. "Now run along, before your mother sends the conductor my way again."

Her face became suddenly quite grave as she stepped forward into my berth.

"You don't still believe that you met my mother before, do you?"

It seems foolish now, but my temper got the better of me and I snapped at her in response.

"Margarita, I not only believe I met your mother before tonight, I know for a fact that she was in this very compartment with me earlier this evening and what is more, I am going to prove it!"

The little girl shook her head sadly and gave me a crooked smile that sent a chill through my bones.

"That is most unfortunate to hear, señor."

Her voice had deepened and she suddenly seemed older, changed somehow. She turned and slid the door shut; then, reaching up to her hair, she pulled a knitting needle from out of the bun into which her black hair was wound.

"Poison on the tip," she said in this unfamiliar low, menacing voice that she had somehow adopted. "This will not take long. Do not struggle for you will only prolong the inevitable."

My mind reeled as I began to accept the impossible.

"Margarita, you're not a little girl!"

"I am no child, señor. I am no girl."

Involuntarily, I took a few paces back as the dwarf advanced on me with the poisoned knitting needle.

56

"Come, come, señor. Do not be difficult. It is time to take your medicine."

The dwarf lunged at me. I arched my back to avoid contact and lashed out with my right leg and kicked as hard as I could.

It felt strange, striking out viciously at what, until moments ago, I believed was but a helpless little girl, but this was now a matter of life and death.

The dwarf stumbled for a moment, but was still blocking the doorway, so I took the only avenue of exit open to me. I stepped onto the little dining table, made a desperate lunge for the ladder, and hauled myself up to the top sleeping bunk. Quickly, I pulled the ladder off the top rung and hurled it to the ground just as the dwarf was beginning to scamper up it to follow me.

"You won't have an easy time of it now," I said. "Let's see you re-attach that ladder by yourself."

I grasped the pillow, pathetic means of defense as it might have been, and held it before me as a shield in case the dwarf flung that poisoned knitting needle in my direction.

The dwarf looked up at me, sighed and replaced the knitting needle in the bun atop its head; then, kneeling down on one leg, he reached into the stocking of his left leg. Carefully, the dwarf withdrew a small curved blade and held it in its hand, testing its weight.

I grimaced as I looked at the sharpness of the blade. There really seemed to be no way out of this now.

Happily, my body did not accept defeat as quickly as my mind. I tore the blanket beneath me off the bed and flung it down upon the dwarf's head, leaping down from the sleeping compartment in the next instant.

I fell heavily with all of my weight upon the dwarf, but impeding its vision did little to aid me, for the creature

57

began slashing with his blade almost instantly. It tore through the blanket and was coming perilously close to me as I rained blows upon his head and chest.

Hurriedly, I grasped his wrist with both hands and squeezed with all of my might in an attempt to loosen his grip upon the blade. Leaning forward, I opened my mouth wide and bit at the blanket where the outline of the dwarf's nose was clearly visible.

The dwarf cried in pain and began kicking and punching at me as my teeth crunched down on cartilage.

The door to my berth swung open and I looked up in amazement to see the conductor with his white walrus moustache staring down at us in shock.

"Just what the Devil do you think you are doing, Dr. Houghton?"

He reached down to haul me off the still covered form of the dwarf. As he did so, the dwarf struck out with the blade and sliced into the conductors arm, puncturing an artery. The man doubled over in pain as blood sprang forth as if from a fountain. Rising, the dwarf began to gouge savagely into the poor man's back while pulling the blanket off with the other hand. I saw the look of uncomprehending shock on the conductor's features as I stumbled out into the corridor and fled.

"Meee-ster!"

My God, that little monster was following me already!

I glanced behind me once and saw the tiny fiend, barely four feet in height, running on his stubby little legs in an effort to catch up with me.

This was a nightmare. A child that was no child, but a homicidal dwarf dressed as a little girl armed with a deadly blade, a poisoned knitting needle, and God knows what else, concealed in every spare pocket or orifice on his person.

I swung through the door and entered the restaurant coach. Startled looks on the faces of the staff as they were cleaning up stopped me in my tracks.

"I realize this will sound ridiculous," I started to explain, pointing behind me, when the door flung open and the dwarf let loose an animalistic snarl as he leaped upon the serving tables, blade in hand, and sped forward in a desperate bid to overtake me.

Anticipating his leaping upon me, I turned and flipped the nearest serving table up on its end and rammed it into the table behind it just as the dwarf reached it. Both tables collapsed in a tumult of shattering glass and smashed pottery. I bolted back the way I came in my effort to avoid the angry staff as they rushed to subdue me.

I had little hope that the dwarf would be down for long. The demonic imp would probably slaughter everyone in the restaurant coach before picking up my trail. As I passed through the outer door on the way back to my car, I felt the burst of night air upon me and came to a sudden halt. That was it! The opening between cars might afford me the only avenue of escape left to me.

Grasping the edges of the opening, I hauled myself out of the train and onto the top of the restaurant coach. I had seen this trick performed many times at the picture show. Sadly, the picture shows never took wind into account when staging daring stunts such as I had now foolishly attempted. The speed of the train made movement almost impossible. I clung to the side of the coach for dear life.

I held on tight, clueless as to how I was to proceed when I felt something hit my heel. Grimacing, I twisted my neck to look down and saw that hideous misshapen brown face staring up at me. The dwarf had found me and must have thrown his blade at my leg. Happily, the wind had spared me a crippling injury, but I now was faced with the challenge of having to press on, for there was still the matter of the poisoned knitting needle, at the very least, to consider.

Grasping the ridge on the top of the coach, I strained and felt the muscles in my arms pull uncomfortably taut as I struggled to hoist myself up. For one dizzying moment, the wind nearly knocked me backward before I managed to fling myself down hard upon the roof of the car.

The rush of wind against a speeding train is deafening. Absolutely nothing else can be heard. If I lived to survive this ordeal, I swore I'd write a letter to every studio mogul in Hollywood exposing them for the frauds they were, but at the moment, I had greater worries on my mind.

I twisted my head with great difficulty to look behind me. I could just see the dwarf's head and arms as he fought to gain the top of the car and reach me. Unexpectedly, the deafening rush increased until I thought I would go mad. The force from the wind made it almost impossible to hold on. I was aware of a light shining down upon me, but there was no way for me to turn and look up and ascertain its source.

I thought I heard two cracks above the roaring din and, the next thing I knew, an enormous shadow had covered me, nearly obscuring the mysterious light. I screwed my eyes shut tight as the noise and wind were overpowering. I believed this was the end and the rushing sound in my ears heralded my passing from this life to the next.

Then it abruptly ceased. There was still the wind assailing me, but its intensity and volume had decreased unexpectedly. Half fearing what I might find, I craned my neck to look up and my jaw dropped in amazement.

There, on the coach in front of me, was an autogyro. How it had come to rest atop the train, I could not fathom, but it was obvious the light and the rushing, deafening wind were caused by the vehicle's perilous descent. A man was stepping down from the front of the autogyro and half-crawled, half-scrambled his way to my side. Cautiously, I tried to rise. He held an arm out to hold me in place.

"Professor Knox?"

I nodded my head in amazement. All thought of my assumed identity was immediately forgotten.

"There's a dwarf...an assassin..." I stammered, shouting to be heard.

The man nodded.

"I took care of him. Not to worry. I doubt very much he survived the fall. At the risk of sounding rude, I suggest we continue this conversation inside."

He held out a hand. As I grasped it, I felt tears welling in my eyes. I had been spared. Not for the first time, forces seemed to intervene when I had no hope for survival. I was not a man who believed in miracles, but I began to wonder if Spiridon's patron saint hadn't come to my aid after all.

Hunched over, we scooted our way to the autogyro. I gazed in amazement at the machine as we made our way to the front. He climbed in the passenger side and clambered over behind the controls while I pulled myself in next to him and half collapsed in the seat, gazing frightfully at the rushing trees whirling past us as the train barreled along.

The man said not a word as the autogyro's engine roared to life. The cabin shook madly as the propellers built up speed. I thought my heart might burst as, jerking madly, we took to the night sky. A wave of nausea over-came me as I saw a stone tunnel roar beneath us and real-ized just how narrow our escape had been.

I glanced over at my rescuer. He was tall and thin. I was gladdened to recall from his speech that he was British as well. His hair was gray with streaks of white at the temples. His skin was tanned and healthy, and belied his age.

"What is this machine?"

He smiled, but did not make eye contact with me as he responded.

"It's a prototype of a new autogyro that Henrich Focke is developing. It represents a significant advance-ment upon the design of the Fw 61 and seats two...which is certainly fortunate for you."

"How did you get your hands on it?"

"You can thank the Crown for that. British Intelli-gence. Happily, Chancellor Hitler was agreeable and ap-proved our borrowing it or else you would already be a dead man, Professor."

"Chancellor...Hitler? Why me?"

The thin man laughed and I noticed for the first time that his eyes were an uncommonly clear blue, like the ocean on a sunny day. Somehow, the hawk-like nose and hard mouth had previously hid those strangely calming eyes. They immediately softened his otherwise severe features.

"The Si-Fan killed Professor Simos and you were next on the list. You have information that is vital to them. So vital that we can't afford to let you die. Hitler is no friend of the Si-Fan, so he was willing to support us. You don't honestly believe that I intercept the Orient Ex-press every day in this contraption, do you?"

"The Si-Fan?" I repeated. "I heard that name mentioned before. I don't understand any of this. Why should anyone want Spiridon dead...or me for that matter? Who are you anyway?"

For the first time, he held eye contact with me as he nodded in greeting.

"Forgive my lack of manners. Sir Denis Nayland Smith. British Intelligence. Once we set down in Budapest, and I work on getting you safely back on British soil, I'll fill you in on all that's been happening around you. I have to warn you, Professor, whether you like it or not, your life is never going to be the same again."

Good God, it was Sir Denis Nayland Smith. This was all I needed! Not that I wasn't grateful, but why him of all people? One thing was certain, I was in a mess and the best thing I could do was feign ignorance on all points.

As I looked down from the autogyro onto the darkened treetops below, I reflected that things couldn't possibly get any worse. Of course, in hindsight, I can honestly say that my run of bad luck had barely begun.

6. CONVERSATIONS WITH SIR DENIS

The morning sun had newly risen in the sky when Sir Denis and I were shown into Sir Patrick's unoccupied office at the British Legation in Budapest. The Minister was likely still asleep in bed in the residential portion of this grand building on the Varhegy in Mihaly Tancsics Street. Buda Castle was built on the southern tip of Castle Hill and Sir Patrick's office afforded an excellent view of the Danube.

"First off, Professor," Sir Denis began to restlessly pace almost as soon as Sir Patrick's secretary departed, "I need you to relate every detail, no matter how seemingly insignificant, leading up to the death of your colleague, Professor Spiridon Simos, in Corfu."

I puffed my cheeks out and sighed, realizing I was imitating that poor unfortunate conductor aboard the Orient Express in my desire to appear bewildered by what had occurred.

"Regrettably, there is precious little that I can add, Sir Denis. I arrived in Corfu just a few hours before Spiridon was killed. I had dinner with Spiridon and his fiancée, and one of her friends who was to serve as Matron of Honor. I was to be Spiridon's Best Man. After dinner, we went back to the hotel. Spiridon and I had a few drinks at the bar and the next thing I knew was the disturbance in the hallway the next morning when Spiridon had been found, murdered in his room. I believe Japanese thieves were responsible...at least, that was the speculation based on the peculiar weapons that were used to kill him. That's really all there is to tell."

Sir Denis stopped in his tracks and turned to glare at me with those intense eyes of his.

"Professor Knox, how do you think that I came to be aware of your plight?"

I struggled to think of a reply. Damn it, I had blundered already.

Sir Denis held up a hand.

"Don't bother. I will make you aware of certain facts that you could not possibly know. Greba Eltham and her late father were both very old friends of mine. Greba's employer is the oldest friend I have in this world. He is also Kara's husband. I know for a fact that you were aware of what occurred in Cairo to Dr. Petrie. Kara told you, along with Spiridon and Greba, when you arrived back at the hotel."

He paused just long enough for the point to sink home that he knew I was deliberately withholding information from him.

"You may possibly be aware that Kara was abducted sometime later that same night from the hotel. Greba discovered that she was missing and confronted her fiancé. She is alive today only because he attempted to shield her from the Si-Fan. You have seen what happened to him as a result. They have tried to kill you twice already. These people will not cease until they succeed. Do not imagine you are safe. They have the Petries, but you represent something else altogether. You either possess knowledge vital to their cause, or you were a witness to events they wish to keep secret. In either case, they will not halt their efforts to silence you. You have been fortunate to have lived this long. You would likely have died last night had Greba not put me on your trail."

"Where is Greba now?"

"She is safe...under the protection of British Intelligence."

"Will you do the same for me?"

He smacked his fist into his open palm.

"Your safety is predicated on your cooperation. Why did you flee, Professor? What do you know that made you turn tail and run when you saw Professor Simos' body?"

Oh God, I didn't know what to say. If I told him the truth, it could be worse for me in every way. Alternatively, if these people that had killed Spiridon and abducted Kara and her husband learned that I had revealed nothing to the authorities, they might determine that I posed no threat to their plans and need not be eliminated. If I did cooperate, my protection would surely be finite and the assassins would gain their revenge at some later date if they could not reach me now. That settled it. I would not fully cooperate. I would do my best to deceive wherever possible.

"You are correct, Sir Denis. I was aware of what had happened to Mrs. Petrie's husband. When I saw Professor Simos lying there, I panicked. I felt certain there was a connection between the two incidents and I'm afraid my nerves cracked. I'm not proud to admit the fact, but it is the truth."

Smith bent over the desk where I was seated and smacked his palm down upon it.

"Rubbish! You are still lying. Why would you connect what you described as a robbery and murder by Japanese thieves in Corfu with Petrie's abduction in Cairo? You know more than you are letting on. I cannot help you if you are not honest with me. Tell me about the dig you and Professor Simos were working on in Luxor."

Damn you, Spiridon, why did you have to open your

mouth about the dig? I thought. I knew the moment it came up that night at dinner that it would come to no good.

"I'm sorry, Sir Denis, but that is a confidential matter that I cannot disclose. I can, however, assure you that the dig has nothing whatsoever to do with this organization you mention."

That hawk-like nose was mere inches away from mine as he leant forward across the desk.

"You are in no position to judge the Si-Fan and their intentions. There is a connection. Professor Simos had some association with the Si-Fan. Greba learned that much from him only a short time before he was murdered. I am quite prepared to accept that you have been duped and have bitten off more than you can chew as a consequence, but I cannot help you unless you help me first. Again, I say to you, what is the nature of the dig in Luxor?"

I remained silent and forced myself to return his steely glare.

He broke away first and, straightening, sighed in frustration as his hand tore through his silver-streaked grey hair.

"Have you ever heard of Dr. Fu Manchu?"

I nearly laughed when I heard the name.

"Some sort of Chinese gangster, isn't he?"

He nodded in response.

"Something of the sort, yes. He is possessed of the most brilliant scientific mind our world has ever known. He is a genius and, in his own way, he is also a man of great integrity. That is not to say that his activities are not criminal, but rather that he is fighting for what he believes to be a just and noble cause."

He sat down across from me and pulled his pipe

from his jacket pocket and began stuffing it with tobacco as he spoke.

"I have spent my life fighting him. Thanks to perseverance and good fortune, I have survived this long despite being outmatched at nearly every juncture. Our war began nearly thirty years ago, although it sometimes seems as though time has stood still for us."

"Why do you tell me this? Does China have some involvement in this matter?"

Sir Denis lit his pipe and waved the match until the flame was extinguished.

"China is not the enemy, Professor Knox. They are but one tentacle of the Si-Fan. That venerable secret society claims members across the globe from the lowliest criminal classes all the way up to statesmen, doctors, barristers, amd even archaeologists, it would seem."

I leaned back in my chair and held his gaze.

"This sounds like some sort of Masonic business. What of it if Spiridon was involved with them? Is it illegal to join a secret society? I didn't take you for a hysterical old Papist, Sir Denis."

He smiled ruefully.

"I am not hysterical, I assure you. The Si-Fan's ambitions are many. They seek to undermine the British Empire and remove Western missionary as well as military presence in the East. They seek to abduct and coerce, through any means possible, the greatest scientific minds in the West to aid their cause. They seek to assassinate world leaders to shape the political landscape to best suit their own goals. You may find it hard to believe, but I recently saved both Chancellor Hitler and *il Duce* himself, Signor Mussolini, from assassination by the Si-Fan. This was merely the latest of many scores that Dr. Fu Manchu now has to settle with me."

"I'm not so certain that the world might not have been better off if you'd left well enough alone," I laughed.

"You're not the first person to make that suggestion and I daresay you won't be the last. By the way, I understand that Professor Simos was a member of the KKE."

I nodded in the affirmative.

"Yes, Spiridon was admittedly a Communist. The University had no difficulty with this. He certainly wasn't a dissident, if that's what you're suggesting. Of course, it's rather academic now that Greece's Prime Minister has banned all political parties. I'm afraid that Mr. Metataxas is a bit too eager to follow in Mussolini's footsteps. Apparently, his memory is spotty when it comes to recalling what that foul pig did to Corfu. That said, I can assure you that we would never have received clearance for the dig if there was even the slightest reason to doubt Spiridon's patriotism."

Sir Denis chuckled and shook his head.

"You must not have had much experience of secret societies, Professor, if you believe a man may not serve two masters. That is precisely the case with members of such groups until...one day...unexpectedly, they are forced to choose. That spells tragedy for anyone who is associated with these individuals, either socially or professionally. An aberrant behavior pattern that results in chaos and death, and it's all attributable to membership in the very secret societies you consider to be so harmless. Do you think such talk is far-fetched? I assure you that I speak the truth. Oh, the press may be counted upon to convince the public that such tragedies are an Act of God, or mere human error, or the sad results of a solitary disturbed individual who lost his nut, but once you've been around this business for as many years as I have, you begin to recognize the telltale signs. There are few accidents or coincidences in this world, Professor, and seemingly insane actions are usually carefully orchestrated down to the slightest detail."

He nodded knowingly to me as he puffed at his pipe. The man was a certifiable loony. Precious wonder he was friends with Sir Lionel Barton. Two peas in a pod and they were both as mad as hatters.

"All right, Sir Denis, supposing I accept what you say is fact. Why would this Dr. Fu Manchu of yours have any desire to kill Spiridon or to abduct the Petries? What is his motive?"

He smacked his palm down on the table once more in irritation.

"That's just it! That's why I must know about your dig in Luxor. It is the only possible link to explain this business. Don't you see how imperative it is that you trust me and confide in me?"

My mind was racing. What did I have to fear now that I had squandered most of the money to complete the dig in fleeing Corfu? He already knew the location. Surely, he would have contacted Sir Lionel by now. He would rely on his vast knowledge of Egypt to determine the significance of Luxor. Was he simply toying with me, or was Barton not the expert his reputation suggested?

"I don't understand...why would this secret society of yours be interested in a routine archaeological dig?"

Sir Denis slapped the desk again.

"We both know very well that routine is hardly an apt description of your dig in Luxor. Professor Simos was looking for something specific and knew where to find it...something that no one else seems to suspect even exists."

Ah, so Sir Lionel was in the dark about Luxor!

"Where did he get his information from, Professor?

Has it not occurred to you that this dig was arranged by the Si-Fan? What is their purpose? What do you expect to find?"

Now I was concerned. Spiridon had revealed that he had obtained the information from this Si-Fan organization, just as Sir Denis was suggesting. What if he had deceived me as to the real purpose of the dig? What if Spiridon had been the one who was deceived? Now that the dig was approved by the University, and Cairo had agreed to allow us to excavate, had Spiridon outlived his value to this group? I was beginning to let my imagination run wild as I considered the sobering thought that Sir Denis might be correct after all.

"I want to help you, Sir Denis, truly I do. I assure you that if I knew what you were looking for, I would tell you, but I cannot for the life of me answer any of your questions."

He didn't react badly this time; perhaps he was considering that I might be telling the truth for once. I resolved to press on.

"Here is my dilemma. I need funding to complete the dig. I was forced to spend most of what I had when I fled Corfu with those maniacs after me for goodness knows what reason. I have an idea...if British Intelligence can find a way of restoring my funds, you could come along and join the dig yourself, and then if you find anything of interest, you'll be on the spot to handle the situation as best you see fit."

He smirked a bit, looking like the cat that ate the canary.

"What a splendid idea, Professor. I'm sure you won't mind if I bring along two more to the party. Chap called Kerrigan who has proven quite useful to me recently, and an old friend of mine that you may already know, Sir

71

Lionel Barton."

I felt sick and suspected my face betrayed the same. Just when I thought things couldn't possibly get any worse. Sir Lionel Barton! Oh, Spiridon, what had I done?

7. PASSAGE TO AFRICA

"Don't mind Fey, Professor Knox, he's my valet. Been with me for years...I trust him with my life. That should tell you everything you need to know."

The tall silent olive-skinned figure stepped up the ramp leading to the open doors of the small aeroplane that Sir Patrick had arranged for Nayland Smith's use. We followed him into the cramped cabin and seated ourselves across the aisle from one another while Fey climbed into the cockpit. I pulled the seat's strap taut and buckled it as I watched the wing propeller kick into life outside my window.

My eyes screwed tight as the aeroplane lurched forward beneath the engine's roar. My heart rate began to decrease once we had climbed to a sufficient altitude and leveled off restoring a sense of normalcy inside the cabin.

Glancing across at my counterpart, I saw Sir Denis smiling at me in evident amusement. I looked around the otherwise empty cabin. My eyes turned toward the cockpit where Sir Denis' peculiar valet was visible in the pilot's chair. I could not hazard a guess as to the man's nationality and that disturbed me greatly. How a man such as Nayland Smith could trust his life to a foreigner was utterly beyond me.

"We have not yet identified the Greek assassin shot dead in the back of the taxi cab. I don't suppose you were aware of his name?"

I swallowed hard as I recalled the unpleasantness of the details surrounding the incident.

"Neapolis...his name was Neapolis. I did not know his first name."

Sir Denis nodded grimly and jotted the name down in a small notebook resting in his lap before continuing. "What about the assassin on the train? A dwarf, I believe you said."

I felt a wave of nausea roll over me and knew our altitude would only make things worse if I did not succeed in putting it out of my mind.

"That's right. It was a dwarf disguised as a little girl called Margarita, who was posing as the daughter of a woman who..."

I stopped myself too late. Sir Denis' eyes were staring at me intently.

"Go on, Professor. Tell me all about this woman on board the train with the dwarf posing as her daughter."

I sighed and launched into my explanation with a sense of encroaching doom.

"She said her name was Helga Graumann and she was quite simply the most exquisitely beautiful woman I have ever seen. She stepped into my berth and claimed that the rail had inadvertently placed us in the same compartment. It was a mistake obviously, but I was not about to let her slip away. We chatted for a bit, not for very long I am afraid, before I...well, I am rather embarrassed to admit the fact, but I fell asleep and when I awoke, she was gone. Terribly rude of me I know. The damndest thing was, when I did find her on the train...I went looking for her, you see...she claimed not to know me and that her name was emphatically not Helga Graumann. She had a little girl with her...her daughter...except, of course, she was not anything of the sort...I mean he, not she! Oh, I do not know what is right and what is wrong, Sir Denis. All of this is absolutely mad."

He could barely manage to contain himself in his seat.

"Describe this woman to me. Do not leave out any detail no matter how trivial it may seem."

I leaned back in my seat and pictured her.

"Full red lips...a perfectly sculpted face...jet black hair. She was the very image of some alabaster goddess from the classical world."

"You say you fell asleep whilst she was with you. This is extremely important, Professor, so please answer truthfully. Did you experience any queer dreams while you slept? Again, I beseech you to omit no details, however slight they may be."

My face reddened at the memory.

"I dreamt that I was making love to her. I cannot explain how this came to happen, but we were in my sleeping compartment together. It was wonderful...like nothing else I have ever experienced. She...she knew my name..."

"Well, I should certainly hope so!"

"No, you don't understand. I was using a false name when I boarded the Orient Express."

"...and she knew your real name...in your dream?"

"Correct. What is more, she was asking me questions."

"What sort of questions?"

"Personal questions."

"Questions about the dig in Luxor, perhaps?"

I swallowed hard and nodded my head.

"I thought as much. Tell me, Professor...by chance, did Miss Graumann light a cigarette before you fell asleep?"

I felt the hair on the back of my neck rise.

"Yes, but how did you possibly guess?"

Sir Denis smiled sympathetically.

"I would hazard to say that your Miss Graumann would also answer to the name of Koreani."

"Koreani?"

"When I first met her many years ago, she was called Fah lo Suee. Like her father, I never knew her true name."

"Her father?"

"She is the daughter of Fu Manchu and you may count your blessings that I rescued you in time. Any assassin traveling with her is certainly among the deadliest that the Si-Fan employs."

My mind was reeling as I tried to take in all that I had heard.

"This is fantastic. Why would I have attracted the attention of these people? I swear to you that there is nothing in Luxor of interest to anyone but a student of the past."

Sir Denis stared at me and I wondered if he suspected that I was still lying.

"Perhaps there is more to the site than you suspect. Something bound Professor Simos to the Si-Fan. They led him to the site for a purpose, whether it was one understood by you or not. However, there is another possibility that we may have overlooked..."

I raised an eyebrow as I waited for him to elaborate.

"There may be something in your background that is of interest to the Si-Fan."

I sputtered speechlessly and raised my hands in exasperation.

"Do not trouble yourself trying to recall, Professor. We already have an idea of what this may be about."

My eyes widened in disbelief.

"You have been investigating my background?"

Sir Denis smiled once more and I began to gather that I was playing into his hands just as he had intended.

"Indirectly, as it happens. It was your sister who first came to our attention when Sir Lionel Barton met her in Abyssinia several months ago."

"My sister!"

I had not seen Anna in years. The thought of her mixed up with Sir Lionel made me ill.

"You don't understand about my sister, Sir Denis..."

"I understand that she's a brilliant zoologist," he shrugged.

"Yes, but she's also..."

"Oh, I know, she's a bit eccentric. She would have to be if Sir Lionel is smitten with her. I understand that he's also rather fond of Monkey."

"Monkey?"

"Yes, Monkey is her constant companion. Apparently Sir Lionel is the only other person allowed to touch her...Monkey, I mean."

"Yes, well thank Heavens you clarified that. Monkey!" I shook my head in disbelief. "I can just imagine what Anna must be like these days."

"We will pick up Barton and your sister before continuing on to Cairo to meet up with Kerrigan before the lot of us head to Luxor."

"Hang on a tick! No one said anything about dragging my sister along on this expedition!"

Sir Denis' face betrayed none of the guile that I knew was lurking beneath his sincere expression.

"Well, we can't very well leave her to her own devices. She has already survived several assassination attempts on her own life. "

"What?"

Sir Denis nodded.

"I'm afraid so, Professor. It seems that the Si-Fan has reason to hold you both in contempt. Now perhaps you understand why I was reluctant to trust your word when you told me that you had no idea why the Si-Fan took notice of you in the first place. He who tells falsehoods is fated to come a cropper. Pity you didn't learn that lesson as a boy."

Yes, I thought, *a pity indeed that I failed to learn that lesson and many others beside, it would seem.*

8. STRANDED IN THE JUNGLE

Remaining seated as the aeroplane came to a rough landing amid the heavy foliage that surrounded General Quinto's private airfield was a nerve-wracking experience. I was grateful that the airfield had outlasted the General, but I feared the aeroplane would tear apart from the force of the heavy branches that scraped past the window at the front. Fey hung onto the wheel for dear life while Sir Denis and I watched the branches rip past the windows to the right and left of us.

My knuckles were white as they gripped the arm of my seat. It was several seconds before it dawned upon me that the engine had stopped and the wing propellers had ceased to revolve. I glanced at Sir Denis and managed a weak smile.

"Perhaps not the way that the University would prefer that you travel, Professor, but we got you here in one piece all the same."

He stood up and made his way toward the cabin where Fey was climbing out of the pilot's seat and turning in our direction. Smith said something quietly to him, but I could not make out the words clearly enough to be certain what language he was speaking. For his part, Fey only nodded his head and pulled his cap down closer to the bridge of his nose. The man made a point of never making eye contact with me. I found him terribly unsettling.

Fey swung the thick metal door open and a breath of heavy humid air struck me instantly. The cawing of birds and the buzzing of insects drowned out the silence of the hollow aeroplane.

"So this is Italian East Africa," I said looking around from the doorway.

"Here," Sir Denis said as he handed me a rifle. "You may have need of this yet."

He and Fey pushed past me to lower the ladder to allow us to clamper down from the aeroplane. A few seconds later and the three of us were on the ground, rifles held at ready as we looked expectantly toward the surrounding jungle. Fey removed a battered and creased map from the satchel that hung round his right shoulder and handed it to Sir Denis.

Smith unfolded the map and studied it for a bit. Squinting, he stared off in the distance with a hand held above his eyes to protect them from the sun. I could see nothing but trees and grass no matter which direction we faced. I could not imagine what he was expecting to find.

"There. We head that way. That should be the path that leads to Barton and your sister."

I was surprised there were no soldiers to greet our arrival and said as much to Sir Denis.

He shook his head. "The Governor wouldn't risk sending his troops out here. The locals are no friends of Victor Emmanuel. Their loyalty lies with Halie Selassie."

I thought of Anna living among such people. Sir Denis appeared to read my mind.

"Your sister is safe enough from his followers. From what Sir Lionel tells me, she is given a wide berth by the natives."

I wondered at such a thought. When last I had seen Anna, she was still at school. She was so like our mother in every way; she disapproved of nearly everything about me while, at the same time, behaving in the most singular fashion herself. Her behavior attracted attention wherever she went, yet she seemed to pay others no mind.

We were not compatible as siblings, and I had no desire to be henpecked by a sister three years my junior, so I made no effort to keep in contact with her. After a year or two, the letters stopped and, quite honestly, I had let the memory of her die in my mind, along with everything else from my past. The world provided history enough to pour over and of far greater import than my own life.

A zoologist...that was no surprise, I supposed. Still, I wondered what she was like these days. Once, when we were both very young, she had meant nearly everything to me, but time changes all things and we had proved no exception.

Presently, Sir Denis and Fey finished pushing through the dense foliage and a clearing appeared containing a simple granite structure with a few windows and an open doorway not fifty yards from where we stood.

"This should be it," Sir Denis spoke in hushed tones. "Keep your rifles at ready in case we run into any trouble."

I wished the incessant trilling and buzzing around us would cease. It was nigh on impossible to concentrate on anything else as we approached the crude building. Nervously, I watched the windows and doorway for some sign of activity, fearing a shot would ring out before we had time to react.

We reached the doorway without incident. Sir Denis poked his head in and glanced quickly around before stepping inside.

"It appears to be empty," he said in hushed tones.

As Fey and I stepped through the doorway, Sir Denis motioned with his rifle for the three of us to separate and explore the house. There was a table and a counter, but the rest of the large room that comprised the first floor was overflowing with heaping piles of papers, trinkets, books, maps, and God knows what else. It looked as if someone had raided a library and strewn its contents haphazardly about the room with no thought of whether they were at risk from exposure to the elements.

Fey climbed the creaking staircase to the second floor. Nothing had been visible from the two windows when we had approached, and I was beginning to suspect that whoever had been living here had hastily abandoned the house.

That was when we heard the sound of a terrible commotion, as if a heavy weight had fallen across the floor. There was a ghastly scream and, before anything else could register, I saw Sir Denis bounding up the stairs. Hurriedly, I followed him, ready for whatever terrible scene might greet our eyes...except for the actual horror that the room held.

Fey was fighting for his life. The torn shirt hung in shreds from his arms and chest like ripped flesh. He wrestled to break free from the hulking bestial form that filled much of the room. My mind was trying to block out all else, and it was a palpable effort to concentrate and recognize what it was that Fey was struggling to overcome.

It was the towering form of a gorilla. That monstrous mockery of a human being, whose very presence here, in this house, made acceptance of reality so challenging, was the creature that now gripped Fey like a child holding a doll. Saliva dripped from its bared fangs. Muscles rippled in those obscenely long arms. The beast pulled Fey's arms backwards until I felt certain his spine was about to crack. Sir Denis lifted the rifle to his shoulder and took aim.

"Monkey, no!"

The voice rang out and, at last, silence fell. The gorilla released its hold on Fey and the poor man slumped forward, nearly unconscious. The beast's entire demeanor changed to one of sedate calmness as if it were actually tame.

I rushed to Fey's side and helped him to regain his feet. Again, I found myself struggling to focus and forced myself to recognize the next threat to reality in the room. Stepping forward to the gorilla's side was a woman. She was pretty, with dark brown hair pulled back behind her head, and deep red lips dominating fair features that had somehow avoided the punishing jungle sun. She was dressed in a man's safari uniform and wore a fedora upon her head. Only the glasses, resting delicately on her nose, looked decidedly feminine. It actually took me several seconds before I recognized her.

"Anna," I cried in amazement.

"Hello, Michael," she said matter-of-factly. "I see you shaved your head. I must say that I do not like it...or the beard, for that matter. They make you look like an old man."

She stroked the gorilla's arm and turned her full attention to the savage beast, cooing at it quietly and acting as if seeing me after all this time, was the most normal state of affairs imaginable.

Sir Denis lowered his rifle and turned towards me.

83

"Your sister, I presume?"

"Forgive me. Anna, this is Sir Denis Nayland Smith. Sir Denis, this is Anna Knox."

"That's *Professor* Anna Knox. You aren't the only one who went to school, Michael," she flashed the briefest of smiles and patted the gorilla on the arm. "This is Monkey."

"You call that a monkey?" I snapped.

"Hush," she scolded, "you'll hurt her feelings."

"Her feelings?"

"Yes, her. You have two perfectly good eyes, Michael. Use them. Poachers killed her mother when she was an infant. She has been with me for over eight years now. She is perfectly tame, but very protective. I am sorry about your friend, but he should not have blundered up here unannounced. Lionel is terribly weak and Monkey was only trying to protect us in case you were sent by the Viceroy."

"Sir Lionel Barton is here?" I asked, incredulously.

"Of course, you don't think that I would let him leave in his present condition, do you?"

"I've never known anyone able to prevent Sir Lionel from doing exactly what he pleases," Smith chuckled.

"Oh, fiddlesticks," Anna's brow furrowed as if she were cross with Sir Denis because of the remark, "his bark is worse than his bite. The old bully only needs someone to stand up to him. The trouble is so few people are willing to try. Follow me and I'll take you to him."

As she turned toward the back of the house, the gorilla twisted its gargantuan frame and followed her, leaning forward and using its long arms to swing its mighty body forward to follow in Anna's wake.

Supporting Fey's sagging form between us, Smith and I followed at a safe distance.

"Your sister is quite a girl," Sir Denis smiled, wryly.

"You have no idea," I replied.

In truth, I realized that I had no idea either. We were strangers to one another and I felt a pang of guilt for having severed our relationship. We had been so close once...twins separated by three years our father used to tell us. That had all changed ever since...I did not want to dwell on the past anymore.

Presently, we reached the cramped backroom of the second floor of the house where Sir Lionel rested upon a bed in a darkened room with no windows to illuminate it. Anna and that massive gorilla she insisted on treating as a pet stood on the right side of the bed. She looked down at Sir Lionel with concern.

His eyes opened as Smith and I approached, supporting Fey between us. He stared up at the ceiling above him as if determined to ignore his visitors. Sir Lionel breathed laboriously through his mouth. While watching his chest rise and fall, I noted that his ribs had been heavily bandaged, which hampered his breathing greatly.

"What happened to him?"

"He was attacked while returning from the village. He had gone there to send you a telegram. I'm sure that you appreciate the fact that we cannot operate a wireless from here."

"Was it the Si-Fan?" Sir Denis asked.

Anna shrugged.

"It's possible, I suppose, but he will not speak of it. One of the natives that come round regularly to peddle vegetables found him in an alleyway. He was lying in a puddle of blood. They had left him to die, but Lionel is a tough old bird. He'll pull through, won't you, darling?"

Sir Lionel's head moved almost imperceptibly and his eyes came to rest on Smith. He flinched as if to convey some sort of meaning. It was clear that he was struggling to speak. Anna reached a hand out to calm him.

"Please, don't strain yourself, my dear. Sir Denis, I may have to ask you to leave the room if he will not calm down. I can give him something to make him relax if need be, but we must conserve our supplies, for I cannot be certain when we will be able to replenish them."

"I understand," Smith replied, nodding his head. "We may be able to transport him to a proper hospital in Cairo once Fey is back on his feet."

Sir Lionel shook his head vociferously to indicate his disapproval of the idea.

"There's your answer," Anna said, gesturing toward Sir Lionel.

"Barton, be reasonable, please. If we leave you here, you are in grave danger." Smith was earnest in his appeal. "Cairo has facilities where you would be comfortable and well cared for. Weymouth could arrange for a round the clock guard to be posted."

Unexpectedly, the gorilla went into a rage, snarling and throwing its heavy arms about, smacking into Sir Lionel's bed in the process. At the time, I thought it was in reaction to Sir Denis' behavior, but Anna quickly explained.

"It's the Abyssinians! They're back."

The gorilla had obviously detected the sound first and Anna was used to trusting its acute hearing. She rushed from the room with the agitated gorilla following close behind her. The entire incident was starting to take on the quality of a nightmare. Smith had maneuvered Fey into a chair that rested against the wall just a short distance from Sir Lionel's bed. The two of them were speaking in hushed tones.

"This is madness," I exclaimed. "Here we are surrounded by a bloody bunch of savages with two of our party injured. We may as well surrender now."

Sir Denis spun and shot me a deadly look of warning.

"Your sister has managed to hold the natives off by herself while trying to nurse Barton back to health. Try and live in the moment and perhaps you'll find that life is somewhat easier to survive when one actually puts forth an effort."

Suitably chastened, I followed his rapid gait out of the room and into the main area where Anna was peering out the edge of a window. I approached as near as I dared and saw down below a group of perhaps two dozen black men gathered outside of the house.

I had imagined the Abyssinians to be an unruly mob of barbaric cannibals, but I was severely mistaken. The group below were dressed in pants and shirts. They stood armed with rifles rather than *assegais*. There were no shields bedecked with colorful representations of their pagan deities. One of the black men stepped forward and, to my surprise, he addressed Anna in thickly accented English.

"We return, missy. Will you give us the man, Barton? Our master's patience grows thin. Soon we will have no choice but to take him by force. We would rather have you see reason and give him up willingly. I promise no harm will come to you if you capitulate."

Anna turned toward Sir Denis and whispered: "He gives the same speech every day. It is growing rather tiresome."

The gorilla's lips curled in a menacing growl as she looked down at the man shouting up to her mistress.

"We know you have company, missy. We saw the aeroplane land. We have left men to guard it. There will be no escape by air for you. You and your friends are stranded here until we consent to let you go."

Anna kept staring down at their leader while quietly hissing a response to Sir Denis: "So much for your plan to get us to Cairo."

Smith stepped forward to the window and addressed the men:

"There are many of us and we are heavily armed, with more friends coming to join us soon. If you do not disperse at once, or cease your attempts to hinder our departure, I promise you that the casualties will be high on your side, if indeed any of you survive the conflict at all. You have no business with us, so go now while you still can."

There was a murmur of anger through the crowd at Sir Denis' appearance at the window. I suspected the majority did not speak English, but they certainly understood that Smith's answer did not constitute an agreement to the terms their chief had proposed.

Their leader's brow furrowed. "We have no quarrel with you. We require the man Barton to take to Luxor. We have no wish to harm any of you. Even he will return...provided he cooperates."

"Precious little chance of that," Smith muttered under his breath.

I looked at Anna and the woman my younger sister had become. I thought of Sir Denis' words and tried not to think about the gorilla that stood among us as if it were a person. I stepped forward to the window and leaned out, resting my arms upon the sill.

"I am Professor Knox. The excavation of the High Priests of Thebes' burial chamber at Luxor is my responsibility to lead. Your master will doubtless know of me. Leave these people in peace. I shall accompany you willingly."

"Knox, what are you saying?" Smith hissed at me, laying a firm grip upon my shoulder.

"Michael, no!"

It was the first time in years that Anna showed me any feeling approaching concern. I did not wish to ruin it by saying anything more. If I were to meet my death, I would do it bravely, knowing that my sacrifice had spared the lives of those who were my betters. Thus far, my own hand had brought down everything that had come upon me, whether directly or indirectly. It was time that I took responsibility for my actions.

For the first time in my life, I would face my fate like a man.

9. THE DEMON'S TOUCH

Once I stepped outside into the clearing, I realized that it had all been a dreadful mistake. I had handed my rifle to Sir Denis mere moments before, and had just surrendered myself over to a group of armed Abyssinians. My eyes sought for their leader, the one who spoke English. Instinctively, I felt I would be safest if I stayed in his close proximity.

As I approached, two of the Africans converged to block my path. They thoroughly searched me for any weapons I might have concealed on my person. Satisfied that I posed no threat to their leader, they stepped aside and allowed me to approach him.

"You go to Luxor. No tricks, Englishman, or you die."

The chief gestured at my face with the butt of his rifle.

I gave my assent and followed him as he turned to lead the way. Two of the Abyssinians walked alongside me, while two others were following so close behind that I could feel their breath upon the back of my neck as we walked.

We made our way through the foliage until we had returned to General Quinto's private airfield. A second aeroplane had landed not more than 150 feet from the one that had brought us to this God-forsaken jungle. There was a small band of Orientals gathered in front of the second aeroplane. They were dressed identically in black robes with bright crimson bandanas tied around their heads. Their bodies were muscular and agile, and their identical dress suggested that they trained together as a group for some common cause.

My mind turned to those dreadful *shuriken* devices that had killed poor Spiridon. I wondered if they carried the same implements for death. After a few moments of tense staring in our direction, they seemed to reach some sort of conclusion about us and they parted.

That was when I saw her.

At first, I did not recognize her. I simply was awestruck by the exotic beauty standing before me. She wore an ornate headdress of a fashion I had never before seen. Bejeweled bracelets and armlets covered her soft skin. Long hoops hung from her earlobes that glistened in the sunlight. Loose bits of gossamer that somehow clung in defiance of all gravity from her breasts and hips were all that covered her modesty. She was a goddess and when at last she spoke, I recognized her as the woman I knew aboard the Orient Express as Helga Graumann.

"You may allow Professor Knox to approach me," she said imperiously.

I turned and noticed that the Abyssinians had prostrated themselves before her as if she were royalty of some sort.

I stepped forward with some degree of trepidation. How was I to address her? I was not even sure of her true name. What sort of treatment should I expect from her this time?

She fanned herself languorously as she watched me approach beneath heavy-lidded eyes.

"Good day to you, Professor. I am glad to see that you sustained no serious injury aboard the Orient Express. I did so fear that Margarita would deprive me of your future company."

She pronounced the name with a mocking emphasis.

"So you do know me!" I exclaimed in disbelief.

I had not time to register her reaction before one of the Oriental men stepped forward and dealt me a smashing blow to the side of my head that literally knocked me to the ground. My ears were ringing for a moment as I fought to remain conscious.

Two of the Orientals grabbed me roughly by the arms and, hauling me to my feet, brought me to stand before her.

Her thin, delicate hand reached out and roughly grabbed my chin and twisted my face upward toward hers.

"I do not know you yet, Professor, but very soon I shall."

She twisted my head to the left and shoved me backwards as she turned and, with but a few short steps, climbed the ramp up into the aeroplane.

She left me to ponder the meaning of her words as I was trundled up the ramp behind her and thrown roughly to the floor in the back of the cabin. They bound my arms and legs tightly with heavy rope. Any attempt to struggle would have been futile.

Despair overtook me. As the aeroplane's engine kicked to life, and the buzzing of the propellers drowned out all other sounds, I felt as is my consciousness had separated from my mind. The relief provided by this astral severance proved to be short-lived. As the aeroplane rolled forward and lurched off the ground, my stomach emptied its contents on the floor in front of me.

I was unable to move as gravity sent the refuse back toward me as the aeroplane climbed toward the Heavens.

I lay there in my humiliation until the aeroplane leveled off and two of the Oriental men made their way back to check on me. They laughed vulgarly upon seeing my unfortunate predicament.

"Silence!"

Their laughter ceased and they stepped aside to allow Helga Graumann to approach and look down upon me. Her face betrayed no emotion whatsoever as she beheld my sorry plight.

"Get him cleaned up!"

She turned and stalked back to the front of the cabin. The Orientals went away for a short time and then returned with several wet cloths. They placed the towels upon the floor nearby as they bent down and lifted me upright. One of them brandished a sharp blade. I gasped as he brought the blade down quickly in long arcing sweeps along each shirtsleeve and then down each side of my shirt.

The man was a professional with the blade for, in little time at all, they were pulling the shreds of my clothing free. The sharp blade he held firmly in his right hand had not left a single scratch upon my person. The wet towels felt rough against my mouth and the skin of my neck, arm, and chest as they made quick work of cleaning me as their mistress had directed.

I was helpless as a child and felt like a shadow of a man as they hoisted my arms above my head and shackled my outstretched wrists to a metal bar that hung just out of range of my sight, straining my head toward the ceiling of the aeroplane. Shackles affixed my ankles to a plate at the base of the wall.

Satisfied with their work, the Orientals stood aside at full attention awaiting further instructions. Presently, Helga came to check on their progress. She smiled lasciviously as she looked me over from head to toe. For the first time, I was aware that I was stripped of both my dignity and my clothing.

"There, that is much better," she cooed at me as if I were an overtaxed child needing motherly affection before falling into a fitful sleep. "Bring me the box," she said, snapping her fingers irritably.

Presently, one of the Orientals returned with a metal box, perhaps eight inches long and three inches high. This he handed to her. She seemed to study it with some interest before releasing the small catches on each of the corners and unfolding it into sections until it had virtually tripled in length and width.

She placed this strange puzzle box around my waist gingerly, as if she were dressing an infant in a diaper. I shut my eyes in humiliation and tried not to notice the warmth of her breath upon my stomach. She was looking up at my face, but I averted my eyes, lest I should see her and react as a man to the nearness of her body.

The box snapped shut as she fastened each of the clasps on its four corners. I glanced down and saw the rectangular box had locked in place about my waist and around each leg. There was a locking mechanism on the front of it and I watched, squirming with extreme discomfort, as she twisted the lock clockwise two full rotations.

"There is a spring release contained within that is activated by tensile movements," she said, looking up at me and smiling. "The intent of the design is to release the tension, should the contents of the box place stress upon its constraints. However, the locking mechanism that I have just activated is a modification of the original design that counteracts this operation, so that the opposite reaction is produced by stress."

"What does that mean?" I asked in a hoarse whisper.

She smiled again as if explaining something very pleasant and very simple to a tot.

"It means, my dear Professor Knox, that unless you remain quite still, the spring mechanism will tighten as the length and width of the box recede in direct proportion to your movements. Do you understand my meaning?"

I managed a short humorless laugh in the face of this latest development.

"I am strung up by my arms and my ankles are likewise bound. I shouldn't think that there is much fear of my tensing my muscles any time soon."

She sucked on her lower lip as if she found my demeanor to be displeasing.

"Oh, you do make me sad. I thought we were going to have such fun together."

As she pronounced the word "fun," she slowly etched a circle around my right nipple with the nail of her forefinger.

My breath caught in my throat in harsh reaction to her touch. There was a ticking sound like a metronome and the spring within the metal box began to recede. I was immediately aware of my pinched flesh. I winced in pain. Several more ticks followed and, along with them, came even greater discomfort.

That musical laughter, so like an innocent child at play, rang in my ears.

"You see! I knew you would not disappoint me. Let's try again!"

This time, she leaned forward and extended her tongue just slightly between her teeth—just enough to moisten the circle her finger had traced on my chest. Then she grasped my ribs roughly between both her hands and bit hard on my tender flesh.

I let loose an anguished cry at the pain she inflicted and the even worse torture that followed that damnable ticking sound.

"Please, no more! I beg you!" I pleaded.

She laughed and hugged me, leaning her cheek against my abdomen.

"Why, Professor! You surprise me! We have hardly even begun to play!"

I shook my head vigorously from one side to the other.

"No, please! No more! I'll tell you everything I know about the Theban Necropolis."

Her laughter stopped instantly and she gazed up into my eyes with the hungry look of a tiger.

"I'm afraid you don't understand this game at all, Professor. The object is not so much to see what you are willing to tell me as it is to insure that you are unable to repeat what you know to anyone else after I finish with you."

Her lips twisted into a contemptuous sneer as she reached for the lock with her left hand and turned it clockwise two more times.

A terrible scream tore from my throat as I slipped away into darkness.

Time had passed. I was in terrible pain, but my torture had ended. My arms and legs were free. I was lying somewhere, bent and broken and covered in sweat. Everything hurt. Every breath was a new pain wracking my bruised and battered body. I was no longer in the aeroplane. I was on solid ground again. I did not hear the sounds of the jungle, but it was dark and I could not determine my location. The awful torture I had endured from that witch had doubtless impaired my senses.

"Michael! Oh, my poor Michael, what have they done to you?"

My mouth hung open as I fought to remain conscious.

It was Anna! She had found me at last! Thank God! O, Thank God! I needed family. I needed someone who knew me, the real me, not the failed man that I had become. I needed someone who cared. The punishment for my sins had been brutal, and I needed to know whether anyone cared enough to find out if I would heal, or whether I would languish and die in torment.

I saw Anna as she knelt before me, brushing the dark brown hair from her eyes. For the first time, I realized how little she had changed over the years. She was still beautiful. It was easy to overlook that fact because she was my sister, but also because it was her nature to be as unaware of herself as she was of others. Her only concern was for animals, and yet here she was, tending to my wounds just as our mother would have done all those years ago.

"I am sorry, Michael, but this is going to hurt," she said as she rubbed an ointment into my wounds. "Tell me about the dig in Luxor."

"The dig?" I repeated the words, shakily.

"The Theban Necropolis, of course. Tell me all there is to know. It will help keep your mind off the pain while I tend to your wounds."

I did not once consider that I was violating any confidence by doing as she bid. Anna was my sister. I would trust her unto the end of time.

"Spiridon found the Theban Necropolis. It exists in Luxor."

"Who is Spiridon?" she asked.

"Spiridon Simos, the archaeologist who helped me find a teaching job at the University of Athens after Christ College washed their hands of me."

"You lost your position at Christ College?"

I shut my eyes to block out the memory.

"Conduct unbecoming a professor, they said. It was doubly worse that I was an alumnus, I suppose. They were right, of course. I should have known better."

"Was she worth it?"

Anna's question held a note of mockery that was uncharacteristic of her. It stopped me in my tracks and made me actually reflect on the question.

"They're never worth it, Anna. Women are just a way for me to drown out the memories. It is no different than men who drink to excess."

"I have known many uses for copulation, but I must admit that I have never considered its effectiveness as a palliative."

Her bluntness was jarring, but I tried to remind myself that my sister was no longer a child. What is more, she was a child who had known the same terror as me. It was only reasonable, if somewhat disquieting, to consider that her experiences had been similar to mine. Perhaps the truest sign of maturity was recognizing the similarities one held in common with those who once engendered such intense feelings of estrangement.

"Spiridon Simos was a well respected Professor of Archaeology at the University of Athens. He exerted considerable influence in convincing the University to bring me on board and offer me a position. Several months ago, he claimed to have deciphered some ancient runes indicating a hitherto undiscovered Theban Necropolis buried at Luxor. The significance of which could serve to overturn all that was accepted as fact concerning Ancient Egypt."

"What was the significance of this Necropolis?"

She had ceased mending me, but I was not concerned. I felt overcome with the fever of having shared my secret knowledge with someone I could trust at last. The many months of silence had finally broken like a draught ending at last in a glorious downpour.

"The runes pointed to an unknown religion practiced only by the Pharaohs. The Pharaohs kept the Egyptian people deliberately in the dark with their pantheistic belief systems, the sole purpose of which was to control the people and keep them from suspecting the truth."

"What was this truth?"

"That the Pharaohs belonged to an order of elect scholars who practiced a form of black magic that enabled them to shape world events on a mass scale."

"That is utter rubbish," she laughed derisively.

"I know it sounds like it and Spiridon was reluctant to share the runes with me, but I saw the proof that he was correct."

"What proof did you see?"

"Our initial dig brought forth the ruins of a temple of Anubis and further penetration showed an older subterranean structure directly beneath it. That is where the Theban Necropolis lies. That is what I am going to unearth that will finally allow me to regain a position of respect and authority within the field."

Anna shook her head in dismay.

"Your only proof is that there is another structure further beneath the ground that the newer structure was built upon. That is not so amazing. You have no reason to suspect there is anything to your friend's fairy tales."

I reached out a hand and grasped her arm.

"My proof lies in the fact that this damn secret society murdered Spiridon, kidnapped a close friend of his fiancée and made two attempts on my own life. It is reasonable to conclude that these people are taking his claims quite seriously."

"Why should they?"

"The night before he died, Spiridon confided in me that he never translated the runes to uncover this secret knowledge, but rather that the knowledge was revealed to him by a high-ranking member of this same secret society. They wanted him to uncover the Theban Necropolis for them."

"Then why did they kill him? None of this makes the slightest bit of sense, Michael."

"I have given it a great deal of thought and I believe it actually is quite logical."

"Well I would certainly be interested in hearing how you think you've sorted it all out."

"Thanks to Spiridon's intervention, the University of Athens was able to obtain Cairo's permission for the dig at Luxor to occur. He told neither the University nor Cairo anything remotely close to the truth concerning the real reason for the dig. Once he had set everything up, including hiring the crew for the excavation, Spiridon was suddenly not only expendable to these people, but his removal was now highly desirable. Had I kept a civil tongue in my head when Spiridon and I were drinking in the hotel bar the same night he was murdered, I might not have attracted their attention. Not only may I have precipitated Spiridon's murder, but they now have reason to suspect that I learned the truth from Spiridon, and therefore believe that I constitute a direct threat to their activities."

"Why should this secret society of yours care about the Theban Necropolis in the first place?"

"That is the simplest part of the entire puzzle, Anna," I replied. "The secret society is part of the same elect group of scholars that directed Egypt's rise to greatness three thousand years ago."

I paused for a moment as she stared at me with a queer look upon her face.

"Do you know what I just realized, Michael? I realized that you are nowhere near as stupid as one would suspect, judging only by first impressions. Sadly, that also means that I cannot afford for you to fall into Milagro's hands."

I was about to ask who this Milagro person was, when I was struck by how very different Anna suddenly appeared to me. It was as if a veil was lifted from my eyes, and I now saw her for the first time. Her hair was jet black, her eyes shone like emeralds, high cheekbones tapered into full, sensuous lips and her proud chin suggested a regal bearing. Her skin was dusky, but the shape of her eyes betrayed a trace of Oriental heritage. This was not to my sister that I had revealed my secrets, but to Helga Graumann instead! I was still a captive in the aeroplane. They must have drugged me at some point.

"You...you tricked me, you witch!"

She clicked her tongue at me and set her face in a pout.

"No, no, no, no, Professor. I would never do such a thing. You must believe me."

She leaned close until her lips were almost touching mine. Icy hands pressed against my chest and slithered down my torso. Once, my desire for her would have overwhelmed me, but I could conjure no passion for this demon's touch. I shut my eyes and tried to let the moment pass. Any pleasure given me now was surely a precursor to greater pain once the aeroplane reached its destination.

10. DAUGHTER OF THE DRAGON

My eyes opened to sunlight streaming in through the windows of the aeroplane even to the rear of the craft where I lay bound and helpless. We must have been near Luxor. What fate would await me now that I had revealed all there was to tell about the dig?

Presently, Helga made her way to the back of the craft. She carried a small black case in her hands. Her hips swayed gracefully as she walked. The smile that played upon her lips made it evident that she was aware of the lust that burned in my crippled and injured frame for her, despite all she had done to me.

She knelt down before me, opened the case and removed a needle.

"Do not worry, Professor Knox. It is not an opiate this time. There is no need for such drastic measures now."

"You're going to kill me, aren't you?"

She looked into my eyes and laughed delightedly at my earnestness.

"Of course, we are not going to kill you, Professor. We are not barbarians. You have much important work to accomplish in the coming years...under the proper guidance and influence, of course. Soon, you shall meet your new master and your perspective will change. You will not find your new station in life unpleasant."

She plunged the point of the needle into my forearm.

"This will prevent you from speaking or struggling when it is inadvisable. You will remain conscious, but will suffer from a temporary paralysis. All motor activity will cease. Do not fear. The drug will last only a short time."

It was as she said. Almost immediately, I was aware of a numbing sensation spreading rapidly throughout my body. She smiled in satisfaction at my condition.

"You will receive perhaps some psychological comfort from the fact that it will no longer be necessary to keep you bound like some wild beast of the jungle that we have just left."

So saying, she motioned for one of the Orientals to reach forward and release me from my bonds. Free at last, I slumped over the man's shoulder, unable to control my own body. He lifted me easily off the ground and carried me a few feet to the far left corner of the craft where he placed me inside of a small bamboo basket.

I was cramped, but able to see through the small slits in front of my eyes. I guessed correctly, as it turned out, that the bamboo stalks hid me from outside view, unless one peered closely into the basket. The man fastened a lid on the top of the basket. I found myself plunged into darkness. Mute and helpless as an infant in his mother's womb, I stared out of the basket and waited to see what would happen next.

As it happened, I did not have long to wait for the aeroplane banked sharply and began its descent. From my vantage point in the bamboo basket, I was unable to determine anything about our arrival until I felt the shudder and sudden jolt as we reached the ground once more.

The aeroplane taxied on the runway and at last came to a halt. At least, we were on a proper airfield this time! Presently, Helga and the Oriental men began to rise from their seats. Two of the men came into the back of the cabin and, lifting the bamboo basket to their shoulders, carried me off the aeroplane.

The North African sun was hot and pierced through the openings between the stalks. Unable to move, I lay there in a crumpled heap with the hot sun nearly blinding me while the Orientals carefully set the bamboo basket down upon the ground. After a few moments, they returned with a pair of long, thick rods. They affixed the rods to the sides of the basket, leaving the same length free at either end. In this fashion, four men bore my weight, two in front and two in the rear.

They carried me to a nearby truck and, lowering the rear gate, they carefully placed me inside before securing the gate once more. Throughout all of this, I had no glimpse of Helga. How long I sat in the back of the truck, I could not hazard a guess. In my current condition of immobility, I was certain all events seemed far more time-consuming than they truly were.

The noise of the wind and the indistinct shouting of voices filled the air and made thinking difficult. The sound of voices eventually grew nearer and soon, I could discern footfalls approaching. The metal doors at the front of the truck screeched as they opened. The weight of the truck dipped as the driver and passenger climbed in and came to a rest.

The engine turned over and, with a sudden lurch, the truck started forward. I had a brief view of the airfield as we departed. I felt certain that we had landed in Cairo. Shortly thereafter, the truck came to a halt. The engine idled while I heard the sound of chatter, but was unable to discern any words above the noise. Soon enough, there was a creaking sound of metal lifting and the truck surged forward again. From my view within the bamboo basket, I watched as the gate to the airfield descended once more next to the sentry station as we departed, kicking up a cloud of dust as we made our way down the dirt road.

The sun was starting to set by the time that we reached our destination. I had a good view of the location as the truck backed into the driveway up to a large iron gate. Arab guards stood posted by the gate. They set aside their rifles and opened the gate to allow the truck to back in and move up close against the great house.

The front doors of the truck clanged as they opened, and I felt the vehicle bounce as the driver and passenger climbed down. The Arabs were watching the new arrivals with anticipation. They made a queer gesture, touching their forehead, lips, and heart with the tips of their thumb and forefinger pressed tightly together. Presently, they prostrated themselves before their visitors as if these new arrivals were some saintly religious figures.

My amazement grew when I saw the individual who inspired such awe was none other than Helga Graumann. I realized that the Arabs' reaction to her presence was identical to that of the Abyssinians. Her driver was one of the Orientals, apparently the only one to have accompanied us from the airfield. Immediately, I learned that my assumption had been incorrect as several Orientals emerged alongside the truck. I realized that they must have arrived sooner in a separate vehicle. The Orientals formed a front and rear guard for Helga as she made her way past the prostrate forms of the Arabs and entered the great house.

The gate on the back of the truck lowered and two of the Orientals who remained behind grasped the wooden rods and dragged the bamboo basket out of the truck.

Two of their fellows grasped the rods from the rear and the four of them bore my weight as they made their way into the house behind Helga.

The basket shook from side to side and I feared it would burst open beneath my weight. I watched in a state of shock as the Arabs inside the house gathered quickly on either side of the Orientals and, likewise, anointed their foreheads, lips, and heart and prostrated themselves on the marble floor as Helga passed them by.

As we approached the Grand Staircase, a tall and powerfully built Arab, whose turbaned head blended with the thick ebon-colored veil that hid his features, descended to the ground floor and stood before us, barring our way with his arms folded in a gesture of defiance.

There was no way for me to tell if the Orientals were bracing themselves for a conflict for only their backs were visible to me. Helga did not falter in her step, but instead marched past the powerful and mysterious Arab with only the slightest nod of acknowledgement from her proud head. I watched as his arms dropped to his sides and his hands clenched in seething rage. I regretted my helplessness, knowing that whatever happened next, I was unable to raise my arms in my own defense or the girl's.

My bearers marched up the staircase behind Helga and followed her down the winding corridor and into a large and richly furnished flat. The bamboo basket that contained me was set down against the far wall, just inside the doorway. Helga dismissed the Orientals with the briefest of commands. They bowed and left the room. I sat slumped in the basket, watching her as she walked around the flat, inspecting the room to see if it met with her approval.

She stepped out of view briefly, likely to examine her bedroom or the restroom. When she returned, she had dispensed with the exotic headdress and her top. She walked about the flat in this shameless state as if it were perfectly natural to do so. Her brazenness must have meant the undoing of many a good man in her day.

I heard the door to the flat open. Helga froze and turned to stare at the doorway, just out of my line of vision. She failed to attempt to cover herself or protect her dignity in any fashion.

"It is customary to knock upon a lady's door before entering," she said with a withering look and turned aside to review some papers on the desk in front of her.

The powerful Arab, his face still hidden from view, crossed the room in four great strides. He seized her by the arm and spun her toward him.

"Insolent whore! You dare to treat me with such contempt in front of my servants! I should have you flayed!"

She wrenched her arm out of his hand and shot him a look of barely restrained fury.

"I have no wish to play games with you, Esteban. Besides, those fools believe me to be Our Lady of the Si-Fan. You wouldn't expect Our Lady to bow to you, a lowly president of the Council of Seven, would you?"

He grabbed her other arm and spun her around violently, like a spiteful child taking his fury out upon a rag doll.

"You forget the debt that you owe me. Were it not for me, you would still be Koreani, the simpering slave girl whimpering at the feet of the dog she could not recognize for her own father."

She broke free of his grip a second time.

"And you forget the debt that you owe me," she spat. "Were it not for me, think of what your fate would have been all those years ago, had my father been left to treat you like a fly whose wings were ripe for removing."

He reached up with barely restrained rage and tore the veil from his face. I could only catch a glimpse of one side of his face, but it was enough to see the grisly smile slit into what had once been his mouth. There were numerous scars alongside his permanent grimace, indicating failed attempts to correct this terrible disfigurement.

"Do you think that you need to remind me of this? Do you think that I do not recall the agony I endured at his hands every second of every minute of every hour of every day since that time?"

I dread to relate this, but a faint smile played across Helga's face as if she somehow were enjoying his pain as he continued to address her.

"Do you also think that I do not recall your humiliation of me? Do you think that I forgot how much you enjoyed treating me like a toy in front of anyone who cared to watch you indulge yourself?"

"Esteban, be fair," she said, shaking her head indignantly. "I am not the same person. Whatever I did then was the result of my upbringing by the man we both have reason to hate. When my father wiped my memories, I lost my entire identity, including the reprehensible traits that you have recounted many times since, to my lasting shame. Imagine hearing the awful exploits of a despicable person, and then being told that they were your own actions. There is no way for me to respond to such recriminations for the woman I am now is truly innocent of any wrongdoing."

He stared at her for a moment and then raised a shaking fist to her face.

"If I thought for even a second that you were deceiving me..."

She put her arms around his neck and began pressing her full lips against that awful disfigured mouth.

"How can you accuse me of such things after all we have meant to one another?" she murmured to him softly. "We are like two young lovers together, Esteban. Both of us are starting anew with no pasts, no guilt. Think of all that is good in our lives. You are Khnum-Khufu reincarnated, and I am Our Lady of the Si-Fan. Together, we will eradicate the last vestige of influence my father has over the Council of Seven, while you work to bring the new Fascist powers rising in Europe to heel at our command. Munich will be our victory, darling; for it is in Munich that you will finally claim your destiny. Can you taste it? It is so close, my love, so very, very close."

They slipped down to the carpeted floor together and Helga rolled on top of him with an unexpected animal abandon that still shocked me after all I had witnessed from this young hellion. I shut my eyes; the only action I could still easily accomplish, and wished sleep would overtake me so that I did not have to listen to the fury of her insatiable passions again. The memory of her pleasure was one that still caused me pain.

Presently, I became aware of a new sound, not of their frenzied lovemaking, but rather of the two of them sighing out of something other than exhausted release.

"You are sure?" Helga asked him, her voice betraying her frustration.

"There is nothing...I cannot..." he stammered in response.

"Perhaps if I were more like a boy..."

Her words cut off as the man she called Esteban began to throttle her before quickly regaining control of his emotions. He swore at her ceaselessly with a foul torrent of blasphemies directed upon her character and her heritage. Yet, for all of her protests, her face betrayed a look of genuine amusement that did not match her plaintive words, begging his forgiveness for having offended him.

"Consider how I must feel?" she implored him. "A woman prides herself in these areas, and your inability to respond as a man makes me fear that something is wrong with me. I never meant to hurt you by bringing up your past just now, but it was all that I could think of by way of an explanation for..."

"Yes, yes, I know," he snapped. "I have had enough of this talk already. What did you learn of Sir Lionel Barton? What happened while you were in Abyssinia?"

He dressed hurriedly as he spoke and was quick to re-attach the veil that hid his scarred visage from sight. Helga did not appear the least bit bothered by her nudity and continued to converse with him while lying upon the floor, staring up at him while he fumbled to regain his dignity.

"You have nothing to fear from Barton. The dacoits nearly killed him when they made their last attempt on his life. He is a sick old man and cannot interfere with our plans again."

"What of the girl?"

His voice sounded anxious. It was a fact not lost upon Helga.

"What of her? What is she to you? Should I be jealous? You are developing quite a taste for the opposite sex now, aren't you? How very peculiar. One would have supposed it was not in your nature to change."

He shut his eyes to escape the torment of her words.

"Stop that, please. Do not make me ask you again. We will not talk of the past. It is done and I am free from it."

She sat up with her back arched and her elbows supporting her weight. She was a magnificent sight in spite of herself.

"Are you truly free, Esteban? I wonder...deep down, at night, in the moments before dawn drives away the darkness, do you ever turn and watch me as I sleep and wish..."

"Stop it!" his hands were covering his ears. His voice shook with emotion as he spoke. "Do not do this to me. Why must you taunt me so?"

"I did not taunt anyone," her voice sounded as innocent as a toddler at play. "I merely posed a question that I think needs to be answered sooner or later. That isn't so bad of me, is it?"

"The girl," he snapped. "I asked you about the girl. What has become of her?"

She clicked her tongue at him and shook her head.

"I don't think I want to discuss this with you. What does that smelly young thing with her pet ape matter to you anyway? Perhaps I had her killed and roasted on a spit. The Abyssinians eat human flesh, you know."

"They do not, and we both know it," he was in control again. "Now stop being morbid, Fah lo Suee, for I am growing tired of playing these games of yours."

"First, tell me why you are so interested in this girl."

She set her face in a pout and stared up at him with her nose lifted in the air.

"Many years ago...before the War, that smelly girl, as you called her, was one of three children that blundered into my plans. I foolishly trusted a...an under-ling...to dispose of them. It proved a fatal mistake for it was the beginning of a series of setbacks that cost me centuries of work."

She shivered with excitement as he emphasized the word, "centuries."

"So you want her dead then? Let me handle it for you. I will not falter."

I felt my blood boil as she spoke of murdering my sister as if Anna's life were of no real importance. I was still unable to move, trapped as I was in a basket, as if I were one of the living dead.

"No, not now...not after all these years...she has survived, but what of her scars?"

His voice trailed on the last word as if he were sa-voring it.

"What of her glorious scars? That is always the in-teresting part...to observe what form the scars have taken after a couple of decades of a petty mortal life, with all of its pain and disappointments. It always shows, you know. If one knows what to look for, one can always spot them. It is as if they were my own children. One need only look for a resemblance."

I hated him more than I did Helga, for all of her cruelty and wantonness. I wanted to see him dead. After all this time, here was the man who was responsible for what I had been through...for what we had all suffered. He was just a few feet away from me, and I lacked the strength to end his miserable life as justice demanded. If there was a God in Heaven, He was not just or merciful for He would not aid me now.

"So that's it then?" Helga spat the words as if an obscenity. "This is just about satisfying your idle curi-osity?"

He shook his head slowly from one side to the next.

"It is about Fate, my dear. Fate cast those three children as obstacles in my path, lo those many years ago. Fate returns one of them to me again when I am so close to achieving my destiny. It is Fate that conspires against me, but as with my vanquished enemy, Time, it is I who shall ultimately prove victorious."

He was a certifiable loony, I thought.

"If Barton is well enough to travel, have him and the girl brought here. I will deal with them later. They have yet a role to play in this game. I must return to the Great Pyramid. Khunum-Khufu must rest and prepare his mind for the gambit to be played in Munich shortly."

So saying, he turned and strode proudly from the room without a further word to her. I heard the door shut. Helga had rolled over to her side to watch his departure. Her face broke into a smile once he had gone. I watched with a mixture of dread and anticipation as she crawled along the floor to peer into the bamboo basket that had become my prison.

"Do you begin to understand, Professor? Do you see how kind I can be when I wish it? I could have given you to him as a plaything. It would make him so happy to have found you again, all grown up...and you being unable to move or speak...why, surely it would have been a dream to him. Yet, I did not betray you despite the hate that burns in your breast for me. Soon, your re-education will begin and you will learn that in my own way, I love you. Best of all, you will come to return my affections."

She collapsed against the basket laughing in that beguiling chiming fashion of hers.

"Soon you will have the honor to learn what it is to be loved by a daughter of the dragon."

I felt a creeping dread overtake me. I could not control my body and began to quake in helpless fear for what might yet be done to me in my paralyzed state.

11. THE DEVIL DOCTOR

Sleep did not come easily, yet I must have finally managed to fall into a deep slumber, for I awoke to find the bamboo basket rocking from side to side as a pair of Orientals bore me down the stairs. Doubtless, two more were bearing my weight from the rear, but I was still unable to turn my head to glance behind me. The evening sun was just starting to set in the sky above as we departed the great house. I was immediately aware of the smells and sounds of Egypt and longed to be free to move once more.

The bearers placed the basket on the ground before the back of the truck that had brought us from the airfield. The Orientals lowered the gate at the back of the truck before they lifted the basket that had become my cramped cage and pushed it roughly into the back of the truck. The gate closed with a metallic slam as, first one pair and then, the second pair of Orientals clambered over the gate and seated themselves on either side of the basket.

The engine turned over and the truck made its way kicking up dust all around us. My eyes stung with sweat and sand. It was then that I realized sensation was slowly returning to my body. I could only guess that Helga was travelling with us once more for I had not seen her. That she had spared my life was undeniable when it was easily within her power to turn me over to a man whom I had never before seen, but whom I had vowed to kill were he ever within my power.

Esteban Milagro was the name that had seared itself into my brain. I would not easily forget that horribly scarred visage. There were many questions that I would put to Helga were I given the opportunity to do so.

The truck drove for well over an hour. I began to recognize the area and realized that we were approaching the site of our dig at Luxor. We came to a stop and I lurched forward, realizing at last that I was master of my body once more. The Orientals reacted immediately to my unexpected movement and began chattering among themselves animatedly. One of them stuck his head out the back of the truck and hollered something in their foreign tongue.

Shortly thereafter, I heard the screeching of the doors opening in the front of the truck and Helga and the driver approached the rear of the truck. She was dressed in a deep blue evening gown with heels. Her hair was lightened and curled and draped across her bare shoulders seductively. I could not imagine a more inappropriate garb for our surroundings, but she did look stunning. I puzzled the reason for her change in hair color. The driver pulled the gate down with a loud clang. The other Orientals quivered in fear, lest Helga accidentally touch their person or make eye contact with them. I did not understand the status she was falsely claiming as "Our Lady of the Si-Fan," but they appeared to treat her with the greatest reverence. The thought crossed my mind that Mut would surely object to this blasphemous deception.

Presently, they removed the lid from the bamboo basket and two of the Orientals helped me to climb out of it. My limbs, neck, and back felt exceedingly stiff and the act of standing straight was terribly uncomfortable.

The sun felt strange on my skin and my eyes burned from its rays as I climbed down from the truck and felt the hot sand beneath my feet. I was dressed only in a light blue tunic and could not recall receiving it. Evidently, I had been dressed while I had slept. I shuddered to think of my vulnerability among these people whilst paralyzed by that damnable drug.

I was aware that Helga's eyes were upon me and that the Orientals at my side were serving as guards as much as they were aiding me in regaining my balance. My thoughts were not with any of them, but rather with the awesome sight before us. I gazed up into the towering twin statues of Ramses II that kept their silent vigil before the Karnak temple complex.

It was a truly captivating spectacle and one whose breathtaking majesty never diminished despite the number of times I had gazed upon its magnificence. Egypt, in its revealed glory, stood like another world before our ignorant modern eyes. The vision and artisanship of her splendid designs were without peer in this 20th century of the Christian world. The bewildering scale of the enclosure wall was beyond compare with anything else I had gazed upon, anywhere on Earth.

"You are at home, Professor," Helga spoke.

I did not even turn to meet her glance as she strode to my side and continued addressing me.

"It is good to see you come alive at last. I had begun to worry that nothing could stir you. I have little use for men that cannot be aroused."

She was a purely carnal creature, doomed to see her intellect dwindle over time as her base nature superseded all higher impulses. The dawning recognition that I was walking the same path was not lost upon me as I stood

118

before this towering reminder that man had higher aspirations than the satisfaction of his own wanton nature.

"We are before Amun, the father god," my voice wavered as I spoke. "Amun was one of the eight gods of Hermopolis and became the chief god of Thebes. During the 18th Dynasty, Amun became associated with Ra of Heliopolis, and so became Amun-Ra, the father god. The conflict between devotion to the pharaoh and Amun-Ra remained a sore point thereafter. The temple of Amun-Ra's consort, the vulture goddess Mut, is where my team is excavating. Amun-Ra and Mut's son is Khonsu, the Moon god, who watches over this temple at night."

My heart was racing with anticipation at the thought of returning to the dig after all I had come through.

"I must warn you, Professor," Helga said taking my hand, "this dig is no longer under your direction."

I recoiled at her touch and pulled my hand from her grip.

"Of course not…I've been gone for weeks. I left Hassan in charge when I joined Spiridon in Corfu for his wedding."

My mind reeled as I thought of all that had occurred since that time.

"The official purpose of this dig, as far as Cairo and Athens are concerned, is the excavation of the Temple of the Solar Disc which Akhenaton constructed in defiance of Amun-Ra. The real temple is likely located right where we are passing now."

I glanced behind me at the stone-faced Orientals who followed in a straight line next to one another, barely a step behind us in case I tried to flee, or worse, harm Helga in some fashion.

"Horemheb had Akhenaton's blasphemous temple torn down as well as the temples he constructed at

Thebes. Horemheb was loyal to Amun-Ra and restored the father god to his place of prominence here at Karnak. Just a little further…past the ram-headed sphinxes…we will come to the temple of Mut. That is where Hassan and the men should be hard at work. Beneath Mut's temple is the older construct of the Hermetic Order that I mentioned earlier. That is what Spiridon came to find…or rather, that is what this Si-Fan group wanted him to find for them."

"You will prove an asset to my father," Helga smiled as she spoke.

"I don't understand. I thought you told Milagro that you hated your father."

"You have a keen ear, Professor," she said with a shrug of her shoulders. "Had I not taken the precaution of leaving the only dacoits with a command of English behind at the house, you would have caused me great embarrassment just now."

"I prefer to be direct with people and expect to be treated in kind. You could start by explaining that which I do not understand. Who are you? Are you Helga Graumann, or is that a false identity? It is not the name that Sir Denis calls you by, nor is it the name Milagro calls you, nor is it the title by which these dacoits know you. What is the truth?"

"Need I remind you, Professor, that you were using a false identity when I first met you? You had shaved your head in a further effort to disguise yourself."

"Yet, you knew me in spite of my efforts to elude my pursuers. The difference is, I do not know you. Are you truly the daughter of Fu Manchu?"

"Might I ask where you became acquainted with Sir Denis Nayland Smith?"

My face flushed as I realized I had foolishly let my guard down in my pursuit of knowledge. I only prayed that I had not endangered Anna further by speaking.

"You said you were direct, Professor, I admire that quality. Your silence suggests to me that Sir Denis has come to the aid of his old friend, Sir Lionel Barton. That explains your disappearance from the Orient Express. I presume that Sir Denis was also responsible for the loss of Margarita."

I said nothing. My mind raced to think of what I could possibly respond with that would not do further harm.

"Never mind, Professor, it is just as well. Your loss would have been regrettable. I did not have sufficient knowledge of your worth at the time, and Margarita was so enthusiastic that I feared reining her in would have proven...difficult."

"How can you pretend that...that thing was a little girl?"

She laughed mockingly at my outrage and stole a glance at me as we continued walking past those magnificent ram-headed statues.

"You do have trouble accepting that identities may be adopted and discarded at will, don't you, Professor? What one is at a certain time is what best suits one's purpose. There is no law, no right and wrong to follow. You children of the West are so rigid in your thinking. It is remarkable that your culture has not already collapsed from your inability to embrace the fluctuations of this world."

As I looked up at the sphinxes before us, I wondered if there was some truth in her words. I considered the tense situation in the world, with the Fascists rising to power throughout Europe, and wondered if I were already living through the collapse of Western civilization. What had we to show for ourselves? Certainly nothing to rival Egypt in its splendor.

Presently, we came upon the Luxor Temple. The sound of my team hard at work with their picks and shovels grew louder as we approached. We passed the shattered colossal statue of Ramses II, he who reconsecrated the temple to Amun-Ra, Mut, and Khonsu, the Theban Triad of Hatshepsut. Finally, the sound of Hassan and his men laboring filled our ears as we reached the entranceway to the Temple flanked by the statues of the great Pharaoh and his Queen.

As we entered the Temple, Helga's eyes drifted to the large mural depicting Mutemwia, Tuthmosis IV's Queen, engaged in sexual congress with Amun-Ra.

"The Pharaoh was responsible for overseeing fertility rites," I said, pointing to the mural. "The custom of the Ancients was to follow the schedule of the annual flooding of the Nile. The Pharaoh was both son and earthly counterpart of Amun-Ra. Therefore, conceiving his heir involved a fertility ritual in which Amun-Ra would allow his ka, his life force, to enter the Pharaoh's body and pass through to his Queen to sire his own divine heir. Rather similar to the European concept of divine right, I suppose, although the act of divine embodiment would likely strike many Westerners as more akin to demonic possession. Unsurprisingly, most of my predecessors have chosen to suppress that bit. No one wants to put museums or universities off where funding is concerned, hey?"

Helga did not return my smile, but rather merely glanced at me and turned back towards the mural. I broke away from her and made my way to the center of the room where the flooring had been broken and a rope ladder descended to the excavation below ground from whence the sound of the team emanated.

I began my sure-footed descent with Helga following closely behind me. When I reached the end of the rope, I dropped the few remaining feet to the ground below. Dust swirled about the room as the deafening clanging of picks and shovels rang blows upon the ground. All about the room were to be seen tombs ornately decorated with the startling likenesses of Ra, Anubis, and Osiris. I recognized Hassan among the group and approached him cautiously.

"Hello, old man," I said as I clapped a hand on his shoulder, "how are things progressing?"

Hassan turned to face me and I gasped at the sight of his eyes. They held a dull expression, without as much as a glint of recognition of me. He held my gaze with no expectations of what I should want by interrupting his work. The men around us kept digging as if my arrival was of no importance.

I was stumbling for words when Helga reached my side. At the sight of her, Hassan fell to his knees and prostrated himself upon the ground. Noting his response, the other men laid down their tools and likewise did the same.

Helga lifted her head to gaze upon the roof and pronounced a guttural sound in a tongue unfamiliar to me. At her command, the men rose and, bowing, returned to work, except for Hassan who rose to kneel upon one knee with his head lowered. Helga gave another command in what sounded like a series of barks and grunts. Hassan rose and, nodding his understanding, set off toward an antechamber. Helga followed him and after pausing a moment, I did the same.

Hassan stood at attention by the entranceway to the antechamber. I looked into his eyes as I followed Helga. There was not even the slightest indication that he was even aware of our presence. The man behaved as if he were under a spell.

As we stepped through the entranceway, I noted two Nubians standing guard just inside, with large scimitars held at ready. The tip of their blades rested upon the ground in front of them. Inside the antechamber stood a small table, filled with chemical apparatus and, next to them, ancient tomes were stacked high in a pile. Small statuettes, doubtless recently unearthed, stood on the ground next to the table. A pair of Mushrabiyeh screens formed a border against each anterior wall, as if to give the illusion of windows in the chamber.

Behind the table stood a tall, thin man wearing a deep purple skullcap upon his head. Wrinkled features that appeared to be made of papyrus leant his face a mummified appearance upon first glance. Bright green eyes of a peculiar luminescence shone like jade from their sockets. Long, thin skeletal hands extended from the sleeves of his purple robe and stroked a marmoset that he held cradled in his arms. The creature chirped sharply upon our arrival. Helga rushed to the old man's side and knelt before him, staring up expectantly like an obedient dog in a manner reminiscent of the reverence that the Abyssinians, Arabs, and Orientals had displayed for her presence. Slowly, the old man's magnificent green eyes rose to meet mine as I stood in the entranceway facing him.

"Good evening, Professor Knox. I am Dr. Fu Manchu. Fortune smiles upon us this day for allowing our paths to cross."

Speech was difficult when faced with such an inexplicably powerful presence, but somehow I found the will to respond.

"What business do you have here? This is a private excavation by the University of Athens with the special permission of..."

He lifted his right hand and snapped his fingers twice while the marmoset darted up his left arm and came to perch upon his shoulder. The Nubians stepped forward in response to his gesture and one of them grabbed me roughly and pinned my arms behind my back. Dr. Fu Manchu bent forward and lifted from the table a small black case just large enough to hold a pair of eyeglasses. He opened the case and withdrew a needle from within.

Demonstrating meticulous care, he filled the needle with an amber-colored fluid from a beaker on the table. More of the peculiar fluid bubbled in the apparatus that rested nearby. He crossed in front of the table with slow, precise steps until he had reached my side. He raised his right hand in which he grasped the needle.

The Nubian quickly released one of my arms. His companion grasped and pulled the sleeve of my tunic back to expose the skin. Showing no hesitation or emotion whatsoever, Dr. Fu Manchu plunged the needle deep into my forearm. I winced in pain as if fire had touched my veins instantly upon contact. Almost immediately, I felt my equilibrium falter. My knees buckled as the Nubian tightened his grip upon me to prevent my falling.

"Professor Knox, can you hear me?"

The voice sounded distant. The accent was peculiar, alternating as it did between a sibilant lisp and a guttural snarl. My vision was blurring badly as I struggled to remain conscious.

"Professor Knox, this is your Master speaking."

The voice paused for a beat before continuing.

"Who is your Master?"

"Dr. Fu Manchu..." I heard my voice answer in a dull monotone.

"Excellent, Professor, you have done well. I have a task for you. A very special assignment tailored just for you to perform. Do you recall the name Alexandra Dunhill?"

A vision of a fair-skinned girl with blonde hair flashed before my eyes.

"Yes," I replied in the same dull-witted monotone.

"You shall renew your acquaintance with her in a short time. She, too, has an important role to play, but she requires your assistance to complete her task. When the time is right, Helga will come to you and you will do as she bids, without question. You shall recall nothing of these instructions until that time. Do you understand your Master?"

Someone was dropping pebbles in a pond. My face was so very close to the pond that I could see the ripples in the surface spread out further and further as each pebble fell. I shook my head to clear my brain as my vision returned to me.

There was a purple robe covering a pair of dark green slippers. My eyes climbed up the robe until I found I was staring up into the face of Fu Manchu!

"What business do you have here? This is a private excavation by..."

He lifted the palm of his right hand while the marmoset that sat perched on his shoulder lunged forward and screeched at me. I pulled my head back, fearing that the creature would bite me.

"Save your words, Professor. You have been relieved of your duties here. A power greater than any you recognize is at work. You Europeans are but children playing soldiers for names upon a map. The fate of the world rests under Egyptian skies and not in any of your passing monuments to Europe's vanity and fleeting glory."

Turning from me, he returned to the table and gestured with an outstretched hand toward the objects upon it. The Nubian that had held my arm rushed forward. Rising, Helga joined him and they both set to work. The Nubian packed the ancient tomes into a large trunk upon the floor, while Helga busied herself dismantling the chemical apparatus and placing it in a second, smaller trunk that lay beneath the table.

Thus completed, each bore their respective trunk and made for the far corner of the anteroom where the intimidating figure of the otherwise frail old man stood waiting for them to finish their tasks. The second Nubian who had pinned my arms behind my back hustled me along to follow. As we nearly caught up with them, the old man reached out a thin skeletal hand and touched the wall. This simple gesture had a remarkable effect, for a panel slid open in the wall, several feet away from him, and revealed a hidden doorway. I could see a stairwell leading down to the lower level that Hassan and his team were furiously working to uncover in the outer chamber.

The Nubian with the trunk was the first to proceed down the steps, followed by Helga, and then Dr. Fu Manchu. The second Nubian, the one who held my arms pinned behind my back, shoved me roughly to the ground. Stepping forward, he likewise touched the wall and quickly ducked through the opening as the panel slid shut behind him.

Regaining my feet, I rushed to the wall and felt along it in the same fashion that I had observed both Fu Manchu and the Nubian manipulate the hidden controls scant seconds before, but I could not find the release. Frantically, I ran my fingers along the cold stone where the panel had magically appeared at their touch, before it just as quickly disappeared, but I could find no trace that it had ever existed.

I looked about the empty antechamber as the sound of the picks and shovels of Hassan's team rang loudly from just outside the entranceway. I was alone in the room with no proof that all that had occurred was anything more than a fevered dream. Fearing for my sanity, I slid to the floor and wept as the very real possibility of madness, that terrible affliction that threatened to claim me since childhood, raised the specter of its awful head once more. I had gazed into the face of insanity this day and had learned that it answered to the name of Dr. Fu Manchu.

12. COUNCIL OF WAR

Gunshots rang out somewhere in the distance. I was covered in sweat and shivering at the same time. Memories cascaded through my mind of a crocodile...Prince Abard...hanging on for my life...being told to climb...my little sister...and Alexandra...something about Alexandra...I hadn't seen her in years...the sound of gunshots once more, closer this time...where was I?

"He's here!"

A voice called out quite close to me. I could see nothing but faces blurring in and out of the darkness...a snowman...bits of human flesh sticking out through the snow...the nightmare that never ends...the reason I can never know peace...Milagro, that was the name...he was the one who must pay.

"Professor Knox? Can you hear me, Professor?"

Someone was holding me up. A hand slapped me across the cheek hard, once...twice.

Instinctively, my hand reached up and grabbed the wrist.

"Don't do that again."

I was staring into the face of a man I had never seen before. I let go of his wrist and pushed his arm away from me.

"You are Professor Knox, aren't you?"

I nodded to the stranger and felt an intense pain in my head for my trouble.

"Last time that I checked, I still answered to that name. Who are you?"

The man's face broke into a broad grin as he extended his hand in friendship.

"The name's Kerrigan, Bart Kerrigan. I am here with Sir Denis Nayland Smith. We've come to get you out of here, Professor."

Sir Denis! Here? I shook my head in bewilderment.

"No, I can't leave. This is my dig."

"If we leave you here, it will also be your tomb. Here comes Sir Denis now. He'll sort you out."

I turned and saw a figure descending from the rope ladder and recognized that it was indeed Nayland Smith. A rifle hung from his shoulder and he seemed more vigorous and alert than when we had parted in Abyssinia. He dropped to the ground as he reached the last rung of the ladder and turning, crossed the chamber in a few long strides until he reached my side.

"Good work, Kerrigan. I did not think we would be fortunate enough to find Knox still in one piece. Glad to see that I was wrong for once."

"Anna, where is Anna?"

"Your sister is fine," Smith reassured me, "or at least out of harm's way for now. When we heard and subsequently saw the aeroplane that carried you here make its departure, we decided that we had best make our move. Your sister stayed behind with Barton, but Fey and I charged the Abyssinians. Happily, the battle did not last long. A great number of them were killed, due in no small part to the help of Monkey."

"Monkey..." I repeated the name feeling slightly dazed at the thought of that creature fighting side by side with civilized men.

"Any zoologist who tells you that a gorilla is a gentle creature is either a fool or a liar. Tame as that animal may be, it is still very much an animal, as she proved among the Abyssinians. We saw backs being broken and arms torn from their sockets. Sheer unfettered bestial savagery is the only way to describe the mayhem unleashed, and thank God for it, for, without Monkey, we would not be here now. I hesitate to imagine what she would be like if someone had actually managed to harm your sister."

"Where is Anna? You didn't leave her in that bally jungle I hope?"

"I'm glad to see that you're starting to think clearly again. No, we did not leave her behind. Once we felt certain that the remaining Abyssinians had scattered for the time being, we decided to waste no time allowing them to regroup. Fey and I carried Barton in a sick bed while Anna and Monkey followed close behind. Anna was heartsick at the thought of leaving Monkey behind, but there was nothing else for it. It was imperative that we get to Cairo as soon as possible. Once there, we met with Kerrigan and the local police superintendant, who is an old friend of ours. Fey stayed behind to safeguard Barton and Anna. We have had Greba under police protection for the past few weeks and we intend to get your sister and Sir Lionel shipped out as soon as we can arrange it."

"You have to act sooner than that, Sir Denis," I grabbed his arm in desperation and held on to the sleeve like a drowning man. "The Si-Fan has already given the order to capture Anna as well as Barton. My sister's very life is in jeopardy. Every second's delay could mean her death."

Smith said something in reply, but my vision blurred as the chamber began to spin before my eyes. Drained beyond all reasonable endurance by all that had occurred and half-starved, I collapsed at last.

I awoke to soft sheets and heavenly pillows, with warm sunlight streaming through an open window down upon my face. This was bliss, and I knew it for the world I had dreamt of discovering my entire life. I was aware of another's presence and looked over to my side where Anna sat in a chair facing me.

"Good morning, Michael," she smiled kindly.

"Anna? Is it really you?" I lifted myself up on my elbows and shook my head to clear my mind of the cobwebs as I recalled my earlier drugged deception.

"Of course, it's me," she laughed. "Who else would it be?"

"Helga...or Koreani...or Fah lo Suee...," I stammered.

Anna rolled her eyes, "No, Michael. It is only your sister and not any of the other women you've been occupying your time with instead of doing honest work."

My head sunk back into the pillows and I shut my eyes in relief. "Oh, thank God, I'm finally free."

Anna reached forward and touched my hand. "You've been through a great deal. Are you able to get some breakfast in you? Sir Denis and the others have much to discuss with you and you will need to get your strength back."

Oh God, I thought, *not more questions.*

Two hours later, and I was dressed, clean-shaven, fed, and feeling reasonably like my old self. My hair was growing back nicely, and I no longer felt like a ghost of the man I had been. When I came downstairs, I found Sir Denis and Kerrigan waiting for me in the front room with three other visitors. There was a middle-aged official called Weymouth, who was the local police superintendant and an old friend of Smith's, the silent and brooding Fey, who I still mistrusted, and an ailing Sir Lionel Barton, who walked very stiffly with the aid of a cane, but had otherwise seemingly recovered to his usual unpleasant self. I noted, with more than a little apprehension, that Anna had seated herself next to Barton and was playing the part of his attentive nurse to the fullest.

As I took my seat before them, I felt very much like a condemned man appearing before an Inquisition that had long since decided his fate.

"You're looking much better, Knox," Nayland Smith said after introductions were completed and the lot of us had settled down to enjoy our tea and a relaxing smoke. "Now why don't you start by telling us the purpose of your excavation in Luxor?"

"We were excavating the Temple of the Solar Disc," I said with a shrug. "Naturally, we wished to keep this fact from other interested parties who might otherwise wish to...how shall I put it? Steal our thunder?"

I looked pointedly at Sir Lionel who bristled with contempt.

"Bollocks," the unpleasant old man erupted. "You were excavating Luxor Temple and your team had nearly penetrated a third level underground. That is nowhere near the Temple of the Solar Disc as any fresh-faced novice would tell you."

I shifted uncomfortably in my seat. It seemed that Barton's reputation as an Egyptologist was no exaggeration. He knew more by talking with Smith about the site than many men who had been there would have themselves.

"We're aware that the Temple of the Solar Disc was the excavation that the University of Athens believed they were funding," Smith stated. "It should come as no surprise to you that, after Professor Simos' murder, I contacted both the new department head and the board of regents. Presently, you will tell us the true purpose of your excavation. We need to know the reason that the Si-Fan has been so interested in this site. I will not hesitate to hand you over to Superintendant Weymouth if you refuse to cooperate. I assure you that life in a Cairo prison would not be to your liking."

I glanced at the official seated in the armchair on Smith's left side. The man sat there, taciturn, smoking a foul-smelling Turkish cigarette and staring at me stone-faced. Apart from brushing aside the ash that had fallen into his lap, he appeared completely unmoved by our discussion. I had little doubt that he was enough of a bastard to lock away a man for life if it suited him to do so. Such men often occupied colonial posts.

I thought of Hassan and the rest of the team that Smith and Kerrigan had scared off with a few rounds fired above their heads. The Si-Fan had drugged the men to make them their slaves. I had some experience of their methods myself. That Fu Manchu had already penetrated to the lowest level, there was no doubt, although I could not understand the purpose in having them continue to dig when he had already gained access. In any event, there was little reason to continue to deceive Smith and the others. Fate had removed me from a decisive position in this particular drama, and I had too much to lose if I failed to disclose all that I knew.

I realized that all eyes were upon me as I struggled with my conscience. It was clear that my window of freedom was closing rapidly. Weymouth had a predatory look in his eye. I really had no desire to see the inside of a Cairo prison.

"Spiridon was contacted by the Si-Fan some months ago with information about a lost Theban Necropolis that had been built upon the Luxor Temple. Supposedly, beneath it was a secret chamber of the Theban priests containing information about a secret Gnostic faith practiced by the Pharaohs. There exists a tradition about a secret society which worshipped an older faith unknown to the Egyptian people. This society had members located around the world in positions of the highest power. As incredulous as it may sound, this group literally wielded power that Alexander and Napoleon only dreamt of in their wildest fantasies. Once Spiridon arranged for the excavation to proceed legally, he was no longer indispensable to the Si-Fan's plans. Unfortunately, he had taken me into his confidence, and I was likewise marked for death."

It felt strange to discuss such matters as fact.

"Yet, that has changed apparently," said Smith, puffing contemplatively at his pipe. "They have had ample opportunity to rid themselves of you since the incident on the Orient Express. How do you account for this seeming change of heart?"

I sat back in my seat and sighed.

"There is some sort of struggle for dominance within this Si-Fan group. I cannot say that I fully understand it, but I witnessed enough of it to have some notion of the politics involved. Helga, her father, and a man called Esteban Milagro, seem to be at the center of the conflict."

I felt decidedly uncomfortable discussing Milagro, but there was little choice in the matter.

"Esteban Milagro?" Sir Denis reacted as if I had struck him. "After all this time? I wonder...I believe I'm beginning to understand something. Kerrigan," Smith said turning to his right. "I do believe that Professor Knox may have inadvertently uncovered the reason for the Si-Fan's change of direction lately."

"I'm grateful to hear that I've made myself useful to someone," I said. "Now, perhaps you would care to explain it to me, because, frankly, I've never felt so lost without a trace in my whole life."

Smith smiled and set his pipe down in the ashtray that rested on the table in front of him.

"The Si-Fan is an ancient secret society, older than the Buddha himself, it is claimed. They are based in Tibet, but have loyal followers found on every continent. I first encountered the man known as Fu Manchu nearly thirty years ago in Burma where I was stationed as a colonial administrator."

How appropriate, I thought as Smith continued.

"Dr. Fu Manchu was an agent of the Si-Fan at the time. Later, he rose to become president of the Council of Seven, its ruling body. Last year, two failed plots to assassinate both Adolf Hitler and Herman Goering cost him the presidency. Since that time, the Si-Fan has made a dramatic shift and become supportive of Hitler and Mussolini's policies. Obviously, the change in direction is attributable to the new president of the Council of Seven, but until now, the identity of Fu Manchu's successor was a mystery to us."

"Esteban Milagro is the president of this council that you mention," I confirmed. "I overheard Helga say as much during an argument I witnessed between them."

"Who is this Helga he keeps referring to?" Sir Lionel thundered.

"Helga Graumann," I added to Barton's further annoyance.

"You will remember her best as Madame Ingomar, Sir Lionel," Smith declared. "Whereas Kerrigan knows her as Koreani, and I knew her as Fah lo Suee. By any name, she is the daughter of Fu Manchu and is the most dangerous woman in the world."

"She has a title as well," I added, feeling emboldened that my contributions were restoring me to their good graces. "She is known among the Orientals as Our Lady of the Si-Fan."

Immediately, I was aware that I had misspoken. Nayland Smith's face fell and he started forward in his seat as if he were about to grab me.

"Are you certain that you heard the Orientals refer to her by that title?"

I stammered for a moment, thinking of what could possibly be wrong with what I had said.

"Of course, I'm certain. I heard it used to refer to her several times. Helga even excused her offending Milagro by stating that her title justified treating him with disdain in public."

"This is puzzling," Smith said as he retrieved his pipe from the ashtray. "When last we saw her, Fah lo Suee was unaware of her identity as Fu Manchu's daughter. Her father had wiped her memories."

"Yes," I said, recollecting what I had heard. "That is what they discussed. Apparently, Milagro restored her memory somehow, but her father is unaware of this."

Smith puffed at his pipe. "This does make for an interesting development."

"Who is Fu Manchu?" I asked, "Why is he so dangerous?"

"He is the most brilliant man alive today," Smith snapped, "of that, I have no doubt. He possesses all the secret knowledge and cunning of a dozen Eastern races and several lost civilizations to boot. He also holds degrees from at least four Western universities. Our earliest record of him dates from Lord Kitchener's conflict with El Mahdi. We know he was Governor of Ho-Nan province under the Empress Dowager at the time of the Boxer Uprising, and that he fell from grace with the Royal Family at that time. We do not know his real identity or his actual age. Suffice to say he is far older than he looks, thanks to his *Elixir Vitae* with which he holds death at bay, and may continue to do so for several more decades to come, if not longer. He is privy to many of the secrets of the priesthood of Thebes and of the infamous Cult of the Black Scorpion. Countless numbers of lives have been lost, and many more enslaved, because of his machinations. It is no exaggeration when I tell you that Dr. Fu Manchu is the single greatest threat to Western civilization alive today."

"That is impressive, considering the recent developments in Europe."

"Yes, Professor, it is. That is why the Si-Fan's shifting allegiance had us puzzled, but if Esteban Milagro is now president of the Council of Seven, I begin to understand. I first met the man just before the Great War. He was an occultist eager to infiltrate the Si-Fan at the time. He ran afoul of Fu Manchu in the process and was left terribly disfigured as you doubtless noticed."

I nodded my head in agreement as Smith continued.

"Do not make the mistake of underestimating him, as I fear Fu Manchu must have done. Esteban Milagro was very nearly responsible for unleashing a devastating supernatural power upon the Earth. There are times when I have wondered whether the Great War would have occurred at all without his invoking sinister forces from beyond to conspire against mankind."

I cleared my throat, somewhat reluctant to speak. "What is so significant about the title, Our Lady of the Si-Fan?"

"It is a title that is reserved for the human incarnation of the goddess Kali. The traditions of the Si-Fan state that the goddess' human incarnation is reborn each generation and remains in the care of a secret lamasery in Tibet where she rules over the Si-Fan, perpetually young and inviolate."

I exploded with laughter at the ridiculousness of his words.

"That seems a bit off whether one is talking about Kali or Helga, doesn't it?"

"You need to remember, dear boy," Barton warbled beneath his bushy white moustache, "while traditions and customs change as one group of people comes in contact with another, allowing their mythologies to develop in a similar fashion, Gnostic beliefs remain rigid because of their failure to mix with other spheres of influence. What remains is the remnant of two conflicting goddess myths, combined into one matriarchal figure who is equal parts whore and virgin."

"Rather sounds like the ideal girl if you ask me, but I'm quite sure that it has been an awfully long time since anyone has accused Helga of being a virgin, let me assure you."

"On the contrary," Smith replied, "it is the role she was born to play, and has played before quite successfully. That was the identity she had adopted when I first learned of her. She was still a teenager and beguiling members of the Si-Fan's Council of Seven, while her father plotted his advancement. Now, it seems she is working to advance her own interests, while pretending to serve two masters. We have seen this behavior from her before with the Mandarin Ki-Ming. She is taking an enormous gamble that her father will not learn the truth. I fear his mercy for his own flesh and blood has its limits."

"What I still don't understand is the interest in the excavation. While I was their prisoner, I saw Fu Manchu gain access to the lower level that my men were busy digging out in the very next chamber."

"What? Do you mean to say he was present at the dig when we found you?" Smith exclaimed. "Great Scott, man! Why did you wait so long to tell us this? We might have captured him."

I shook my head and explained: "I did my best to find the release for the secret panel in the wall, but to no avail. There must be a lever activated by some other means to prevent its discovery. I searched quite thoroughly for some method of activating it. Believe me, it is not there, and yet, I saw them leave by the very same secret panel with my own two eyes."

"Blast!" Smith swore, striking his fist in the palm of his hand. "If only we had known at the time. Do you have any idea where Milagro's base is located?"

I shook my head again. "I was driven to his headquarters and I know it is some miles from Cairo in the middle of the desert, but I could not find it if I tried. I could not even hazard a guess as to which direction it lies from here. It shouldn't really matter, I would think, as they were heading to Munich...or at least Helga and Milagro were."

"Munich?" Kerrigan jumped from his seat with a start. "Did you say Munich?"

"Yes, it is supposed to represent some sort of victory for Milagro. I'm sorry but if I heard more concerning it, I'm afraid that it was beyond my comprehension."

"Smith, that's it!" Kerrigan was nearly bursting with excitement. "This Milagro character is obviously going to Munich to meet with Hitler. He plans to manipulate the tense situation in the Sudetenland to press the Si-Fan's advantage!"

"You may be right, Kerrigan," Smith snapped. "It would also explain what confused Knox at the dig. Fu Manchu has already gained access to the secret chamber. We already know that he is an adept of the secrets of the Theban priesthood. His catalepsy-inducing drug, and likely the *Elixir Vitae*, are both products of the priesthood's Gnostic skills. It stands to reason that Milagro is trying desperately to match and exceed Fu Manchu's arcane knowledge. That is why he, or one of his subordinates, used Professor Simos to arrange the dig for them. The question now is, which side is Fah lo Suee favoring? She is obviously deceiving both of them in an attempt to seize control of the Si-Fan for herself. Since her father has already been deposed as President, her time to act would be after Milagro allies the Si-Fan with the Nazis."

My head was spinning, but I realized that Smith was beginning to make sense of the disparate strands of information that I had accumulated.

"We have to get back to London, Smith. It is imperative that the Prime Minister initiates Plan Z as soon as possible," Kerrigan seemed barely able to breathe as he spoke.

"You're absolutely correct, Kerrigan. We will appeal to the highest diplomatic level necessary to arrange a private flight to London," Smith said, chewing agitatedly on the tip of his pipe. "Meantime, Weymouth will use every means possible to conduct a search of all desert installations near Cairo that might conceivably house Si-Fan operations. It's as good a bet as any that the Petries are being held at the facility where Knox was taken. Professor, I will ask you to accompany the Superintendent. You may not know how to find your way, but you would certainly recognize the location when you see it. Fey, you will continue to safeguard Sir Lionel and Anna here until we return. You will be responsible for insuring that neither of them leaves this house under any circumstances."

"Now wait just a minute..." Barton and I spoke in unison. I sat back in my chair and nodded for the old man to speak first.

"Fu Manchu makes the find of the century over in Luxor and you expect to keep me locked up here like some pathetic old invalid? Have you taken leave of your good senses, Smith?"

"You will get your chance to turn up every nook and cranny at the site in Luxor, Barton, I promise it. For now, however, the safest place for you and Anna is right here, as far removed as possible from the Si-Fan's notice. Once this business in Munich is concluded one way or the other, we will certainly need your expertise to make a proper survey of the site."

I felt miffed at his obvious slight, but saw a chance to speak up for myself.

"I rather think that I would prove more useful if I were to accompany you, Sir Denis. I was unable to get a very good look at Milagro's headquarters since I was

142

locked inside of the back of a truck, and was then contained in a basket day and night once we were inside. Alternatively, if I were to accompany you, I could provide an eyewitness account, if one were needed, of all that I had seen and heard among Milagro, Helga, and Fu Manchu. It would certainly seem prudent to take me along in the event that the Prime Minister would have questions only I could answer."

Smith puffed at his pipe for a moment as he mulled my offer over in his mind.

"I have a feeling that I may yet have cause to regret this, but I'm going to let you come along, Professor. We could use another man and you've managed to survive thus far. You may be correct, you may yet prove useful. You, of course, will submit to being under my direct command at all times."

I nodded my head in agreement.

"Splendid, then we've not a moment to spare. First we start with the embassy..."

I didn't realize it at the time, but our first council of war against the Si-Fan had just concluded.

12. INCIDENT AT 10 DOWNING STREET

"The situation in the Sudetenland is extremely complex, but I will try to summarize it in as little time as possible," Kerrigan was speaking across the aisle of the aeroplane to Smith and me as we glided barely 100 feet above the Atlantic.

"There are more than three million Germans living in Czechoslovakia today; the majority of them are in the Sudetenland. President Benes has been at loggerheads with the Sudeten Nazi Party for the last several months. You may have read in the papers that the Nazis are demanding the Sudetenland be granted autonomy from Czechoslovakia in order to ally itself with Germany. Benes has steadfastly refused to comply with these demands because the Sudetenland houses most of Czechoslovakia's border defenses, and many of its banks, as well.

"The Prime Minister, with the support of the French, has advised President Benes to accede to Hitler's demands in order to avoid further escalation. Lord Runciman was appointed mediator to prevent a full-fledged German invasion. Benes gave in to nearly every demand the Nazis made a couple weeks ago, but the Sudeten Nazi Party still organized a demonstration which led to the usual violence, provoking the expected police action. Consequently, Chancellor Hitler is now demanding that the Sudetenland be turned over to Germany to prevent the continued slaughter of Germans by Czechoslovakia."

Kerrigan paused for a moment and smiled. "In my view, the Nazis are determined to have their war and let diplomacy be damned. That is the situation that the Si-Fan regards as ripe for exploitation."

"Is this your specialty with the Home Office?" I asked.

Smith snorted in amusement. "Kerrigan is a journalist, Professor. He doesn't work for British intelligence."

"Not directly anyway," Kerrigan added with a smile.

"That's true," Smith said after a moment's consideration. "I suppose I've always found it useful to rely on civilian resources ever since I first dragged Petrie into this business all those years ago."

For a moment, I detected a hint of sadness across those suntanned, weather-beaten features of his. It was evident that, whatever fate had befallen the Petries, Smith held himself responsible. I didn't envy him that particular burden.

"Like Petrie, Kerrigan has put his journalistic talents to good use chronicling our ongoing conflict with the Si-Fan," he chuckled, as if we were discussing a particularly involving game and not a matter of life and death. "Petrie was a frustrated author and enjoyed sensationalizing our exploits, whereas Kerrigan has a more polished and refined approach as befits a veteran Fleet Street reporter."

Kerrigan smiled at the compliment. "Sir Denis is far too generous, I'm afraid. My first two efforts were the result of my interviewing the parties involved some months after the fact, and the results were somewhat less than ideal accounts as a consequence. My most recent narrative has the advantage of chronicling events that I witnessed first-hand. Regrettably, the Home Office has been redlining my manuscript for months. I daresay, if they ever allow it to be published, I shan't recognize many of the names or incidents."

Smith laughed and nodded his head in agreement. He sat and puffed at his pipe for a moment, contemplatively.

"Fu Manchu has one consistent weakness that we have been able to successfully exploit time and again."

I raised my eyebrows expectantly.

"Women," he said simply. "I don't mean for his own amusement; he reserves his ardor for something higher than the pleasures of the flesh. Rather, he employs female agents to seduce and subsequently blackmail prominent men into compromising their integrity to aid the Si-Fan. Failing that, the fairer sex regularly serves as bait for their unwary prey's capture or elimination."

"I don't understand how this constitutes a weakness? It would seem to be quite an effective tactic on his part."

"It is effective, Knox, but women...and men...are human, not automatons. Eventually, one of those irresistible tools of his becomes emotionally involved and then..."

He snapped his fingers to indicate the evaporation of all that Fu Manchu had worked to achieve.

"That undoing has saved my life, and those who assist me, many times over the years. From Petrie to Kerrigan, a great number of men in my company have been fortunate enough to survive their encounters with these Mata Haris of his, and most of them have come out ahead for their troubles..."

146

I glanced across at Kerrigan and noted the pained expression on his face. I realized that he was among those who had not been so fortunate. Smith's callous disregard for the man's feelings reminded me that the reason he had likely persevered for so many years against Dr. Fu Manchu was largely attributable to their many commonalities. It was an interesting thought, considering that I was placing my life in his hands.

"I suspect Fah lo Suee, or Koreani, or Helga Graumann, as you know her, has likewise developed an attachment to you. Do not be too flattered, Knox, you are hardly the first and her infatuations are always fleeting. We may be able, if fortune smiles upon us, to put this attraction of hers to good use, however. That was the principal reason that I agreed to bring you along."

Kerrigan settled back in his seat and sighed. "It will be nice to be home again."

My mind turned to how many years it had been since I had left England. Now, I was not only returning home, but being granted an audience with the Prime Minister. My life had turned decidedly surreal ever since I had joined Spiridon in Corfu in what seemed a lifetime ago.

England had not changed in the intervening years. September was still wet and dreary. We took a taxi straight from Heston Aerodrome to Westminster. The leaves on the trees in St. James Park were just changing color and had not yet begun to fall with the autumnal death that would soon settle upon the land. Nature seemed sadly out of step. The rest of Europe had already embraced a final autumn and was waiting for the curtain to close on the continent one final time.

I had passed by 10 Downing Street many times, but had never been privileged to step inside that 200 year-old monument to the Empire's glory. Three large town-houses had been joined together by William Kent, through the generosity of Sir Robert Walpole. I had memorized the facts of its construction as a schoolboy, and now found myself welcomed inside its majestic interior in the company of no less a personage than Sir Denis Nayland Smith and Fleet Street journalist Bart Kerrigan. These were strange times indeed.

Past the wrought iron spiked fence, the narrow white Georgian door of Number 10, with its lion-face iron knocker, opened into a house with black and white marble tile containing somewhere around 100 rooms accessible from the stone triple staircase with its wrought iron balustrade and mahogany handrail. The sheer size of Number 10 was easy to believe, given the dazzling scope of its interior. Offices, conference rooms, sitting rooms, reception areas, and dining rooms abounded. The third floor was the Prime Minister's private residence, and the kitchen was located in the basement. These, and other facts, sprouted dryly from our aged escort's mouth as if he were conducting school-children on a tour.

The interior courtyard was mentioned, but not glimpsed. Happily, we did see the terrace overlooking the sprawling half-acre garden. For the first time in many months, perhaps longer, I felt a thrill of childlike happiness, and began to suspect that my innocence could be reclaimed after all.

We were led into the White Drawing room where, we were told, the Prime Minister would join us shortly. The room was decorated in Turner's gorgeous land-scapes and sat in sharp contrast to the dour portraits of our nation's former Prime Ministers that looked down upon visitors from the walls as they climbed the staircase. A bronze statuette attracted my eye. It was a miniature version of Florence Nightingale from the Crimean Memorial in Waterloo Place. My recognition of the piece did little to stem my curiosity of what sort of woman she must have really been.

"Gentlemen," a voice boomed as the door opened unexpectedly. I turned and found myself facing Prime Minister Neville Chamberlain. He looked older than I had expected from his photographs, but it was more the fact that he was standing before me, and not simply a picture, that was the most unsettling. "Good afternoon..." he paused and checked his pocket watch, "...almost. I haven't much time for this meeting, Sir Denis; you will kindly come directly to the point."

He put his fist to his mouth as he cleared his throat with a mighty rumble and seated himself at the head of the table. I quickly took my place next to Kerrigan, who sat opposite Nayland Smith.

"Of course, Prime Minister, I would not be here if circumstances did not demand your attention. Thank you again for making time for us and at such short notice. You, of course, remember Bart Kerrigan, a journalist friend of mine...he has complete clearance from the Home Office...and this is..."

The Prime Minister turned to regard Kerrigan and interrupted Smith before he could introduce me properly.

"Yes, George briefed me about Mr. Kerrigan and this latest book of his. This is very unorthodox, Sir Denis, very unorthodox, indeed."

Smith smiled uncomfortably. "Yes, Prime Minister, indeed. This is Professor Michael Knox of the University of Athens. We have the Professor to thank for bringing the facts of the current Si-Fan plot to light."

"Yes, I'm quite aware of your longstanding obsession with the Si-Fan, Sir Denis. You will presently come to the point."

"The point, sir," Smith said, testily, "is that the Si-Fan is seeking to use the current unstable situation in the Sudetenland as a tactical move to cement their alliance with Germany. The point of said alliance will be for the Si-Fan to direct the Nazis in increasingly greater acts of aggression. They mean to conquer the world, sir. I do not believe you can afford to delay another hour. You must put Plan Z into action."

Smith's agitation was evident as the Prime Minister coldly stared at him. I could not hazard a guess whether he was carefully considering Smith's warning, or preparing to storm out of the room in a fit, believing his time had been wasted. Finally, he sighed and took a deep breath.

"Heaven knows we don't need further trouble from the Si-Fan, Sir Denis, but these people need to make up their minds. First, they try to assassinate Hitler, and now they want to lie in bed with him. Perhaps it was short-sightedness on our part in demanding that you prevent those assassinations," the Prime Minister slowly shook his head. "There is so much to be done here at home that I cannot attend to because of these damned foreign policy matters. Speaking of which, I understand you caused a bit of a stir in Abyssinia recently. Need I remind you that we don't need Italy breathing down our necks because of your failure to respect their jurisdiction?"

"That was regrettable, Prime Minister," Smith said, choosing his words carefully, "but my focus, as always, is on the larger picture if you follow me."

The Prime Minister grunted indicating that he did no such thing.

"The world, sir," Smith explained. "There is more at stake here than just Britain."

"Thunderation, Mr. Smith!" The Prime Minister exploded with rage, pounding the table with his fist. "If I wanted a lesson in idiocy, I'd be meeting with Anthony Eden instead. Britain's welfare is paramount. Preserving peace is the one and only reason for us to meddle in the affairs of other nations. If the Si-Fan has the good sense to decide to stop upsetting the applecart, perhaps it is time that you did the same."

Kerrigan exchanged a concerned look with me.

"Sir, with all due respect," Smith began, "I fear that you fail to appreciate the gravity of the situation. The Si-Fan's recent decision to support Germany and Italy is not indicative of their apprehension over Europe being a tinderbox at the moment, but rather a reflection of the man who has succeeded Fu Manchu as President of the Council of Seven. He is an Englishman, sir. His name is Thomas Valley. You can pull his file. He was presumed to have died just before the War, but he lives, and has now risen to prominence in the Si-Fan under an assumed alias."

"Yes, they seem quite fond of those," the Prime Minister added, rolling his eyes. "Perhaps some English sensibility is just what these people need. It seems it's what the whole world needs to set things to right. I have no intention of plunging Britain into a war she can ill afford, nor do I have any desire to allow History to re-member me as the man who did so. It has been said, Sir Denis, that you have allowed this situation with the Si-Fan to turn into a private war of sorts. You would not be the first official in British Intelligence to make the mis-

151

take of considering himself the British Government incarnate. Now, I personally have never doubted your patriotism, but..."

"Prime Minister," Smith interrupted, "such scurrilous talk has plagued me throughout my career, and has doubtless hampered my advancement to even greater heights," he paused pointedly. "Fu Manchu still sits on the Council of Seven. We have every reason to suspect that he will do whatever is possible to sabotage his successor's plans to regain control. That could mean anything, but another attempt on Chancellor Hitler should certainly not be ruled out. We cannot afford to allow the Si-Fan to gain the advantage on either side. There is too much at risk to allow them to sway the situation one way or the other. The very war you are working so hard to prevent could be the inevitable result if you continue to do nothing but wait.

"You may choose not to heed my words. You would certainly not be the first to do so, and I daresay you won't be the last. I have said before that I am no stranger to others discounting me as a hysterical alarmist. I will also note that I have generally been proven correct in hindsight, as my survival through the years should attest. Consequently, I concern myself with doing what is right, rather than worrying about how others will perceive my actions in the future."

The silence in the room was deafening and I wondered whether Smith's last remark had not gone too far. The Prime Minister's face showed no emotion, which only made me more uncomfortable as I waited for some reaction. Presently, he spoke with surprising calm as if he had not just been dressed down by a subordinate.

"As it happens, Sir Denis, recent events have already made it necessary for me to take drastic steps regarding the situation."

"You speak of the Nuremberg Rally, I presume?" Smith asked, lifting his eyebrows with interest.

"Excellent, Sir Denis," the Prime Minister nodded, smiling faintly. "I am pleased that you have not neglected your duties while you were abroad. I count on your personal attention should the situation demand it."

"Of course, sir," Smith answered, brusquely.

"Splendid. Then if there is nothing else..."

The Prime Minister rose from the table and the three of us followed suit.

"Did you have an opportunity to see the view from the terrace, gentlemen?"

The Prime Minister addressed Kerrigan and me as if we had come along with Smith as sightseers.

"Yes, sir, thank you for asking," Kerrigan said, forcing an uncomfortable smile, "it was simply breathtaking."

"Wonderful, wonderful," the Prime Minister said as he turned and exited through the door that Smith held open for him.

No sooner did we step into the hallway than our aged escort reappeared in a very agitated state. It struck me that he rather resembled a penguin with his large eyes, beak-like nose, and long strands of hair plastered to either side of his otherwise bald head. The tuxedo he wore only completed the image of the comical flightless fowl.

"Prime Minister, please pardon this intrusion. Sheikh Saleh has just arrived unannounced and is demanding an audience with you immediately."

The Prime Minister sighed and glanced at his pocket watch. "Very well. Show him to the White Room and offer him refreshments. I can spare him five minutes after my briefing."

The old man nodded with barely concealed relief as the Prime Minister moved off, paying us no further notice. Evidently accustomed to such behavior, he gestured for us to follow him as he stiffly showed us the way out.

As we descended the massive stone staircase, my pulse quickened at the sight before me. There, at the foot of the stairs, stood a man dressed in a white suit. The keffiyeh he wore upon his head and the dark grey scarf that was wrapped around his mouth stood in sharp contrast with his Western dress. I recognized him instantly.

Visions of the terror I underwent as a child flashed before my eyes...being abducted...fearing that I would never see my mother again...fearing for what would become of my little sister...half-starved and beaten by an Englishman and then Arabs...finally, the realization that the abuse we suffered was for naught as we dangled helplessly above a crocodile pit...I was certain the end was upon us and there was no one in Heaven or on Earth who would come to our aid...all because of him...the man now standing before me...

I was conscious of the obscenities escaping my lips as I pushed past Smith and Kerrigan and threw myself upon the man in a frenzy that I cannot rationally explain. Smith and Kerrigan were at my side pulling me off almost instantly.

"Knox, what the devil has come over you, man?"

"Good Heavens! Oh, Sheikh Saleh, please forgive this outburst! What is the meaning of this outrage?"

"I have him! I have him!"

"Knox, just what the Hell do you think you're doing?"

The voices jumbled in my head as a wave of dizziness overcame me. I could see that hated figure, hands grasping his throat as he coughed violently. My arms were pinned behind my back. Hands roughly grasped my shoulders.

"That's him, that's Milagro, I tell you!"

My head stopped spinning. Nayland Smith was staring at me with a look of bewilderment upon his face.

"Have you gone mad, Knox?"

"My apologies, Sheikh Saleh," our aged escort was saying.

"Let me tear that scarf from his face and you'll see that I am correct!"

"Knox, stop this at once," Smith hissed through gritted teeth.

"Sheikh Saleh, please forgive me. If you will follow me, please," the escort's voice was quivering, but I could no longer see the man as Smith and Kerrigan bundled me toward the exit.

13. WORLD GONE WRONG

"Do you have any idea how much effort it took to keep you from being arrested? I don't care who you thought he was. Behaving like a madman in Number 10 was simply asinine. You have single-handedly destroyed whatever credibility I managed to retain after our disastrous meeting with the Prime Minister."

I was sitting in Sir Denis Nayland Smith's study in Whitechapel receiving as harsh a dressing down as I'd received since I was...well, since I was dismissed by Christ College for conduct unbecoming a faculty member. That incident concluded with my leaving England for a number of years. The current incident followed my return to England by a matter of hours. I was working on convincing myself that the problem was England, and not my own behavior.

"I took the trouble to inquire into the background of the gentleman you assaulted..."

"That gentleman was Esteban Milagro," I interrupted, but Smith was just as quick and was emphasizing "was *not* Esteban Milagro" at the same time as I was speaking. I sat silently for a moment as we stared at one another. Smith was fighting the urge to pace.

"Esteban Milagro...or Thomas Valley, as I first knew him, is an urbane and dapper man of slight build. He was most definitely not the muscular Arab gentleman that you very nearly throttled."

"You didn't even bother to remove the scarf. He has the exact same hideous smile carved into his face as you described. That was the man I saw in Egypt with Helga Graumann. I am certain of it."

"Sheikh Zahi Saleh," Smith sighed, "comes from a very old and very wealthy Egyptian family. He is renowned for his exotic menagerie and has, by all accounts, no criminal or political affiliations. He is a peaceable, if eccentric, collector of rare birds, animals, insects, plants, and flowers. He has become a common visitor to 10 Downing Street in the last few years, and has been actively involved in dressing various functions with choice selections culled from his private collections. Does that sound anything like the President of the Council of Seven to you?"

I opened and shut my mouth. I was so positive it was him, and yet what Smith said gave me cause to doubt. Could I have been so affected by the paralyzing drug that my memory was no longer reliable? I resolved not to argue the point any further.

"What next?" I asked after a moment of silence. "Do we return to Egypt?"

"You will remain here in London and confine yourself to my flat. It is likely that the Prime Minister will be requiring my services imminently. It seems that he was correct. The world does need a British mind to sort things out. Let us hope that if it comes to it, he is up to the task."

"Plan Z?" I asked.

Smith nodded, but said nothing else and began to busy himself with a file before him on his desk.

"If I may ask, what exactly is Plan Z?"

Smith looked at me a moment before he rose from his seat and began to pace about the room.

"In the event that war with Germany appears inevitable, the Prime Minister will fly to Munich personally to negotiate with Chancellor Hitler."

"That doesn't seem so startling a decision to make under the circumstances. Why is there a need to shroud the plan in such secrecy?"

"The reason, Professor, is not that the Prime Minister is willing to personally negotiate directly with *der Fuhrer* so much as the lengths he will go to insure that peace be maintained. That part of the plan, I am afraid, must remain strictly confidential. Needless to say, I shall be required to accompany him in the event that the Nuremberg Rally goes as poorly as we expect. Kerrigan will join me, but I am afraid there is no possibility of your obtaining clearance after that incident with Sheikh Saleh. I regret that I must insist that you confine yourself indoors while we are gone, Professor. It is for your own safety; we cannot take the chance that the Si-Fan has tracked you here from Cairo."

The next four days passed slowly and without incident. Smith and Kerrigan were both absent much of the time, leaving me a prisoner in Smith's flat. I listened to the BBC's coverage of the Nuremberg Rally and was anxious to learn what additional information Smith or even Kerrigan had been able to glean from either the Home Office or in Kerrigan's official capacity as a member of the press.

There was little doubt that we were indeed on the verge of another war as the Rally progressed. The BBC reported that troops had mobilized on the border. A corresponding sea of bodies gathered outside 10 Downing Street on the closing night of the Rally. There was naught I could do to rectify this world gone wrong had I been at liberty. Consequently, spending my hours sitting by the radio at least seemed more sensible than shivering in the cold among a mob that were as helpless as me to turn events, in spite of the bravado their numbers inspired.

Chancellor Hitler's voice crackled mechanically through the speaker before rising to its practiced fevered pitch that drove his frenzied followers to action, even as it instilled fear in the hearts of all sane listeners hearing him speak. My German was a bit rusty, but I was able to make out most of his speech before the BBC announcer translated it into English.

"The condition of the Sudeten Germans is indescribable," his diatribe began. "It is sought to annihilate them. As human beings, they are oppressed and scandalously treated in an intolerable fashion," he paused as the crowd in Nuremberg cheered with one voice. "The depriving of their rights must come to an end," a second pause as the wave of supporters roared again. "I have stated that the Reich would not tolerate any further oppression of these three and a half million Germans, and I would ask the statesmen of foreign countries to be convinced that this is no mere form of words."

Kerrigan returned late that night, but said little and retired quickly to his room, leaving me with no indication whether he was aware of anything other than what was printed in the papers. Sir Denis was gone all the next day as well, and Kerrigan's comings and goings were frequent. with only the briefest contact between us. Finally, two days after I had listened to Hitler's broadcast, Smith returned home at last and quickly called Kerrigan and me to gather in his study.

"Gentlemen," Smith began, "what I say is in the strictest confidence. I brought you back to London with me in an attempt to warn the Prime Minister that the Si-Fan seeks to use the situation in the Sudetenland to their advantage. Regrettably, circumstances have escalated beyond our control, and whether or not the Si-Fan has played a role in the decision, the fact remains that Germany has determined to invade Czechoslovakia within the next two weeks. Unsurprisingly, the French are hell-bent on remaining neutral—although they are willing to discuss meeting with Britain and Germany to settle the matter peaceably.

"Last night, the Prime Minister finally determined to go forward with Plan Z. He has contacted Chancellor Hitler to offer to come to Munich to negotiate. Hitler has accepted the offer and has invited the Prime Minister to meet with him at Berchtesgaden. I will be in attendance. Professor, I am sorry, but I am afraid that you will have to remain confined here a while longer. Kerrigan and I should be back within a few days."

We spoke little for the remainder of the day as Smith and Kerrigan were otherwise occupied preparing for their trip. A depression had settled upon us as we watched our world hurtle toward an inevitable collision that only promised misery for every nation involved. There seemed little enough to stave off the forces of darkness that had arisen to threaten the fragile peace of our world.

It was just before Noon the next day when I found myself staring out the window. The sun was shining and it appeared unseasonably warm. London was finally free of the ever-present drizzle that did so much to reinforce a sense of oppression. Smith and Kerrigan had departed for Heston Aerodrome with the Prime Minister. Sir Denis' apartment was as quiet as the grave. I wanted nothing more than to take a stroll in the sun and get some fresh air. Smith's fears that the Si-Fan would somehow learn that I was in London seemed remote, and it was easy enough to rationalize my decision to ignore his orders just this once.

The temptation was too great to resist and, soon, I found myself walking freely along the Strand, crossing Trafalgar Square, and proceeding up Haymarket to Piccadilly Circus. I enjoyed being as one with the teeming crowds of the City. It was there that I spotted her. The cool breeze and the warmth of the sun only added to the mystifying sight. She was thin with long, golden tresses, and I was captivated the instant that I laid eyes upon her. She was so familiar, and yet somehow different.

Her eyes caught mine and she smiled as if she was unsure whether she recognized me. Her features were charmingly elfin with freckles and a birthmark, so perfect they might have been drawn on, dotting her nose and cheek, respectively. Her eyes were blue as the ocean on a summer day. The splash of brown in her left eye offered a delightful hint of eccentricity to her character.

She seemed about to ask if she knew me when a name entered my mind as if whispered by a spirit.

"Alexandra...Dunhill...after all this time," I breathed the words as if dreaming.

"Do...do I know you?"

I heard her voice, but I only saw the neighborhood girl I had grown up with standing before me now as a woman. She was five years my elder, but looked very much the opposite. Her face had none of the hardness of suffering written upon it. How had she emerged from our nightmarish childhood ordeal unscathed? I thought of my sister and wondered if the better question was, why I, alone of the three of us, had been left so scarred by the experience.

"Michael Knox," I heard myself speak mechanically. "We were neighbors many, many years ago in Herne Hill."

Her eyes widened and she put a hand to her mouth before throwing her arms about me and hugging me. The impulsive gesture ended as quickly as it had begun, but the smile upon her face was genuine.

"How have you been? My Lord, I haven't thought of you in ages. How are you? How is Anna?"

"I'm well...and so is Anna," I said chuckling. Passersby noted our reunion with quiet bemusement. "I'm a Professor of Archaeology at the University of Athens these days. Anna is a zoologist and lives in Abyssinia."

Again, I noted the charming smile prompting the nervous response of a hand covering her mouth.

"I don't believe it...well, maybe I can believe it. I'm a botanist. I work here in the City...at the moment."

She held her left hand up.

"Never married...what about you?"

I saw her glance at my hand, but thought I would save her the trouble. "No, I'm still unattached...the same as you...and the same as Anna."

"Isn't that funny," she said, her smile aglow with interest.

"Perhaps not so surprising, considering what the three of us went through," I said, testing her memory.

For a moment, a look of seriousness crossed her face, but she literally brushed it aside with a hand pushing the hair from her eyes.

"Oh, I never even think of that anymore," she smiled. "Life is too short to only remember the bad times. Do you have lunch plans already? I was just about to stop for a bite at a restaurant just down the road and thought perhaps you would like to join me?"

Ordinarily, my bachelor instincts would have warned me away. An attractive unattached woman over forty was a dangerous lunch companion. Surely, there was someone younger or less serious with whom to while away the afternoon. But for some reason, I didn't want the company of anyone but her. She was a connection to my past. She was genuine, she was beautiful, and, suddenly, I didn't feel like Michael Knox any more, or rather, maybe I felt like Michael Knox again for the first time in years.

Lunch was pleasant, but too brief. We said our goodbyes and a veil of sadness hung over me as I walked back to Whitechapel and considered that, in all likelihood, Alexandra and I would never see each other again. As I approached Smith's flat, I considered how precious my hour's freedom had been to me. Now, I had to return to my cell and a life of solitude.

Several days later, Smith and Kerrigan finally returned from their meeting in Germany. We gathered in Smith's study once more. Despite my boredom over the past few days, I had not attempted to venture outside again after my lone afternoon excursion with Alexandra.

"I fear the situation has changed for the worse," Smith began our meeting ominously. "Kerrigan and I have just returned from a critical meeting with Chancellor Hitler in Bad Godesberg. Hitler has decided that the agreement we reached in Berchtesgaden will no longer suffice. He demands immediate occupation of the Sudetenland, and intends to address territorial claims in Poland and Hungary as well. The Prime Minister is understandably furious with him. The effort he has exerted to convince the French and the Czechs to cooperate with Hitler to avoid war has not helped his popularity at home. He was booed outside 10 Downing Street when we returned earlier today."

"To what do you attribute this sudden change?" I asked. "Is Hitler merely hell-bent on war or do you think that..."

"Oh, I have no doubt that the Si-Fan has somehow managed to succeed in influencing him. I would need to get close enough to Hitler before I could convince the Prime Minister of that fact. It would only irritate him were I to suggest it now. He is simply huffing and puffing that the meeting was 'most unsatisfactory.'"

Smith paused to allow a terse smile at his humorous imitation.

"For now, the two of them are playing a game of politics. Hitler has tried all the usual tactics. He delayed meetings for hours; he submitted written demands in German only, etc. The more power a man wields, the more like a spoiled child he becomes. The more patience the Prime Minister displayed with him, the less Hitler respects him. On and on, it goes...a child's game that may very well end in millions of unnecessary deaths, just as we saw with the Great War."

"Such are the ways of man," I said and was immediately conscious of Smith and Kerrigan's eyes upon me. "Sorry, just an observation from a lifetime devoted to the study of dead civilizations. Nothing ever really changes. You look upon the wonders of the world and puzzle over the fact that man cannot appreciate them and live in harmony with his neighbor. If Darwin is right, and we are descended from beasts, I cannot imagine what goes wrong in our psychology that makes us destroy ourselves. One certainly does not find that phenomenon among the animal kingdom."

"No," Smith mused, "I suppose it isn't predatory instinct that drives man to self-destruction. Still, philosophy will get us nowhere. We are tottering on the edge of war, and the Si-Fan is ready and willing to give us one last push. We need to find some means of getting close enough to stop them. The question is, how do we manage to get closer to the opposition?"

Sir Denis said nothing more of Plan Z. I envied Kerrigan for having earned his confidence, but understood that my weeks of deception would not be undone by the brief period of my cooperation. Was it possible for us to gain closer access to Hitler? Surprisingly, the means was about to present itself to us in the most unexpected fashion.

14. MEETING IN MUNICH

"Sheikh Zahi Saleh is dead," Nayland Smith announced unexpectedly one afternoon upon his return from a meeting at 10 Downing Street.

"Well, don't look at me, I haven't left the premises. Not recently anyway," I said half-jokingly.

We had gathered, as was his fashion, in Sir Denis' study. He held a manila folder stuffed with papers in his left hand and dropped it on the desk in front of him. One presumed the contents dealt with the late Sheikh.

"You needn't concern yourself with an alibi, Knox, for you were out of the country at the time."

"What?"

"He's been dead for four years this November," Smith plopped down in the chair behind his desk and placed his hands together in front of his face so that his fingertips just barely touched.

"How is that possible, Sir Denis?" Kerrigan asked.

Smith turned and rose from his seat and began to pace about the room as was his habit when agitated.

"Sheikh Zahi Saleh was killed in a boating accident off the French Riviera. The Sûreté has a record of the accident, but no bodies were recovered, and yet the Sheikh's family assures us that they believe him to be dead."

"If he is dead, then who did we meet at 10 Downing Street?"

"That is a very good question, Professor. Whoever it is, he has not returned home in all that time. Certainly strange behavior, wouldn't you say? He continues to maintain the Sheikh's menagerie and gardens around the world and, almost immediately following the accident, he replaced every single member of his staff, including his guards. I'm sure you both would agree that is also rather strange behavior."

"The man we met is an imposter?" Kerrigan asked in amazement.

"It is certainly a possibility," Smith replied.

"Why would anyone go to such lengths to impersonate the Sheikh and for so long a time?"

"An excellent question, Professor, but one that perhaps is best explained when one considers the fact that for the past four years, the Sheikh has utilized his personal collection of rare animal and plant life almost exclusively for the purpose of entertaining various dignitaries, both here and abroad. You may recall my mentioning that he had become a fixture at Number 10."

"Then it is possible that I was correct," I exclaimed. "It is Milagro after all."

"The possibility does exist, although he does not in any way resemble the man I met before the War. Admittedly, that was a number of years ago. In any event, the likelihood that the imposter is an agent of the Si-Fan, and quite possibly the man that you met in Cairo, remains a distinct possibility."

"The question is, what do we do about it?"

Kerrigan and I stared back at him in silence.

"What can we do about it?" I asked, believing some response was required no matter how feeble.

"I am glad you asked that question, Professor."

The way Sir Denis smiled convinced me that I was not likely to share his enthusiasm.

"We need a man on the inside. Someone who is unknown to Hitler and his cabinet, but who might very well recognize our friends from the Si-Fan. Kerrigan and I are far too familiar to the Chancellor to prove effective, but you would do quite nicely."

As much as I longed to be in Smith's confidence, I had no desire to do so by infiltrating Hitler's inner circle. I could feel the perspiration gathering upon my brow as my heart began to race.

"Under what pretence would I be introduced? I'm an archaeologist after all. I have no background in espionage work!"

"Nonsense," Smith snorted. "Kerrigan is a newspaperman and he has done just fine in service of the Crown. You mustn't let sensationalistic thriller writers convince you that an intelligent, able-bodied man is ill-suited to the role, lest he first receive specialized training. You ask under what pretence will you be introduced? My response is a very simple one. You will provide security for Sheikh Zahi Saleh, whose services have been requested by the Prime Minister for an imminent conference in Munich."

"Are you mad?" I snapped, "After what happened a fortnight ago?"

"You are doubtless correct," Smith nodded his head. "The Sheikh would never tolerate your presence, were he to see you."

"Am I...am I going to be in disguise?"

I felt a sense of dread creeping upon me.

"Nothing so melodramatic, I assure you. The Sheikh rarely attends these events in person. Doubtless he would consider it gauche to do so. One of his assistants will oversee the event and make certain that everything goes according to plan. Therefore, you should have nothing to fear, save the Si-Fan identifying you before you see them."

"Oh, is that all," I said, feeling rather nauseous.

"Welcome aboard, old man," Kerrigan smiled, clapping me on the back.

The next two days passed by in a blur. I spent much of the time wading my way through a bureaucratic flood of paperwork that I was required to complete before I could obtain clearance to play a role in Smith's charade. I was amazed that no one bothered to question Sir Denis' judgment. It was as if his word was deemed authorization enough to proceed, no matter how ludicrous the suggestion seemed to me.

The third day saw the three of us travel early in the morning by motorcar from 10 Downing Street to Heston Aerodrome. My fragile grip on reality became even more tenuous as I listened to the Prime Minister's speech on the BBC, while the man himself was seated at my side.

"How horrible, fantastic, incredible it is that we should be digging trenches and trying on gas masks here because of a quarrel in a faraway country between people of whom we know nothing," his voice crackled over the radio. "It seems still more impossible that a quarrel that has already been settled in principle should be the subject of war."

I watched the Prime Minister's face as he listened to his own words playing back to him. How strange it must be to occupy his position and know that the few short sentences composed to express one's thoughts on a topic would be scrutinized by millions, and would serve to reinforce or undermine their confidence in you and, by extension, the nation.

"Unless Chancellor Hitler can be persuaded otherwise, the Occupation will commence in just four days."

The Prime Minister was addressing Smith directly, but it was Kerrigan who replied. "Hitler has said he will refuse to allow the Czechoslovakians he is forcing out of the Sudetenland to take anything other than the clothes upon their back. That is unconscionable. Those poor people will lose family heirlooms, photographs, literally everything they have, forever."

"They will not lose their lives," the Prime Minister replied with a shrug. "That is more important and, for that, they have me to thank. Chancellor Hitler has already promised not to continue the Occupation beyond the Sudetenland. If that is the sum total of what we manage to accomplish, it will be victory enough for me."

"You trust his word?" Smith asked in disbelief.

"I must," the Prime Minister replied. "We all must. For if we are wrong, then we know what must happen."

"Is it true what Chancellor Hitler claims," I summoned the courage to ask, "that the situation reached this point because the Czechoslovakians are slaughtering Germans in the Sudetenland?"

The Prime Minister smiled at me as if I were a precocious child conversing with my parents' peers as he replied: "The Czechoslovakian government is convinced that the annexation of the Sudetenland would topple their economy, and that Chancellor Hitler will go back on his word and occupy all of Czechoslovakia, and then Poland and Hungary as well. Their treatment of Sudeten Germans was a direct consequence of their fears for the future. Let us hope that France and Italy will help us to bring this situation under control and soon."

We pulled through the gates of the Aerodrome. All conversation ceased as we were conscious of the momentous import of the journey we were about to undertake.

Our flight to Germany passed without incident. My nerves were frayed and, judging from the Prime Minister's silence, I presumed that he was likewise feeling anxious. We were met by Hitler's Chief of Staff, General Franz Halder, and his Intelligence Chief, Admiral Wilhelm Canaris, upon our arrival. An armed escort accompanied our small party as we drove to the Fuhrerbau at the East End of the Konigsplatz where President Daladier, First Marshal Mussolini, and Chancellor Hitler soon arrived along with their translators.

As they gathered round the conference table in the Chancellor's office, just above the south entrance to the building, Mussolini distributed a draft agreement to the participants. Prime Minister Chamberlain read the draft carefully. Each copy had been prepared in the reader's own language. Unfortunately, there was no way for Smith, Kerrigan, or me to ascertain its contents at present.

The Prime Minister leaned forward on the table with his hands folded in front of him and, staring at Chancellor Hitler, requested compensation for the Czechoslovakian government and people. I noted Kerrigan's face flush with emotion, and I knew that he was eagerly awaiting Hitler's translator to finish relaying the request. Even had I not been able to make out enough of Hitler's rapid-fire response, the explosive reaction from the Chancellor left no doubt that he had rejected the proposal even before the Prime Minister's translator had a chance to interpret his response.

Gratefully, the tension quickly dissipated as the waiters arrived with their lunch carts. Chancellor Hitler sat smiling as a generous spread of delicatessen meats was placed at the center of the table. As the Prime Minister stabbed at his roast beef with a serving fork, the Chancellor began speaking. He smiled pleasantly all the while. Even if I hadn't understood his words, his demeanor made it evident that his disposition had not improved since his earlier outburst. After a moment's hesitation, his translator explained that the Chancellor wondered whether the Prime Minister had ever visited an abattoir. The poor man proceeded to explain in unpleasant detail the deplorable conditions that a cow is kept in and the particulars of the slaughterhouse operation.

President Daladier chuckled. "You forget, my dear Neville, that the Chancellor is a strict vegetarian. Eating meat is perhaps nearly as offensive as smoking and drinking alcohol in his presence."

Then, why serve meat? I wanted to ask. Sir Denis shot me a warning glance as if he had anticipated my question. My eyes wandered to the portrait of Otto von Bismarck resting above the fireplace. *Now, there was a man who enjoyed red meat and all the vices of the world,* I thought.

Following lunch, it was explained that a number of advisers would be joining the conference as the participants would focus on the draft agreement that Mussolini had prepared. Sir Denis discreetly informed me that my security role for Sheikh Saleh's representative would now begin as his representative had arrived. I was to meet him in the lobby. Sir Denis handed me the man's business card. I glanced at the name and was stunned. The Sheikh's representative was a she, not a he, and what is more, it was a she that I knew! Alexandra Dunhill!

I was stunned and looked up at Sir Denis to see if he was trying to gauge my reaction, but he appeared unconcerned as his attention had returned to the conference.

Presently, I made my way down the stairwell to the lobby. My mind raced as I wondered what it could all mean. I had experienced a queer premonition the afternoon that I had chanced upon Alexandra after so many years. It was as if, somehow, we were fated to meet, and finding her here now only reinforced the sense that we were playing predestined parts in this drama.

"You!"

Her voice rang out as I descended the stairs and crossed the lobby.

"Hello, Alexandra," I smiled and reached to give her a warm embrace. She was dressed in a smart white dress and looked simply radiant. I was relieved to see that she seemed genuinely surprised to see me.

"I don't understand, Michael. How could you know?"

I handed her the business card that Sir Denis had given me only a few moments before and explained.

She glanced at the card and laughed. "So you've only just learned then. For a moment, I feared that our meeting the other week was no coincidence."

"I must admit that the thought had also crossed my mind when I saw your name," I replied.

She was so warm, so natural. My heart raced at the prospect of our seeing one another again.

"Shall we get down to work?"

Her question made me immediately conscious that I had been staring at her, smiling. Embarrassed, I turned and led the way upstairs to a smaller conference room down the hall from the Chancellor's office.

"What exactly is it that you do for Sheikh Saleh?" I asked.

She flushed for a moment and I wondered whether her relationship with the Sheikh was purely professional after all.

"At the conclusion of the conference, the Chancellor wishes to release one thousand monarch butterflies over the city as a gesture of victory to the German people."

"One thousand monarch butterflies...at the end of September?"

She laughed. "It is an extravagant gesture, to be sure, but that is Sheikh Saleh's specialty. We're not actually providing monarch butterflies," she lowered her voice to a near whisper. "We're using viceroys instead. No one will be able to tell the difference, but since we're losing a thousand butterflies in a single day, the Sheikh would rather that we substitute viceroys. The butterflies were shipped last week and should already be waiting for us downstairs in the dock."

"A thousand butterflies?"

"Well," she smiled, "there will certainly be enough that it will look like a thousand."

"Do they have a greenhouse downstairs?"

She laughed at my question once again in that delightful fashion I was beginning to cherish.

"You're not far off the mark, actually. Part of the reason that Sheikh Saleh hired me was my background as a botanist. The butterflies require an artificial stimulant to help them weather the change in temperature. It wouldn't do to release that many butterflies only to have them fall to the ground dead because it is unseasonably chilly."

"What sort of artificial stimulant?" I asked.

She glanced at me sharply as if she wasn't sure that she should trust me.

"PR 365 is the name. It is an experimental drug developed in Sheikh Saleh's laboratory in Milan. It is sprayed upon the subject in gradually increasing dosages so that they build up a resistance to it. This event will represent the largest concentrated test group yet."

"That certainly would seem to mark this venture as a tremendous risk. What if it fails?"

She came to an abrupt stop at the end of the hallway and reached out a hand to the door of the conference room that I indicated.

"Failure is not an option. Sheikh Saleh never fails."

"There is always a first time."

She shook her head and opened the door and stepped inside the room, stooping to illuminate the lamp that sat on a table next to the doorway.

"That is why you're here, Michael. The only way that we could fail is an act of sabotage. You are the safeguard against that occurrence."

"Who would want to sabotage butterflies?"

She stared hard at me before answering sternly. "Someone who wished to embarrass *der Fuhrer*."

"You sound like a Nazi," I laughed.

"Is that so difficult to imagine?"

I was startled by her words. I stared hard at that lovely little face and remembered her as a child. How could she have grown up so wrong?

"There is a war coming, Michael. I intend to be on the right side. Eventually everyone will have to choose...even archaeologists."

Did she say 'archaeologists?' It took perhaps thirty seconds for me to realize that her suspicion was aroused because I had told her that I was an archaeologist when we had met in London, and now she found that I had apparently lied to her.

"Yes, well, I couldn't very well say that I work for British Intelligence, could I?"

She smiled and all thoughts of her Fascist beliefs vanished from that pure face framed by those soft golden locks.

"I suppose you couldn't. I wasn't entirely honest with you either, I suppose. Although I am a botanist, I've worked for Sheikh Saleh for over three years now. He is often out of the country, so he relies upon me to be his eyes and ears and manage operations in his absence."

She pulled off the large yellow bag that hung from her shoulder and set it down upon the conference table. Unfastening its latch, she began rifling through it until she produced a map which she proceeded to unfold upon the table.

"This map depicts in minute detail the Ehrentempel which stands next door to the Fuhrerbau and houses the sarcophagi of the martyrs of the Putsch who died fifteen years ago. The security points are highlighted in red on the map. They will be critical to the logistics of the butterfly release."

We worked well into the evening and enjoyed a late dinner before returning to the nearby hotel on the Konigsplatz, where accommodations had been arranged for us. We both had carefully avoided discussing politics, lest it spoil an otherwise enjoyable meal. When I entered my room, I was surprised to find Smith and Kerrigan awaiting my return.

"I understood that the conference was continuing into the night?"

"You understood correctly, Professor," Sir Denis replied. "The Prime Minister and President Daladier declined the offer of joining the Chancellor and First Marshal for dinner so that they could contact their cabinets. In fact, the Prime Minister is meeting with President Benes and Sir Horace Wilson at the moment."

"Shouldn't you be with him then, Smith?"

Sir Denis shook his head. "Not if he doesn't wish to attract undue attention from our hosts."

"Why does he wish to bring Czechoslovakia's president into the discussion?"

"They've read the draft agreement, Professor," Kerrigan pointed out, "we have not."

Smith nodded. "The Prime Minister wishes to determine which districts are of primary importance to Czechoslovakia before finalizing the agreement. Obviously, the complete annexation of the Sudetenland is the crux of the issue. Kerrigan and I will have to leave shortly to meet them in the lobby. The conference reconvenes promptly at 10:00 p.m. Have you seen anything suspicious, or anyone that you recognize?"

I hesitated for a moment before deciding how best to respond to the question. Unsurprisingly, my delay was noted by Sir Denis.

"I am not talking about Miss Dunhill, Professor. I mean anyone that you might have seen while in Egypt."

"Then you knew?"

"Of course, I knew. Did you honestly believe that I would leave you alone in London without security? We had a pair of CID men watching you at all times. The afternoon that you decided to take a walk, you were followed. Initially, we had some concern that your meeting was not by chance, but subsequent investigation into Miss Dunhill's background assured us that it was as innocent as it appeared. Realizing that Miss Dunhill was employed by Sheikh Saleh was serendipitous, and gave us the perfect opportunity to utilize you to your fullest potential."

I felt somehow unclean knowing that Smith had men spying upon us, checking Alexandra's background, and manipulating me as a pawn in their game.

I must admit that I was grateful to be left alone in the hotel room after Smith and Kerrigan had left to re-join the conference in Chancellor Hitler's office at the Fuhrerbau. Having begun my official duties with Alexandra, there was no longer any need for me to stand by with Smith and Kerrigan for the hours that would determine whether our visit was a success or failure. At the time, I was too disorientated from our trip and the rush of events in the past 48 hours to regret my absence from this critically important conference.

My exhaustion was such that I fell into a deep sleep shortly after climbing into bed. My last conscious thoughts were of Alexandra. It was rare for me to dine with a beautiful woman and climb into bed alone afterwards, but somehow she was different...or maybe it was me who was changing. It didn't matter when all I wanted was sleep...glorious sleep.

I was haunted by queer dreams of my past. A pair of brilliant green eyes appeared in the darkness staring at me intently. After a few moments, a peculiar opaque film covered the pupils. The eyes seemed to grow larger until I was swallowed up in the whites of the eye.

Helga Graumann inexplicably appeared, like some succubus of antiquity, and crept upon me in my bed as I lay dreaming. She aroused me and then cruelly inflicted pain upon me in my vulnerable state. I was helpless to stop her. As is often the case with dreams, there were gaps in logic or in the recollection of the exact sequence of events. The next incident that I recall was being downstairs with Helga at the Fuhrerbau's dock while I was showing her where the butterflies were stored. She did not ask me to do so, it was simply understood. My security clearance at the dock was approved and we encountered no obstacles in reaching our destination.

Helga asked me about the exhaust tubes that emptied into the storage crates containing the butterflies. I explained about the PR 365. She responded that it was extremely important that I understood that we were to empty the tanks into the storage crates so that the butterflies received the full dosage before morning. She asked me if I understood and made me repeat my instructions.

The next thing I knew, someone was calling my name from very far away and slowly growing nearer.

"Professor Knox! Good Heavens, I thought you were drugged for a moment. You were sleeping like the dead."

I opened my eyes and saw Kerrigan stretched over me on the side of the bed. The light was on in the room. I struggled to recall where I was and what had happened last. I glanced at the clock by the side of the bed and saw it was nearly 2:30 a.m.

"They are ready to sign the Agreement, Professor," Kerrigan was whispering excitedly. "There was a delay because Hitler's inkwell ran dry. Can you believe that? Knowing his temper, some poor devil will surely catch

Hell for it in the morning. The Prime Minister and President Daladier returned to the hotel to speak with President Benes. They are going to try and convince him to sign the Agreement as the Occupation is scheduled to begin tomorrow. Get back to sleep, Professor. I just wanted to share the good news. It looks like you'll be busy with Miss Dunhill come the morning. Best of all, this cloak and dagger business with Plan Z can finally be laid to rest."

I sat up in bed, feeling the fog surrounding my brain starting to clear at last.

"What exactly is this Plan Z business, Kerrigan?"

"Haven't you sussed that out yet?"

He laughed and then lowered his voice conspiratorially. "Sir Denis has been busy sowing dissension among Hitler's cabinet. Life at the Fuhrerbau is not as rosy as it seems apparently. In the event that the conference does not end amicably, Plan Z would insure that the German people had a new leader sooner rather than later."

"You don't mean..."

Kerrigan nodded. "Yes, Professor, Plan Z was to insure that the assassination of Adolf Hitler occurs by the hand of one of his most trusted deputies."

15. PEACE IN OUR TIME

The morning did not start well. I met Alexandra at the dock beneath the Fuhrerbau just after breakfasting at the hotel. We had begun final preparations for the release of the butterflies at the Ehrentempel next door. As she clambered up on the crates, I heard her curse under her breath.

"What's wrong?"

She ignored my question for a moment as she rose and hobbled over to the adjacent crate and carefully inspected the gauge on the top of the crate.

"They're empty!"

"What is empty?"

"The PR 365...each one of the canisters is empty. How can this be?"

How could it be? I recalled my dream and Helga's command that I give the butterflies the entire dosage, but that was just a dream. It couldn't have actually happened.

"Why would anyone have done such a thing?"

She didn't answer me at first, but instead, she carefully examined the butterflies within the crate.

"They seem healthy enough. The exhaust pipes have been turned aside and disengaged from the crates. Whoever did this only wished to release the PR 365 rather than harm the butterflies."

"Why would PR 365 harm the butterflies? That's what you were using to bolster their fortitude, wasn't it?"

Alexandra hopped down from the crate and stood in front of me.

"Certainly it was, but I said we gradually increased the dosage, not give them an overdose. There's no telling how that would affect the poor things. No, the way the exhaust pipes were disconnected from the crates suggests that we're dealing with spies, not saboteurs."

"What would spies want with butterflies?"

"Not butterflies, Michael, the PR 365. Sheikh Saleh patented PR 365, but the composition, of course, remains a closely-guarded secret. Since the drug is too new to fully understand its uses and effects, its true value is difficult to determine."

"I don't understand how anyone could have gained access to the crates," I said, perplexed. "The dock is secured with a guard posted at all times and the exhaust pipes were still intact when we inspected them last night."

"That's exactly what we're going to find out," Alexandra replied. "The guard post should have a record of who gained access to the dock. They won't share that with me, but we'll go through the proper channels and have the Chancellor approve the request. If this is an act of industrial espionage, our culprit will soon find that the Third Reich is more efficient in handling breaches of security than a British court of law."

A British court of law, eh? How kind of her. It was evident that she suspected me of being the spy. Under ordinary circumstances, I would have been offended, but my dream had left me rattled. Why had I dreamt of showing Helga the PR 365? What had occurred at the Fuhrerbau while I slept?

It was just after Noon when President Benes finally agreed to the terms of the Munich Agreement. He made a point of noting his objection to the decision to annex the Sudetenland, but that point was both expected and moot. There was precious little Czechoslovakia could do to hold back Germany without British and French support. For better or worse, Czechoslovakia had been sacrificed for the greater cause of preventing a second world war.

I enjoyed a late lunch with Kerrigan at our hotel. While I couldn't say that I knew the newspaperman well, I did know that I would have felt lost without him. He was an island of normalcy amidst the rarefied stratum that I had found myself occupying these past few weeks. That fact was brought home to me even more when President Daladier subsequently sat down to join us.

"Good afternoon, gentlemen," the president said in his thickly-accented English. "That was quite a night we had last night, eh?"

I smiled at his attempt to speak in a foreign vernacular.

"What has become of your friend, Mr. Smith?"

"He is with our Prime Minister," Kerrigan answered. "They are meeting with Chancellor Hitler at present."

Daladier shook his head and clicked his tongue, irritably before addressing us in a quiet voice. "I fear that the Chancellor's real aim is to secure a domination of the continent in comparison with which the ambitions of Napoleon would appear feeble. Today, it is the turn of Czechoslovakia. Tomorrow, it will be the turn of Poland

and Romania. When Germany has obtained the oil and wheat she needs, she will turn on the West. Certainly, it is essential that we combine our efforts to avoid war, but the compromise that we have made at the expense of Czechoslovakia may only precipitate the war we have worked so hard to avoid."

"If that is what you really believe, then why did you agree with the Prime Minister's course of action? It was not the only avenue to peace that was open to us."

I glanced warily at Kerrigan, wondering why he was so brazenly alluding to Plan Z as the alternate means of winning peace. I had no cause to worry. He knew what he was doing and was only leading Daladier on by appearing to speak frankly and with authority.

"Mr. Kerrigan, I witnessed the bloodbath that was the Great War first-hand. I have no desire to let history repeat itself."

Before anyone could say another word, the Prime Minister and Sir Denis approached our table and sat down. The Prime Minister slapped Daladier upon the back, much to the Frenchman's evident displeasure.

"I've got it," the Prime Minister gleamed, barely able to conceal his jubilation. "It is right here in my coat pocket."

"What do you have there?" Kerrigan asked.

"Mr. Smith and I have just come from a private conference with Chancellor Hitler," the Prime Minister was breathing so heavily, it was difficult for him to keep his voice low. "I requested that Prague not be bombed if the Czechoslovakians offer any resistance to the Occupation. Since the Chancellor seemed in an agreeable mood, I presented him with the Anglo-German Agreement to review."

"The what?"

"Now, now, Monsieur President, hear me out first. It is merely three paragraphs stating that both Great Britain and Germany consider the Munich Accord to be symbolic of the desire of our two people never to go to war again. I am very pleased to say that the Chancellor executed the Agreement without a moment's hesitation."

I finished my drink quickly and rose from my seat.

"I'm afraid that's my cue, gentlemen. I have a date with a thousand butterflies."

I left to the puzzled laughter of my companions.

My afternoon was a frantic one or, to be more accurate, Alexandra's afternoon was a frantic one. My duties were limited to following her around and keeping my eyes peeled. Promptly at 3:00 p.m. in the afternoon, Chancellor Hitler took the hastily-constructed stage in the forecourt of the Ehrentempel where the crates of butterflies had been moved.

The crates were concealed by curtains from the eyes of the assembled crowd that had gathered in downtown Munich. Alexandra was suffering terrible anxiety over the health of the butterflies, but thus far, they were alive and at least reasonably healthy, as far as I could determine by peeking in on them. Mussolini, Daladier and Prime Minister Chamberlain gathered on the stage with Hitler. The Chancellor's Chief of Staff and his Intelligence Officer were near at hand along with a score of German soldiers.

The Ehrentempel was under 24 hour security at all times because of the sarcophagi on display there, so I did not feel as out of my element as I might have been had I been guarding something other than butterflies. The potential threat posed by the Si-Fan remained in the back of my mind, but it seemed a remote possibility amongst the chaos surrounding the Munich Accord.

Chancellor Hitler addressed his adoring crowd, informing them of the successful conclusion of the conference. The rapidity of his speech made deciphering his words a challenge for me. He gestured toward each of the three statesmen in turn and introduced them to the appreciative audience. As Prime Minister Chamberlain was introduced, he stepped forward to the microphone in front of the Chancellor and began addressing the confused crowd in English. The Chancellor's translator hurried to the stage and stood beside the Prime Minister, nervously waiting for him to finish so that he could interpret his remarks for the puzzled crowd. It was evident that Hitler did not welcome this intrusion.

"My good friends," the Prime Minister addressed his mostly uncomprehending audience, "this is the second time my visit to Germany has resulted in peace with honor. I believe it is peace for our time. It is my fervent hope that a new era of friendship and prosperity may be dawning among the peoples of the world."

The Chancellor's interpreter had not yet finished translating the Prime Minister's comments when Hitler cut him off to announce: "This has been our first international conference and I can assure you that it will be our last. Neville Chamberlain is an impertinent busybody who speaks the ridiculous jargon of an outmoded democracy. Pay him no heed. If he continues to make a nuisance of himself, I will have him thrown off this stage."

The reaction from the crowd was ecstatic. Smiling all the while, Hitler gestured toward Prime Minister Chamberlain who, understanding nothing of what the Chancellor had just told the crowd, bowed graciously.

The small band gathered at the rear of the stage struck up a bombastic piece from *Tannhauser* while Alexandra hurriedly threw open each of the crates and tore the curtains back as an endless sea of butterflies flooded into the afternoon sky. The crowd roared with enthusiasm at the sheer spectacle of their flight. Hitler had earned his extravagant gesture at the Prime Minister's expense and the poor man was oblivious to it all.

The four statesmen returned to the Fuhrerbau next door after their public appearance had finished. Alexandra and I gravitated toward Kerrigan. Sir Denis was nowhere to be seen. First Marshal Mussolini asked the Prime Minister, via his interpreter, what he planned on doing now that the negotiations over Czechoslovakia had finally concluded. The Prime Minister listened politely to the interpreter and then addressed Mussolini directly telling him that there was much to be done at home. The First Marshal nodded as he listened to his interpreter relay the Prime Minister's response.

"Yes, there is much to be done," the interpreter translated Mussolini's latest remarks. "There are public works programs, creation of new jobs, public transportation, and the economy to occupy one's time if one is to provide for the people's welfare."

"The First Marshal does not seem so bad, considering our host. I could almost forgive him his friendship with him," I muttered quietly to Kerrigan.

"Appearances may be deceiving," Kerrigan replied in little more than a whisper. "Our host may sing the First Marshal's praises, but they hold one another in little personal regard. Our host views the Italians as a race of mongrels, while the First Marshal believes the current regime here to be little more than a band of thugs."

"Ah, so he is a fine judge of character as well. I could learn to like the First Marshal given time."

"Don't be too hasty in your judgments, Professor. While the First Marshal may initially appear level-headed when one considers his opposition, in principle, to eugenics and his view that the Aryan nation is a self-serving myth, he also believes that the entire white race is imperiled if colored people are allowed to breed unchecked. What is more, he recently stripped Jews of their Italian citizenship and banned them from holding government positions or professional jobs."

"Obviously a result of the influence of his short friend over there," I hissed.

"Perhaps, or perhaps it is the inevitable path Fascism is bound to take when it is allowed to run its course. In any event, the First Marshal has vacillated in his relationship with the Pope, while simultaneously building strong ties with the Arab nations. He was presented with the Sword of Islam last year honoring him as a protector of the faith. His intolerance toward Christianity grows stronger all the time as evidenced by his regular blasphemous proclamations to the press. His identification with Nietzsche's disease of the mind is all too obvious. Make no mistake about his cheerful demeanor this afternoon, Professor. He would happily see us all lined up against a wall and shot."

"That would also seem to be part and parcel of Fascism."

Kerrigan smiled at my remark. "I'm pleased to find you a kindred spirit, Professor. One never knows who one is talking to these days."

"No, one doesn't," I said, ruefully. "Although it helps to remind oneself of what really matters and not let sentimentality cloud one's judgment."

We were just preparing to leave for dinner for our last night in Munich when all Hell broke loose. There may be nothing more nerve-wracking than being in a foreign land during a time of crisis. The commotion started in the hotel with raised voices denoting panic. I threw open the door to our room and stood in the doorway trying to pick out enough words to understand what was happening.

A hand grabbed me by the shoulder and pulled me back into the room as the door slammed shut in front of me. I spun round feeling my hackles rise and stared into Sir Denis' hard, stern face.

"Just what do you think you're doing, Knox? Something has agitated the public. The last thing you need to do is stick an English nose in the middle of their business. You forget that we are guests here and our welcome is the first thing that will be rescinded if there is trouble."

No sooner did he speak than the telephone rang. It was the Prime Minister calling for Smith and Kerrigan. Sir Denis hung up the phone seconds later and told me to accompany Kerrigan and him to the Prime Minister's suite down the hall.

"Thank you for your promptness, gentlemen," the Prime Minister said as he closed the door behind us. Happily, my uninvited presence did not appear to register with him. "We have a serious problem. Some sort of epidemic has broken out all over Munich."

"What sort of epidemic?" Sir Denis snapped.

189

"At a guess," the Prime Minister sighed, "it sounds like some advanced strain of smallpox."

"Smallpox is easily controlled," Kerrigan noted.

"I said an advanced strain, Mr. Kerrigan. Scores of cases are being reported across Munich. The aerodrome has been closed. I'm afraid that we are stranded in Germany for the time being."

A sudden explosion rocked the hotel. The Prime Minister lost his footing and fell to one knee.

"What the Hell was that?" Smith swore.

I threw the door open and stepped out into the corridor. Kerrigan was at my side in a moment as an excited bellman jabbered at me in German.

I turned to Kerrigan in shock and grasped his shoulder to steady myself.

"There was an explosion down the street at the Fuhrerbau. It is feared that Chancellor Hitler has just been assassinated."

16. POX ROMANA

The next few hours were chaotic. Munich seemed on the verge of violence. The smallpox outbreak was like nothing I had ever seen. Wherever one turned, there were people in agony as their faces began breaking out in terrible blisters. The symptoms were advancing in a matter of hours instead of days. There was no rationale as to who was infected and who was not. Worse still was the situation in the Fuhrerbau.

Chancellor Hitler's office had been destroyed by a homemade bomb, but luckily the Chancellor had stepped out of the office when it was detonated and was not seriously injured. Admiral Canaris, Hitler's Intelligence Chief, was insistent that First Marshal Mussolini, President Daladier, and Prime Minister Chamberlain remain at the Fuhrerbau for the time being. Knowing how narrowly the Chancellor had escaped assassination, confining us to the Fuhrerbau did little to instill a sense of security.

The mood had changed dramatically and we were being treated more like political prisoners than welcome visitors. The inexplicable smallpox epidemic and the bold attempt on Hitler's life had suspicions running high. Sir Denis and Kerrigan said little to me over the next few days. The Prime Minister spent most of his time in heated conversation with President Daladier, whereas Mussolini was rarely seen without Chancellor

Hitler at his side. Understandably in times of crisis, sides had been chosen.

I'm not sure at what exact point that I realized that Alexandra was absent from our group, but I felt guilty for not having thought of her safety sooner. I expressed my concern to Sir Denis. He did not share my surprise to hear of her absence.

"I'm afraid that Miss Dunhill is being held for questioning by the Gestapo."

"What? Why?"

"There is reason to suspect that the smallpox epidemic was spread by the butterflies that she released. A great number of the infected are children who came in contact with them yesterday afternoon. The insects became sluggish shortly after they were released into the air, and a great number came to rest in residential areas nearby prior to expiring. It is known that the butterflies were treated with an artificial stimulant. The canisters containing the stimulant were found empty which makes chemical analysis impossible. Quite understandably, Miss Dunhill is under strong suspicion of deliberately contaminating Germany with an artificially manufactured virus."

"This is wrong. This is all wrong. Alexandra is not to blame for emptying those canisters."

"How do you know that she isn't?"

"She found that the canisters were empty only yesterday morning. She suspected industrial sabotage. The canisters contained a gas called...um...PR 365...that was used to artificially fortify the butterflies so that they would live longer outside of their greenhouse environment. The canisters had been unscrewed from the crates containing the butterflies. Alexandra believed that the PR 365 was stolen by competitors eager to get their hands on the formula developed by Sheikh Saleh. She was going to request that the Fuhrerbau release the security records to find who had visited the dock the previous night. That is our saboteur. We had been there just before 8:30 p.m. and the canisters were still affixed to the crates at that time. I can attest to that fact. She is innocent, Smith."

Sir Denis tugged at his left earlobe as he considered my words.

"It might interest you to know that Miss Dunhill did obtain those security records and the only visitors to the docks that night after 8:30 p.m. arrived at just after 3:00 a.m. The visitors were a man and a woman. The woman passed the man's security badge to the guard and foolishly he let them both pass. That particular lamentable error in judgment will likely cost the poor man his life."

"Whose badge did the woman show?"

Smith sighed. "It was your badge, Knox. Miss Dunhill declared that you were the traitor. Naturally, this was brought to my attention immediately. I vouched for your integrity and innocence and duly noted that Miss Dunhill could easily have obtained a copy of the badge she had only just issued to you. I also revealed that your presence as a member of this security team was because of your past knowledge of Miss Dunhill, and that you had brought to my attention the fact that Miss Dunhill's employer was not Sheikh Saleh as he claimed, but rather a high-ranking member of the Si-Fan posing as the late Sheikh. You were indispensable because of your past experience with both and that you had already conveyed your concern of potential sabotage to me.

"Luckily for you, our German friends were quite interested in Miss Dunhill's association with the Si-Fan. It seems that the Chancellor is not as trusting of them as we feared. Granted, it is questionable whether he trusts anyone, but in this case, his paranoia may actually work to our advantage."

"Smith, what are you saying? Alexandra will be executed as a spy. She is innocent. We must do something to help her."

"Would you prefer that I hand you over for questioning, Knox? This isn't a simple case of espionage. This epidemic will cost countless lives before enough of the smallpox vaccine can be distributed, and that is assuming that the vaccine proves effective at all. There has to be a scapegoat offered, and quickly, or there will be public unrest. At times such as this, one must weigh the consequences of all possible outcomes. If it helps, consider Miss Dunhill our Czechoslovakia, if you like."

I didn't like it at all, but there was nothing more I could say for Admiral Canaris, the German intelligence chief, walked up to Smith. The Admiral's exchange with Sir Denis was brief, but the smile that played upon his lips showed that he relished the news he brought us. We were cordially invited to attend the Gestapo's interrogation of Alexandra. As the interrogation was already underway, it was evident that our attendance was mandatory.

Admiral Canaris led the way down the staircase to the lower level. Briefly, I feared that we were being taken to the dock. I was beginning to worry that my disturbing dream had become reality after all. Somehow, Helga Graumann had come to me in the middle of the night in a locked hotel room and had me lead her to the docks, where she had released the smallpox vaccine on the butterflies. It was utterly fantastic, but it was the only explanation that made sense.

Alexandra was a Nazi sympathizer. It didn't stand to reason that she would have turned against the German people any more than she would have betrayed the man she called Sheikh Saleh. I couldn't honestly believe that she would ever willingly harm anyone. She was misguided, not malicious. The question remained, what if she was likewise misguided about the Si-Fan? What if Sheikh Saleh really was the President of the Si-Fan's Council of Seven I suspected? What if Alexandra was in league with them? Perhaps she was the saboteur and was willing to sacrifice me for her crime? There were so many possibilities that I didn't know what was real and what was imaginary.

The Admiral opened the door to a small darkened room. I quickly realized that it was far larger than it first appeared. A partition wall was responsible for creating the illusion of the small corridor that was visible when one entered the room. The Admiral led us halfway down the corridor to three folding chairs set against a wall. Smith and I took our seats as the Admiral indicated.

As he sat next to Smith, the Admiral leaned forward and rapped once on the wall in front of us. Almost immediately, a panel slid back revealing a window into the larger room behind the partition. The public address system that was set above our heads began to crackle to life. Evidently, the partition wall was soundproof, or else the public address system would not have been necessary. As I looked through the window before us, I realized that we were now spectators at Alexandra's interrogation.

She was seated in a chair facing directly in front of us. The lack of recognition in her eyes as she looked up forlornly made it evident that the window was actually a two-way mirror, and Alexandra was cruelly being forced to look upon her own pitiful reflection rather than the faces of the silent witnesses to her suffering. There was a mechanical device attached to the right arm of her chair that stood five or six inches in height. Two rolling pins were set within the mechanical frame so close together that they appeared to touch. A crank was attached to the outside of the mechanism.

A uniformed Gestapo man stood at either side of Alexandra. It was then that I noticed that she was bound to the chair with ropes across her waist and around her legs and each arm. The Gestapo man on her left barked a question at her in German. There was a momentary delay before his question played over the public address system.

"How did you obtain that strain of smallpox?"

Alexandra just stared straight ahead as if she hadn't heard the question.

"She doesn't speak German. She is a British citizen," I pleaded.

The Admiral laughed. "She speaks and reads German quite fluently, Professor Knox. Obviously, you were unaware that Fraulein Dunhill willingly supplied information to aid German intelligence for the past three years."

I wondered if Sir Denis knew this and had also withheld this information from me. As shocked as I was to learn that Alexandra was a traitor, I realized that her involvement with German Intelligence would make her fate at their hands even worse now that they suspected she was responsible for unleashing the epidemic.

The Gestapo man who had spoken gestured to his comrade. The second man untied Alexandra's right arm and held it steady so that her hand was aligned to the rolling pins set within the mechanical device connected to her chair. Alexandra winced in pain as the other Gestapo man began to rotate the crank, setting the rolling pins in motion. There was a sickening cracking sound over the public address system followed by a gasp and a shrill scream from Alexandra as first her hand and then her arm broke as it passed roughly between the rolling pins, dragging her forward in her seat. Her head lolled against the side of the device while her broken arm sagged limply from its front end.

"Perhaps you will be more cooperative this time, Fraulein," the first Gestapo officer said. "We shall try one last time. Tell us what was in those canisters."

Alexandra was sobbing and trying to catch her breath as she responded in German: "PR 365....I do not know the formula...only Sheikh Saleh knows..."

"You must know something more than that, Fraulein. You are Sheikh Saleh's personal assistant. Come now, be reasonable...or shall we be forced to break your other arm as well?"

Alexandra shook her head in desperation.

"I don't know anything else. PR 365 is an artificial stimulant that we used to fortify the butterflies to protect them from the temperatures. Sheikh Saleh wanted to ensure that the Fuhrer received the glorious gesture that he deserved at the conclusion of the talks over the Sudetenland."

"Yes, by releasing smallpox upon all of Munich."

"No, no, I swear that we didn't. PR 365 is an artificial stimulant developed at Sheikh Saleh's laboratory in Milan. The name refers to *Pax Romana*, Roman Peace...because of the promise the drug held for the betterment of mankind. The 365 referred to the days of the year. PR 365 has the potential to remove the seasonal constraints placed upon plants and insect and animal life.

It has the ability to revolutionize the field of botany for the good of all nations. It did not contain smallpox. I swear it didn't."

"Even from your lies, it is possible to glean bits of the truth," the Gestapo officer sneered. "*Pax Romana* you say? Surely you mean *Pox Romana* as in smallpox, yes? 365 represents the days in a year, eh? Is that how long before this terrible plague spreads over the globe and brings every civilized nation to its knees? Who is the man you call Sheikh Saleh? We know the identity is an assumed one. Our Intelligence has confirmed that the real Sheikh Saleh drowned off the coast of the Riviera years ago. Who do you really serve? It is not Britain. It is not Germany. Whose master plan did you execute? Who is the orchestrator behind this carefully calculated chaos?"

"I...don't...know," Alexandra was shaking her head frantically. "I swear that I have told you everything."

There was a long pause and then the Gestapo officer sighed. "Do you know, Fraulein, that I actually believe you? What is more, it must be said that I honestly regret that you do not have anything more to offer us."

He withdrew the pistol that hung from the holster on his belt and placed the barrel at Alexandra's temple. The panel slid soundlessly down over the window, blinding our view of the interrogation chamber as the sound of a single shot being fired came over the public address system before it crackled once more as it was abruptly shut off.

"My God," I sobbed.

I was overcome with emotion. It was like a waking dream. I was helpless to intervene. Faced with the reality that Alexandra was dead, and that I was likely the unintended cause of her death, I could not keep my grief bottled up.

Admiral Canaris shook his head contemptuously.

"This is why the Reich has nothing to fear against your people. You are weak for being ruled by your emotions. How can such men ever defend themselves?"

His words gave me pause. My tears did not stop immediately, but I fell silent. I had to stop following the path that events took. I had to be responsible for directing my own fate. Smith was not wrong. It could just as easily have been me on the receiving end of that bullet in place of Alexandra. If I were to survive, I would have to take charge of charting my own destiny.

17. MUNICH BETRAYAL

"Smallpox, in its common forms, localizes in small blood vessels of the skin and in the throat and mouth," Professor von Schenkelberg, newly-arrived from Berlin, addressed us in German. "Normally, this results in a skin rash that blisters. In its common form, smallpox has a mortality rate of 30%. Scarring occurs in most cases of survivors, with only a small percentage facing blindness or deformities as a consequence. The majority of fatalities rest with children.

"The incubation period is generally ten to twelve days when lesions begin to appear on the tongue, the palate, and the throat. The virus migrates to the lymph nodes and multiplies. At the conclusion of the incubation period, the lesions enlarge and rupture spreading the virus to the saliva and bloodstream where it multiplies in the spleen and bone marrow. High temperature and severe toxemia mark the final stage of the disease.

"The current strain facing Munich advances that incubation period to within a matter of hours. We have already seen substantially high child fatality rates, and can anticipate higher than average adult fatality rates given the potency of the virus. Happily, those immediately treated with the smallpox vaccine are showing equally rapid signs of recovery suggesting that this epidemic can be contained.

"As you are aware, the butterflies that we examined confirmed the presence of the virus. It is not unknown for smallpox to be carried by air, given its highly contagious nature. Ordinarily, the rate of infection is affected by the duration of the infectious stage and proves highly sensitive to weather conditions. Of course, the strain of smallpox we are dealing with is much stronger than one ever encountered before. This accounts for why it can be transmitted by insects or animals, which henceforth was a scientific impossibility as they possess no natural asymptomatic carrier state.

"Smallpox inoculation can be traced back to China nearly one thousand years ago. A successful inoculation traditionally produces lasting immunity to smallpox. However, the current strain seems to require an additional inoculation following infection in order to combat the virus. In this respect, it is not unlike inoculations of infected persons who suffered severe infections, and subsequently transmitted the virus to others. The fact that the antibodies have initially proven ineffective to the current strain suggests that it is unnatural in origin, or rather, artificially augmented."

Sir Denis rose from his seat awkwardly and addressed a question in English to the consternation of most of Professor von Schenkelberg's audience.

"Your reference to China is suggestive of the Si-Fan's involvement. I was unaware that the virus was so old. Are its origins likewise traceable to China?"

There was a pause and then I rose from my seat and translated his question into German. It was evident that several parties in the room were shocked by my knowledge of their language.

Professor von Schenkelberg listened carefully to my doubtless flawed translation. He nodded and then responded, directing his answer to Sir Denis who, unlike me, had remained standing after speaking.

"The earliest evidence of the virus was found in Egypt nearly 3000 years ago. From thence, it appears to have spread to India and then China. It is likely that traders unknowingly spread the disease. It ravaged that part of the world for at least 2000 years. It reached Japan in the Sixth Century, and nearly a third of the Japanese people perished in the resulting epidemic. Imagining a worldwide epidemic of the current strain, given the limitations on manufacturing and administering sufficient quantity of the vaccine, it is not unrealistic to expect that one third of the world's population could succumb to this disease in a matter of months."

Smith listened intently and then addressed the Professor in English once more. "There is a historical precedence in using smallpox as a weapon. Great Britain did so knowingly during both the French and Indian conflict, and subsequently during the colonies' uprising in the New World. The possibility of developing a biological weapon from smallpox is something that both East and West have been working towards for a number of years now. It appears that the Si-Fan has yet again proven their scientific superiority. Hardly surprising when one considers Dr. Fu Manchu's genius and the large number of Western scientists that have been abducted and brainwashed into serving their cause."

I translated Smith's response with a fair amount of trepidation, not knowing how Chancellor Hitler would respond to his remarks about various European nations working toward cultivating smallpox as a biological weapon. Smith's statement did elicit an almost immediate response from the Chancellor, but not the one that I had anticipated.

202

"Professor Von Schenkelberg," he asked, "what do you know of the folklore that has arisen in the wake of the smallpox incidents that you mentioned?"

"Many superstitions related to smallpox arose, Mein Fuhrer," the Professor replied. "The Chinese believed the goddess, T'ou-Shen Niang-Niang was responsible for making the 'beautiful flowers,' as they called smallpox. It was believed that the goddess passed the disease to children she favored on the last night of the year, so children were sent to bed wearing grotesque masks so that the goddess would pass over them and leave them unharmed...not unlike the Jewish folklore of the Plagues of Egypt. If smallpox was contracted, shrines were erected in the home for offerings to help relieve or cure the disease.

"The Hindu smallpox goddess, Shitala Mata, was worshipped and feared for her habit of inflicting the disease on those who angered her. Hindus worshipped at her shrine and placed plates of food and pots of water on the roofs of their homes in an effort to appease her wrath. The Japanese believed in the *housoushin*, the 'smallpox devil' that resulted from *onryo*, the spirit of vengeance. *Housoushin* were afraid of the color red. Japanese families used red dolls to ward off these devils.

"Medieval France and Britain also believed that the color red could ward off smallpox, and that prayer and a holy life could also prove effective protection against the malady. China, India, Africa, and South America made sacrifices to appease their smallpox deities. Many African tribes likewise believed that the color red would ward off the smallpox god. Throughout Asia, red light is recognized to this very day for its effectiveness in weakening the infection. The truth behind the power of the color red to help battle smallpox has finally been accepted as scientifically accurate across Europe, proving there is often a shard of wisdom to be found in primitive folklore."

"Very interesting, Professor, that is very interesting, indeed," Chancellor Hitler replied. "I should like to reconvene this discussion after lunch. You will excuse me, Professor."

The Chancellor rose and, to my shock, made his way directly towards me.

"Thank you for sharing your interpreting skills. Your German is surprisingly good. Would you, Sir Denis, and Herr Kerrigan be so kind as to meet me in my office in five minutes? I should very much like to discuss a personal matter with the three of you."

Presently, we made our way down the corridor to the Chancellor's office. Even now, I felt so shaken by the recent attempt on Hitler's life that I was reluctant to visit his private quarters for any length of time for fear of a second, more successful attempt.

Chancellor Hitler was a small, but serious man. Seated across the desk from us, he was strangely lacking in the charisma that defined his behavior in front of a larger audience. It was hard to reconcile the dynamic orator that the German people found so compelling with the oddly sedate man before us. The madness that seemed to possess him at times was entirely absent. There was only an unsettling calm that conveyed a sense of the terrible weight upon his shoulders. It was similar to the burden that I felt in moments from our Prime Minister, but it seemed to weigh considerably heavier upon Hitler.

As surreal as it was to find myself in the company of men of such power and influence, I had to admit that none of them compared with Dr. Fu Manchu. There was a hypnotic quality about that old Chinaman that made me fear him. Being in his presence left one feeling drained, as if something had been removed from one's very soul, or perhaps it was one's memories that had been violated.

Sir Denis nudged my shoe with his foot and I realized that my mind was visibly wandering while Chancellor Hitler was speaking. I suspected that Smith and Kerrigan's command of the German language was stronger than my own, since they seemed to listen effortlessly to the Chancellor while I was forced to struggle to catch the meaning of his words.

"I am grateful to you, Sir Denis," Hitler was saying. "Were it not for you and Mr. Kerrigan, I might have perished in that attempt on my life last year by Dr. Fu Manchu. In the months since that time, the Si-Fan has done their best to make amends for his actions. They have been a welcome ally, albeit one who must remain out of view. That is why recent events have taken me by surprise. Releasing this plague and this latest attempt on my life are not the actions of an ally. You have more knowledge of the Si-Fan than any other man alive who is not counted among their number, what do you make of all of this?"

Sir Denis sat back in his seat and tugged at his earlobe in irritation as he carefully considered his reply.

"It is difficult to be certain, Chancellor. Knox here had some involvement with the Si-Fan in Cairo where they are currently based. He believed there is some sort of internal conflict between Fu Manchu and his successor as President of the Council of Seven. There have been similar divisions of loyalty in the past that threatened to tear the Si-Fan asunder. I suspect it is likely that both the biological attack and the assassination attempt are the work of Fu Manchu, but I would not be certain that the new President of the Council of Seven is the ally that you believe him to be."

Hitler smiled faintly and glanced at me for a moment.

"I learned long ago never to expect much from my fellow man, Sir Denis. People are rarely what they want others to believe them to be. It is imperative that I send someone to Cairo to end this threat of a worldwide smallpox epidemic. The chaos such an outbreak would create, and the lives lost before the additional inoculations required to counteract the effects could be distributed, would be catastrophic and would certainly place the world governments in the hands of whoever controls the culture."

That odd little man rose from his desk and began to pace back and forth behind it, punctuating his speech with the pointer he held in his hand.

"I cannot send my own men to do the job. We cannot afford to lose so potentially valuable an ally as the Si-Fan. As you know, all travel is currently forbidden to prevent the plague from spreading. I could, however, arrange special permission for you, Herr Kerrigan, and Herr Knox to travel to Cairo. What I would like is for Dr. Fu Manchu to be eliminated. I would also like the PR 365 formula and any artificially enhanced smallpox virus that may be found in his laboratory to be seized and turned over to the Reich for disposal."

"As I understand it, PR 365 was manufactured in Milan," I interjected.

Hitler came to a halt and leaned forward on his desk, looking down at me as he spoke.

"Signor Mussolini is arranging for a visit to Sheikh Saleh's Milanese operations. He will see to that front for me. Sir Denis, I would prefer it if you were willing to help me as a mutual ally without my having to result to coercion."

"I appreciate that fact, Chancellor. The elimination of Fu Manchu is certainly to our mutual benefit, but I am less enamored of doing anything other than destroying PR 365 or any trace of smallpox that might be found."

"I do not believe that your Prime Minister would agree with you on that point," the Fuhrer smiled.

"With all due respect, Chancellor, I fail to see why that would be the case."

"The reason, Sir Denis," Hitler seemed barely able to suppress his amusement as he spoke, "is that his welfare is dependent upon the successful completion of your mission."

I watched Smith carefully, but he betrayed no emotion whatsoever at the Chancellor's very clearly stated threat.

"When do we start for Cairo?" was Smith's only reply.

Hitler beamed at him in response.

"You leave at sunrise."

18. IN THE SKY

Our last night as guests in the Fuhrerbau was distinctly uncomfortable. The Prime Minister had been removed to another part of the building, or perhaps another location altogether. We strongly suspected that our rooms were bugged, so the three of us resorted to scribbling notes to one another on paper like schoolboys, and then burning the evidence in the fireplace.

We were woken by an armed guard at just after 3:00 a.m. and were escorted to a conference room where a doctor was waiting for us. Herr Schmidt looked to be in his mid-sixties, bald with white-flecked grey hair around his ears. His mouth turned down in a permanent scowl. He wore a white lab coat with the sleeves rolled up displaying thick black-haired arms whose developed musculature stood in sharp contrast to his advanced age.

First, the three of us were administered inoculations for the smallpox vaccine. A necessary precaution if we were to leave the country. We were then given a second injection, but this time of sodium thiopental. Almost immediately, I was aware of a taste of garlic in my mouth and soon swore that I could smell onions...rotting onions.

Kerrigan retched with a shaking hand massaging his throat gingerly while Smith shook his head and gagged, leaning forward in his seat. He turned and stared at me, his eyes watering and his face red.

"Sodium thiopental...they mean to question us, Knox. We won't be able to resist. Sodium thiopental weakens one's resolve...makes us compliant. We can't help but answer whatever question is put to us."

I nodded my head and was aware that I was mumbling incoherently while I continued nodding enthusiastically.

"Sir Denis," Dr. Schmidt asked in halting English, "tell me about the explosion in the Fuhrer's office."

Smith shook his head no, but slowly began answering the doctor.

"Beck...General Ludwig Beck...General Halder's predecessor...and Graf von Helldorf...Police Chief...they were identified for Plan Z."

I shook my head back and forth rapidly, but could only mumble. Try as I might, words would not form from my lips. The smell and taste were too awful to manage. Kerrigan was subject to a coughing fit and was pointing worriedly at the dour-faced German in the corner seated at a table with a typewriter who was clacking away while Smith answered the doctor's question.

"Tell me all about Plan Z, Sir Denis."

Again Smith shook his head, but again he began answering in spite of himself.

"Plan Z...was the plan...to assassinate...Hitler...in the event that the Munich talks...broke down...only means to...prevent war."

"The talks successfully concluded, Sir Denis. Who went through with the attempt anyway and why?"

"Si-Fan...must have been Si-Fan...only possible answer."

Dr. Schmidt frowned in annoyance.

"Your resolve is surprisingly strong, Sir Denis. Mr. Kerrigan, do you believe Sir Denis' answer to be the truth?"

Kerrigan's eyes gazed plaintively for some sort of reprieve, but his lips began to form words against his will.

"Don't know what to think...it could be true...but also...suspect Sir Denis and...one of the Nazis...were behind...the attempt...the Prime Minister...wouldn't agree...but...we know...that Hitler is...too dangerous...to live."

Kerrigan slumped forward in his seat, nearly unconscious. He had fought and lost a heroic battle to win control over his senses.

"And you, Mr. Knox," Dr. Schmidt now directed his attention to me, "do you believe that Fraulein Dunhill was responsible for the plague attack?"

I shook my head vigorously that I did not agree.

"Alexandra...would...never commit...so horrible...an atrocity... positive of it. She is a Nazi, but...the real saboteur was...Helga Graumann."

"Who is this Helga Graumann?" he snapped.

"She is the daughter of...Fu Manchu."

My head lolled against my chest as I watched drool form from my lower lip and stretch towards the floor. There were no further questions that I recall only the endless sound of the German clacking away at his infernal typewriter.

A short time later, the three of us were driven to Friedrichshafen Airfield. I felt nauseous and had a splitting headache. Doubtless it was an after-effect of the sodium thiopental as Smith and Kerrigan looked similarly under the weather.

Presently, we were given clearance to approach Lowenthaler Hangar where the *Graf Zeppelin II* airship was stored. The LZ 130 *Graf Zeppelin II* really was an awesome sight to behold. The sheer immensity of the design was simply staggering. The airship covered over 800 feet in length and well over 100 feet in diameter. I stared in amazement at the tiny tail fins at the rear of the ship and then followed along its length to marvel at the windows set in the nose cone. The airship relied upon diesel engines to power the tractor propellers. I couldn't imagine the freedom one must feel to soar above the world in this most impressive of all flying machines.

Captain Albert Sammt approached and presented a gloved hand to each of us in turn. The pride he felt in his ship was evident, although I detected a trace of uncertainty about his bearing. Perhaps it was due to the unorthodox nature of a flight where he feared that his British passengers were carrying this new smallpox disease to him and his crew (to say nothing of their families) or perhaps it was the recent *Hindenburg* disaster that weighed most heavily upon his mind and the minds of everyone who saw an airship in the months following that terrible tragedy.

Captain Sammt showed us aboard the ship, noting that the passenger decks could accommodate 40 passengers. There seemed to be just as many crewmen aboard, and several of them favored us with suspicious glances. Obviously, the expense of this early morning flight for only three passengers was highly irregular. We were each assigned spacious and well-lit luxury cabins before being escorted to the restaurant in the centre of the gondola.

The view from the promenade windows when air-borne must be breathtaking, I thought as I glanced out at the hangar.

Soon enough, I had the proof I so desperately desired as we strapped ourselves into our seats and the four Daimler-Benz 16-cylinder diesel engines roared to life. I could feel the gondola quiver in anticipation as the propellers moved the airship forward through the large hangar doors and down the strip. Then, at long last, we were airborne. Captain Sammt had assured us that we would eventually reach a maximum speed of 81 miles per hour, but I was in no hurry. The extraordinary view from the window was enough to make one wish that the flight would never end. For several hours, I knew uninterrupted bliss. At long last, I was free to soar among the clouds.

The captain informed us that the engines were equipped with a water recovery system that allowed engine exhaust to be captured to extract water vapor and condense it for storage in the tanks to compensate for the fuel's weight loss during flight. I marveled at the ingenuity the Germans had displayed in its design and execution. I hungrily digested every bit of information that he shared. The sixteen gas cells were made of lightweight silk, instead of the more traditional cotton. The doping solution for the outer fabric covering included bronze and graphite to prevent flammability and improve electrical conductivity. My mind immediately thought of the ill-fated *Hindenburg*, and I wondered how different that event might have played out had it been designed like the *Graf Zeppelin II*.

The captain switched off the intercom and the loud-speakers instead treated us to *Also Sprach Zarathustra* before a pre-recorded piece by the Deutsche Zeppelin

Reederei Company owned by Herman Goring was broadcast, informing us that the Luftschiffbau Zeppelin, the Reichs Luftfahrt Ministerium and Deutsche Lufthansa A.G., Germany's national airline, were proud to jointly own all Zeppelin operations. I was conscious of my throbbing head once more and decided to get up and walk about the cabin to clear my head if possible.

I made my way through the common area to the forward operational spaces where the flight deck and navigation room were contained. I passed by the map room and glanced out the two large windows on either side with interest before passing the main dining room until I came to the main sitting room where Smith and Kerrigan had now settled.

I took my seat on the sofa opposite theirs. They both nodded a brief greeting to me and resumed their conversation. I leaned forward to catch what they were saying above the noise of the engines and the tiresome propaganda about the glory of the Reich piping from the loudspeakers.

"Smith and I were discussing what the Nazis likely learned from us this morning," Kerrigan said, turning to me. "It's quite alright, old chap. They can't have bugged us in here while Goring's endless spiel continues to play at full volume."

"You did speak of Plan Z, Smith. I do recall that," I said.

"I did, but I managed to steer their suspicions back to the Si-Fan so I wouldn't worry unnecessarily," Smith said with a shrug.

"I've been meaning to ask you about that," Kerrigan's voice betrayed his unease as he spoke. "A bomb is the choice of the anarchist and definitely not the work of Dr. Fu Manchu. The man has too much ingenuity and

213

integrity to stoop to such vulgar methods of dispatching an enemy."

Sir Denis stared at him a moment before responding.

"Kerrigan, if you think a veteran government official is going to give a direct answer to your insinuating remark you are sadly mistaken."

My blood boiled to hear his dismissive tone.

"What of Alexandra? You let her die. Did you really believe her guilty of spreading that plague?"

"Really, Professor, we've been through this all before," Smith said with a sigh. "Even if I shared your conviction that she was innocent as charged, and even if I didn't know that she herself was a Nazi, I would still be duty-bound to choose the greater good over the lesser evil. Intelligence work demands that we treat peacetime as war in order to preserve peace for the many. Every war requires sacrifice. There are no exceptions to this rule. Miss Dunhill was a sacrifice, and one I would readily make again to preserve peace. I do not take lightly the loss of human life, but it is my duty to shoulder that burden. You must learn to do the same if you hope to survive this time of chaos."

"I begin to see that the Prime Minister was right about you," I snapped. "You set yourself above all laws and hold yourself accountable to no man. You knew that the Prime Minister wanted Plan Z enacted only as a last resort. He was grateful that it could be safely abandoned when the conference concluded successfully, and yet you decided to carry on regardless and let the consequences be damned."

"You don't know what you're talking about," Smith thundered.

Kerrigan cleared his throat loudly and I turned to see Captain Sammt approaching.

"I trust you are enjoying your flight, gentlemen," he said in surprisingly clear English and in tones that made it evident he was aware that the three of us were embroiled in a row. "Forgive the interruption, but I would ask that you follow me to the radio room immediately. There is something you need to hear for yourselves."

We followed the captain to the radio room. The *Graf Zeppelin II* was equipped with the most modern radio equipment I had seen. Three radio operators were required to manage the various navigational duties as well as monitor weather reports, ground and ship communications, and any private telegrams that came in via the vacuum tube transmitter for low frequency bands and via the 70-watt antenna for medium frequency bands.

Captain Sammt leaned forward over the station and flicked on the receiver. There was a burst of static and then a faintly audible voice repeating the name, "Sir Denis Nayland Smith" every few seconds.

"Are you able to get a fix on the location?" Smith barked.

Captain Sammt shook his head slowly. His furrowed brow betrayed his concern.

"I can tell you that the signal is not emanating from Germany and no one else should know that you are aboard."

"What about Britain?" Kerrigan asked.

"Not possible," Smith frowned. "The Prime Minister is being held in quarantine and any communication he makes back home will be closely monitored to prevent an international incident…at least, until our mission is complete. By then, it may not matter."

"Why not respond?" I asked.

Smith did not look up, leading me to wonder whether he had even heard my question, when, suddenly, without asking the Captain's permission, he leaned forward and flicked the switch to open the channel for a response.

"This is Sir Denis Nayland Smith. Who is calling?"

The line went dead. There was only static in reply. The transmission had immediately ceased.

"How long had you been receiving that message?" Smith asked.

Captain Sammt sighed. "Perhaps twenty minutes, maybe more. It was very faint at first…so faint we were not able to decipher the words and then the signal increased…or rather, we drew closer in range to the signal's source. We were never able to get a fix with the direction finder so we can't be sure of its origin."

"You were correct," Smith said, "we are getting closer. The source is Egypt."

"How can you be certain of that if we cannot locate the signal's source?" Captain Sammt asked.

"I do not need a direction finder to tell me that Dr. Fu Manchu is in Egypt. He detected a German airship en route to Cairo and, knowing full well that all German air, sea, and land travel has been suspended because of the plague that he unleashed in Munich, he was fairly certain that any airship launched in exception to the travel ban would be for my sole benefit to bring him to justice."

"Then, we no longer have the element of surprise," Kerrigan said.

"No," answered Smith, "but Fu Manchu now has a target…a large one that will very shortly be within range. I'm afraid that Germany is fated to lose its second airship in another spectacular disaster…only, this time, it will be intentional."

216

19. THE SKY IS FALLING

Tense minutes passed by interminably while we waited for something to happen. Captain Sammt had sent a telegraph to Munich requesting guidance on how best to proceed in light of our mysterious contact confirming that Sir Denis Nayland Smith was aboard the *Graf Zeppelin II*. The way that Smith and Kerrigan spoke of the Si-Fan, I did not know what we might be facing in retaliation. Captain Sammt and Nayland Smith had retreated to the flight deck, leaving Kerrigan and me alone in the radio room with the operators.

Unexpectedly, the radio crackled to life and a voice, much clearer this time, but recognizably the same voice we had heard earlier, stated:

"You will be directed to land at Giza. You will follow instructions to the letter. Any deviation will result in your destruction."

"*Nein,*" the radio operator responded, flicking the switch to open the channel. "We will land at Cairo as scheduled. Desist in your petty threats or face the wrath of the Third Reich."

The radio crackled with static before the voice replied, chillingly:

"You have been warned."

The line went dead once more leaving us only with empty static and the terror of the unknown.

I glanced nervously at Kerrigan. Neither of us spoke. Was this what life was like for him all the time? I could not imagine anyone choosing such an existence.

We waited for whatever was going to happen. Our nerves were frayed and I visibly jumped when the intercom switched on and Smith's voice came through the speaker asking for Kerrigan and me to join him on the flight deck.

We traced our way back through the forward operational space and stepped onto the flight deck. Nayland Smith was standing next to Captain Sammt staring out into a phenomenal view of the clouds while the airship effortlessly wound its way through their ethereal majesty.

"How extraordinary," I gasped.

Smith and the Captain turned towards the doorway upon hearing my voice. Smith stepped down from the deck and crossed to greet us.

"I'm glad you are both here. I think it best that the two of you witness this first hand," he said.

"Witness what, Smith?" Kerrigan asked.

Before Sir Denis could respond, it happened, and instantly we understood what the strange phenomenon was that had demanded our attention.

A face had appeared in the centre of the flight deck or rather, the image of a face. It was large, perhaps four feet in length and two feet in diameter, and seemed to hang in mid-air like some sort of ghostly apparition. There was no question of it being a projection for there was no possible source of transmission, but Smith, Captain Sammt and his crew saw it as clearly as Kerrigan and me.

The face had a greenish tint, but there was no mistaking its identity. The head was hairless, with a large

218

domed forehead and magnetic eyes that seemed to stare at each of us as the apparition eerily rotated from left to right. I had never wondered what Satan might look like, but this was as good a guess as any, for that face conveyed an unmistakably brilliant malevolence. Past experience had taught me the name that belonged with that terrible visage. Even had I never met the man before, I might very well have guessed that we were staring into the face of Fu Manchu.

"Sir Denis Nayland Smith," that strangely sibilant and guttural voice boomed as it spoke, "if you wish to spare the lives of the crew of the *Graf Zeppelin II*, I urge you and your companions to heed my words. You must abandon this airship or I shall send it crashing to the ground.

"Captain," those magnetic eyes with their queer luminescence sought for the captain as the apparition continued to rotate as if on an axle, "it is within my power to cripple both your generators, your turbines, your batteries, and your auxiliary power generator. I do not make this threat lightly. I give you ten minutes to jettison Sir Denis and his companions from your airship, or I shall be forced to destroy it. Consider the means by which I have already invaded your ship as proof that I possess sufficiently advanced technology to make good my threat. You will not receive another warning."

As he finished speaking, a crewman turned from the bridge and rushed at the apparition, attempting to break through it in his blind rage. There was a crackle of electricity and the man screamed and collapsed on the floor of the deck, twitching for a few seconds before going limp as the apparition faded into oblivion.

"Eichorn!"

Captain Sammt yelled the man's name and rushed forward to kneel by his felled crewman. Cautiously, he placed two fingers to the side of the man's neck and checked for a pulse.

"He's dead," he said simply.

"Good Lord, did we just see a ghost?" I asked.

"That was no ghost, Knox," Smith said, grimacing, "but rather a higher science, quite likely an older one than our own. This was the third time that face appeared in the last ten minutes. I'm grateful that both of you were present as that was apparently intended by Dr. Fu Manchu as his Grand Finale."

"I don't understand, Smith," I asked. "First, we are told to land at Giza and now he instructs us to abandon ship? Why the sudden change of direction?"

"An excellent question, Professor Knox," Smith smiled, ruefully. "I will refer you to the Si-Fan's similar conflicting attitude towards the Reich for your answer."

Kerrigan nodded knowingly to Smith, but I was left quite in the dark as to their meaning when the intercom clicked on from the radio room and a navigator announced that they had received the message again.

"What did it say?" Captain Sammt, hovering over the radio, snapped at the navigator.

"Same as before, Herr Captain. We were instructed to land at Giza and warned not to attempt a landing in Cairo," the navigator's voice paused briefly, awaiting a response. "Please advise further course of action, Herr Captain."

Captain Sammt hesitated and then released his hold on the intercom before turning to Smith.

"What do you suggest that we do, Sir Denis?"

All eyes were upon him, waiting for his decision.

"Bypass Cairo and attempt a landing at Giza as directed."

"And if in so doing, we lose our generators and turbines as Dr. Fu Manchu threatened, what then?"

Smith shrugged. "Either pray or take solace in the fact that the Reich will avenge our deaths."

Captain Sammt gritted his teeth and shook his head. "I cannot simply turn you over to the Si-Fan at Giza as they wish," he declared. "Those were not my instructions from Munich. As we approach Cairo, you will have to parachute out of the ship. It is the only solution and it is the best chance for all of us to be spared."

The Captain bent over the radio and called back to the navigation room. "Inform them that we will land at Giza and release Sir Denis and his companions into their custody. They are not to hinder our landing or departure. Is that clear?"

"But you said..."

The Captain shut off the intercom and spun on me.

"I am aware of what I just said, Herr Knox. You and your friends will hasten to strap on your parachutes and prepare for your jump."

There was a strange humming sound before the lights in the flight deck were suddenly extinguished and then there was only silence. I felt a dizzying sense of the wind rocking the gondola back and forth and looked out that vast window to the bizarre sight of the sky beginning to fall.

Wait, it wasn't the sky that was falling...it was the airship! We had lost all power!

Smith grasped Captain Sammt by the shoulders and shook him. "Hurry, man, you haven't a moment to spare! Command your crew to abandon ship. It is your only hope! Otherwise, you will be dashed to pieces on the rocks."

Sheer panic clouded my memory of the next few seconds as Captain Sammt deliberated on the correct course of action. I recollected Kerrigan shoving a parachute into my chest and handing one to Sir Denis. I followed his example and slid my arms through the sleeves and secured the straps.

Hurriedly, we followed Sir Denis to the entranceway where he was already unlatching the door. As he pulled the heavy panel aside, the strong gust of wind that assaulted us literally pushed us back a few feet further into the ship. Smith grabbed Kerrigan and me by the arm and pulled us close together.

"Count to ten and pull your string," was all that he said as he pushed me and sent me hurtling through the open entranceway.

I experienced the sudden sensation of weightlessness and realized that I was falling through the clouds. I could not see the ground or anything around me save for those intangible white wisps that surrounded me. So fast...I was falling so fast that I could not even think.

"Pull your string!"

I heard Sir Denis' words repeating in my head like a mantra and, finally, I made the effort to reach up to the chest area of my vest and yank the string as hard as I could. I was immediately jerked upwards as if an invisible pair of hands had pulled me back roughly toward the airship, but there were no hands upon my shoulders and the airship was many miles away by now.

The parachute had opened perfectly and my descent slowed to the point where it felt like I was floating once more. I watched in amazement as, far in the distance, I could just make out the airship sailing in a downward arc. Faintly, I could see several dots blossoming and realized that it must be the crew parachuting to safety at last. Sadly, there were nowhere near the 40 parachutes that I was hoping to see. The airship's downward arc placed it directly in the path of a mountain ridge. I saw the bottom of the gondola snap and shatter into shards as the airship banked and disappeared out of sight over the ridge. If there was an explosion after that, happily I remained ignorant of the tragedy.

I looked at the ground rapidly approaching beneath me and realized that it was a sea of sand as far as the eye could see. I brought my legs up as much as I was able, but I still hit the ground hard and rolled, twisting myself up inside the parachute until my body finally ceased moving.

I lay very still and did not make a sound in the hopes that I might somehow evade the notice of both Smith and Kerrigan if they had landed nearby or our potential captors. I did not consider the possibility of desert predators, or how I would manage to reach safety and find sustenance. My only thought was breaking free of this madness that had claimed me ever since I journeyed to Corfu to attend a colleague's wedding all those weeks before.

20. JOURNEY THROUGH THE DARK

The desert air was cold at night. That was my dawning realization as consciousness returned to me. I struggled out from beneath the folds of the parachute and looked around. Sand and darkness as far as the eye could see.

A growing sense of desperation gripped me as I realized that I needed to find my way to shelter soon. I would not last many hours in the blistering heat once the sun rose. There was a very real possibility that I would die in this desert if I did not get to safety soon. I had no way of knowing how far from civilization I was, or how far away Smith and Kerrigan were, provided that they had indeed escaped.

I made for the nearest ridge, wrapped in the folds of the parachute for warmth and dragging the rest of it behind me to wipe my tracks as I walked.

I lost count somewhere after the fourteenth ridge. I had no sense of time. I only knew that the sky was still black, with no hint of dawn yet approaching, when I struggled to the top of yet another ridge and my heart caught in my throat.

There, in the distance, was a fire.

I checked myself from running toward it with wild abandon like a moth to the flame. I was no stranger to the desert and realized that it might only be my mind playing cruel tricks upon me. I continued walking at the same pace, dragging my tattered parachute along behind me. The thought crossed my mind that it might be Smith and Kerrigan, or perhaps it was the surviving crew members from the *Graf Zeppelin II*. I didn't care. I only wanted warmth and sustenance.

As I approached nearer to the campsite, I could see a large tent and two figures, in traditional Egyptian dress, seated around the campfire. They seemed to pay me no notice as I approached. The men appeared lost in thought, staring at the flames. I was very nearly upon them. Worrying what their reaction might be at the strange sight of a bedraggled figure wrapped in a parachute approaching them out of the darkness, I hollered a greeting in their tongue.

There was no reaction.

This was strange. I could have been no more than fifteen feet away from them now. Perhaps they were sleeping or lost in a meditative trance? I shouted my greeting again, louder and bolder this time. Still the men did not move.

It was only when I reached their side that I understood too late.

There were posts in the ground at each man's back, propping him up in a sitting position. Their faces bore the truth of their terrible deaths. Their throats had been slashed. Flies covered their necks where the blood had been washed away. I could smell death in the air, and I knew immediately that they were not the only corpses to be found here.

I stood still, listening to the rapid beating of my heart. No one approached me. Slowly, I made my way forward toward the tent, careful not to let the parachute dragging behind me touch the flames of the campfire.

I pulled aside the flap and peered inside; all was darkness and nothing stirred.

My head spun round and turned quickly, fearing that someone had stolen behind me in the night, but I was still alone in the dark. I went back to the campfire and cautiously removed a burning log from the flame to serve as a torch. I grimaced as I glanced upon the face of the dead man nearest me by the fire. The terrible mask of death he wore chilled me to the bone.

Holding the torch aloft, I re-entered the tent and gasped in spite of myself to see what awaited me in the dim light of the flame inside the darkened tent. There were a score of bodies piled in a heap on the ground. Perhaps six or seven others lay upon a table like sacks of grain. The tent was filled with the smell of death and the buzzing of insects. I did not have to come any closer to know that all of them had met the same fate as their silent companions keeping their last, lonely vigil outside the tent.

"My God! Who could have done such a thing?" I said aloud.

A hand fell upon my shoulder.

Trembling, I turned and looked up into the face of a tall Egyptian. His eyes blazed with a satanic fury. His nose and mouth were covered by a veil which hid them from view.

"You!" was the only word I could manage as his left hand reached up and tore the veil aside revealing that ghastly image of a permanent leer carved into his face.

It was Esteban Milagro! My mind reeled in fear that he would recognize me as the madman who had attacked him at 10 Downing Street.

"Good evening, Professor Knox," he rasped. The knowledge that he knew me by name caused whatever remaining courage I had to falter. "I have been expecting you. Your team has been assembled for your benefit. They have been patiently awaiting your arrival."

"My...team?"

That awful mouth contorted in a terrible wheezing rasp. After a moment, I realized that dreadful sound was an expression of choking laughter from his misshapen lips.

"Can it be that you have forgotten Hassan and his team so soon? Perhaps the University was mistaken in entrusting you with such a responsibility. No matter...I am sure that I can find a use for you."

I turned and peered at the faces nearest me from the light of the dying torch. He was not lying. It was my team. The same men that I had last seen excavating the Theban Necropolis in a near-catatonic state were now discarded as corpses, left to rot in a stinking tent. I felt the anger starting to build at last. I wasn't sure what I was about to do, but as I turned, the torch was wrested from my hand. I felt its flame perilously close to my face as the blunt end caught my left temple with a blow that sent me reeling to the floor.

I awoke in darkness, aware of the sound of dripping water in the distance. I was cold and manacled with my back against a hard stone wall and a cold stone floor beneath me. There was a faint light in the corner. As I stirred, a figure appeared by the light. Blonde hair, fair-skinned.

"Alexandra," I cried. "How can this be? I saw you dead. You were shot."

"You saw me...dead?" she asked.

The memory replayed in my mind.

"The Gestapo officer...he put a gun to your head. Then the panel shut and we could see no more, but we heard the sound... You must have died...didn't you?"

She stared at me, not saying a word.

"They suspected you of sabotaging the PR 365 to launch the smallpox plague. When they were finally convinced of your innocence, they had no further use for you...or at least, I thought that was what had happened. If you're here now, then they didn't kill you, and you must know that Sheikh Saleh is really..."

I blinked and felt my head swimming as Alexandra's features seemed to shift. I shut my eyes to block out the confusion and when I opened them, I saw Helga Graumann's face in her stead.

"Oh, so it's you, is it? I might have known. You tried this trick once before when you convinced me that you were my sister. You're the one who spread the smallpox plague, aren't you? That's the only thing that makes sense of that queer dream I had. It is because of you that Alexandra is dead."

Helga merely looked at me, smiling in faint amusement at my condition and the indignation that I suffered. After a moment, her features seemed to blur again and, as I watched in amazement, her face took on the uncanny likeness of my sister just as it had once before.

"Stop it!" I yelled. "You are not Anna. You will not deceive me a second time."

I screwed my eyes shut to block out the image of my sister's warm expression.

When I opened them again, there was no face and the faint light in the corner had been extinguished. I was alone in the dark with my thoughts and the unceasing sound of dripping water. Relaxation was impossible with that terrible sound echoing around this cold, empty cell.

Presently, I was aware of something moving along behind my back in the dark.

My God, it was rats.

I pulled my legs up close to my chin and braced myself against the horrible feeling of rodents slipping behind my back and sliding along my thigh. I fought to steady my nerves for fear that a sudden movement on my part would antagonize them.

I was still holding my breath when I heard the terrible sound of hissing and of a great weight slowly dragging along the floor nearer, ever nearer to me.

God in Heaven, the rats had attracted the attention of a python. I lost all control and began screaming, pleading for God to spare me from this nightmare. I could feel the warm breath of the snake close upon my face. I heard the slithering hiss as that awful tongue teased my cheek and I knew that death was upon me.

Then, there was only the incessant dripping somewhere near the far corner of the room. There was no python. There were no rats. There was only that damned water dripping. God, this was madness, and I could not stand my loss of sanity. I wanted to die, but I was still manacled to the wall.

I opened my mouth to scream and felt my face stretch out of shape as my chin began to grow rapidly and curl up into my nose. I had swallowed my own face and was lost in the darkness inside myself. I felt my body sailing forward rapidly and heard the sound of an engine purring as my body bounced along with the vehicle.

What vehicle? Why did I sense a vehicle when my body was floating inside myself? Racing ever onwards in the dark toward the inevitable conclusion of awakening from this drug-induced dream into a reality more horrific than any nightmare my subconscious was capable of conjuring.

There is no greater fear than the future. There is no greater fear than the future. There is no greater fear than the future. Round and round, I went inside myself until I was certain that I had become so lost in the labyrinths of my mind that I would never find my way back out again.

21. STOLEN SECRETS

The gate was lowered and sunlight poured through the opening, blinding me.

I blinked and tried to recover my bearings. I was in the back of a truck and experiencing the queer sensation that I had lived through this before. I dimly recollected hearing the screeching of metal as the door of the cab opened and the sound of footfalls along the side of the truck in those hazy moments as I struggled to awaken from my deep slumber.

The gate had been lowered and sunlight was pouring through the opening, blinding me, when, suddenly, a towering figure cloaked in crimson and wearing a heavy metal helmet over his face stepped into view, blocking out the sun. A single eye slit was the only feature of the strange helmet. His muscular arms and legs were bare and it was apparent that he was a white man, not an Egyptian.

He reached into the back of the truck and hauled me out of the darkness and into the light. I dropped roughly to the ground and stumbled as I realized that my hands were still manacled. I was back at Luxor once more, I thought, as I looked around me.

"Do you know me, Professor Knox?" the strange figure asked in a great booming voice.

"Of course," I nodded. "You are Esteban Milagro...alias Sheikh Saleh."

"I have many names," he boomed. "I am the Beast. I am Nikola. I am the Anti-Christ. I am the Apocalypse. The people of this land knew me of old as Khunum-Khufu. By any name, I am your god."

Good Lord, I thought to myself, *he is a complete and utter madman.*

"Fate has delivered you unto me, Professor Knox. It was fate that placed you as a thorn in my side when you were but a child. It was Fate that three foolish children were saved by the enemy of my enemy. It was Fate that entangled those three children, a quarter of a century later, in the same web once more. It was Destiny that allowed me to unravel the scheming machinations of he who sought to thwart me. It was Destiny that allowed me to track your arrival and prevent you from falling into the hands of my enemy. It was Destiny that led you across the burning sands to fulfill your role in the realization of all that I have carefully planned for centuries. It is Destiny that led you to deliver my greatest triumph to me in leading me to unlock the treasures of the Black Scorpion."

There was nothing I could say to the madman. The heat of the sand beneath my feet, and the rays of the sun warming my skin and nearly blinding me, barely registered. I was the captive of a lunatic who had already slaughtered the team I had hired for this dig. There seemed little doubt that I was fated to die here at Luxor.

I looked up at the towering statues of Ramses II that stood before the Temple of Karnak and considered that, at least, I would have the satisfaction of dying before some of the world's greatest wonders of architecture.

"Follow me," the self-styled god declared and strode off toward the Temple of Mut where my team had been excavating the Theban Necropolis.

Briefly, I hesitated while considering whether I might make a dash for freedom if, by some chance, he had left the keys in the truck. Reality came back to me quickly as I glanced down at my manacled hands and, resigned to my fate once more, I set off after the madman Milagro.

I glanced up at the ram-headed sphinxes before the Temple of Mut and wondered what Amun-Ra or Khnum would make of Milagro's blasphemy. What punishment would Khonsu, the Moon god, exact for his defiling his mother's holy temple? If only life were as simple as the Ancients had imagined it. Retribution would be swift and just, and not left to the whims of chance as it was in the modern world.

I passed once more the shattered colossus representing Ramses II and soon reached the entranceway to the Temple, flanked by the statues of that great Pharaoh and his Queen. Inside the Temple, my attention was captured by the mural depicting Mutemwia, Tuthmosis IV's Queen, locked in the embrace of Amun-Ra. Inevitably, my mind turned to Helga Graumann whose brazen carnality was as potent a weapon as any I had yet encountered in this bizarre waking nightmare that I had the great misfortune to stumble into, and from which I seemed fated never to escape.

We made our way to the center of the room where the flooring had been broken by my team and a rope ladder lowered to the excavation of the Theban Necropolis below ground. Milagro unfastened my manacles, as I would need use of both hands, and then first he, and then I, began our descent. We dropped the few remaining feet to the ground below as we each, in turn, reached the end of the rope.

All around us were tombs ornately decorated with the startling likenesses of Ra, Anubis, and Osiris. Picks, axes, and shovels lay discarded upon the ground as the hidden level below this floor had been penetrated. An opening, barely wide enough for an average-sized man to slip through, showed the way down to the secret room where the Theban priests had stored their Gnostic treasures.

Milagro's hand fell upon my shoulder to check my step.

"The privilege I grant you is great, Professor Knox," he said. "We have come this far only through your efforts and so, I shall grant you the honor of being first to descend and behold with your own eyes the forgotten treasures of the priests of Thebes."

He released his grip upon my shoulder and, with more than a bit of trepidation, for I knew that he was sending me first to ensure that there were no traps laid for unwary trespassers, I crouched down and dropped my legs through the hole.

I waited anxiously, but nothing struck me as my legs dangled in the air. I thought of Hassan and his team. They had worked an endless number of hours excavating to this level and had met their deaths without ever reaping the reward for their labor and entering the secret chamber for themselves.

I glanced up at that hideous blank-faced helmet staring down at me and thought there was nothing more to be done. Squeezing my shoulders through the narrow opening, I let myself drop. I hit the ground and staggered, trying to gain my footing.

That awful blank-faced mask stared down at me through the opening, watching to see how I fared. I turned my attention to my surroundings. It was as if I had stepped back in time to pass through the centuries. It may seem a strange observation, considering where I was, and yet, somehow, the secret stronghold of the Theban priests was as if one had passed from one world to the next.

The room was shrouded in darkness, save for the light that shone from the opening I had just passed through. It revealed an ornate gold chest that rested in the center of the room. Its front was decorated with a peculiar design of seven snakes intertwined, each with the other's tail in its mouth. A life-sized statue of a seven-headed Egyptian god stood guard next to the chest. Each head was of a different beast or fowl, with three heads crowning the four that sprung from his neck. Despite my knowledge of Egyptian culture, I had never seen this particular figure before. The statue held a rod horizontally between its hands as if to challenge me. I took a few paces forward and stopped to study the statue. If this chamber concealed any hidden danger to the unwelcome visitor, it would likely come from this strange statue.

A sound from behind startled me from my reverie. I turned and saw Milagro had dropped to the ground. He hurried to my side, evidently reassured that there was no immediate danger in doing so.

"Do you recognize this figure?" I asked, gesturing toward the statue.

Milagro didn't answer me, but instead, appeared transfixed by the gold chest on the ground before us. He leaned forward and grasped the chest. Anticipating what happened next, I attempted to pull him out of range as the staff swung in a downward arc from the statue's right hand and clanged against the metal helmet that covered Milagro's head. Only then did I notice the blade that protruded six inches along the tip of the staff. Evidently the blade and the spring mechanism were triggered by

Milagro touching the chest. Had he not been wearing that helmet, the result would have certainly proven fatal.

Milagro seemed unaffected by the incident. He began carefully unlocking each snake's tail from its neighbor's mouth. Once finished, he carefully grasped each end of the top of the chest and lifted it open. The antique hinges on the box creaked with disuse. Milagro stared inside the chest and then fell backwards as if stunned.

"It can't be," he cried.

Cautiously, I bent down and looked inside the chest. There was nothing but a layer of undisturbed dust.

"It's empty."

He shook his head. "Not empty, stolen. Someone was here before us, but how? There were no other signs of entry."

He threw himself upon the empty box and clawed with his fingernails at its interior corners, hoping against hope to find a false bottom concealing whatever treasures he sought.

I thought of the hidden entrance in the upper chamber from which Dr. Fu Manchu and Helga had descended to this very room. I could see nothing to be gained from revealing this knowledge after the fact. The man was already seriously disturbed; my disclosing that I was aware that Fu Manchu had already beaten him would only antagonize him further.

"The question remains," I said, "how are we to get back out?"

Milagro turned and looked up toward the ceiling of the darkened room where the sole source of light shined forth. So great had been his desire to get at the Gnostic treasure of the Theban priests that he had failed to consider how we would climb back out. I sized the distance to the ceiling and, even clambering upon one another's shoulders, we would still be several feet from reaching the opening.

The helmet that masked his features betrayed no emotion. I had no way of knowing what he was thinking as he stood staring fixedly at the hole in the ceiling. Turning back, my eyes were startled to see a rope, like a serpent uncoiling under a snake charmer's spell, descending slowly from the opening. I could only conclude that it did so upon his mental command.

While Milagro remained fixed to the spot, I moved forward and grasped the rope. It held my weight and so, with great difficulty, I began hauling myself up, one hand at a time, until I was able to wrap my legs around the rope to aid my ascent. Sweat from the exertion stung my eyes. I gritted my teeth and shut my eyes tight as I continued to pull my weight up. A groan escaped my lips as my shoulders scraped against the opening, but secretly, I was relieved to know that I had made my way back to safety at last.

I choked on the dust in my lungs from the darkened chamber below as I lay on the floor of the Necropolis panting for breath. Wiping the sweat from my eyes, I sat up and took in my surroundings. There were perhaps a dozen Egyptians standing above me. Each of the glowering men's arms was folded across their bare ebon-skinned chests. Standing in their midst was a fair-skinned woman dressed only in a long gossamer skirt and jewel-encrusted armlets.

My heart sunk as I recognized Helga Graumann.

22. CHANGING OF THE GUARDS

"Helga Graumann, I might have known."

"You will remain silent until spoken to, infidel!"

The words were spat at me as if poison. I sat there staring at her. Few women could seem so imperious while wearing so little. I decided it was best to remain seated, for it seemed likely that I would need permission to stand. It seemed that I was to remain a captive for the time being.

Presently, the blank-faced helmet that Esteban Milagro wore upon his head poked through the hole in the floor, and then the man's broad shoulders appeared as he twisted to slide through the opening. Two of the bare-chested Egyptians came forward and helped to pull him through. He nodded his thanks as he stood to his feet. All of the Egyptians fell to the ground and prostrated themselves before him as one body bowing in obedience.

Upon seeing Helga standing there, Milagro grasped the side of the helmet between his hands and lifted it from his shoulders. That horrible visage with its ghastly smile carved in a permanent leer looked upon her with barely-concealed emotion. Unfortunately, his terrible scarring made it impossible to read his face properly. Whether it was lust or exultation or disappointment that he felt, one could not say, for his features could only convey the horror of the punishment inflicted upon him sometime in the past.

"We found the chest, my darling," he struggled to catch his breath as he spoke. "There was nothing inside but dust. Whatever treasures the Priests of Thebes had buried long ago, it has long since been removed. Their secrets are not to be ours, I fear."

She reached a hand out and stroked his cheek, smiling fondly at that horrible face.

"Their secrets are not to be yours, my darling. I shall have them in due course, for they are my birthright."

He grasped her hand and twisted it roughly causing her to gasp in pain.

"What do you mean, you witch? You promised me that your father..."

"Unhand me, traitorous cur!"

The second she raised her voice in anger, the Egyptians rose from their servile posture and set upon Milagro. They acted as one possessed, and I felt certain that they meant to murder him. Seizing my chance, I rose to my feet and stole from the room. I reached the rope that led to the upper chamber and quickly scaled it, knowing that every second might mean the difference between winning my liberty or a premature death.

I reached the upper chamber and ran toward the exit as fast as I could when, suddenly, I came to an abrupt halt. Scores of Egyptians had gathered at the entrance to the Temple and, at their head, stood a tall, thin man dressed in purple robes with a deep purple skullcap set upon his head. His wrinkled features gave the appearance of mummification upon first glance. Bright jade eyes that glowed with an otherworldly force offset the lined face. Long, thin skeletal hands extended from the sleeves of his purple robe. It was Dr. Fu Manchu and, at that instant, I knew that all was lost.

"Greetings, Professor Knox," he said in that peculiar voice that managed to be at once both guttural and sibilant. "I am pleased to see that you have completed all tasks that have been set before you with satisfaction. Your reward will be great."

What did he mean? I thought. *What tasks was he talking about?*

"Do not look so puzzled, Professor," he cooed. "There are no coincidences in this world. There is only Fate, that is controlled by the gods, and Destiny, that is controlled by me."

There was a tremendous row and I turned to see Helga striding triumphantly before the dozen or so Egyptians who dragged a bloodied and battered Milagro in their midst. I tried my best not to let my eyes play upon the movement of her magnificent features as she strode toward us.

"What have we here, daughter?"

Helga placed the metal helmet before Dr. Fu Manchu's feet and knelt before him like an obedient servant with her head lowered and her eyes to the floor.

Milagro ceased his cursing and stared in bewilderment at the old man who stood before him.

"You called her daughter...then you know?"

Fu Manchu nodded sagely.

"I know that you have restored my daughter's memories to her. You have made much progress from your days as an Adept of Mesmer. I bear you no ill will for that particular action, for in so doing, you have restored my daughter to the faithful and obedient child she once was. My Fah lo Suee, she is the flower whose blossom remains untouched by time."

"You old fool!" Milagro spat upon the ground in contempt. "You dare speak to me as an elder. You are no longer President of the Council of Seven. Can it be that, in your senility, you no longer recall that it is I who now hold that title?"

Dr. Fu Manchu shook his head sadly.

"It is you who are mistaken. The Council has stripped you of your position. Your fate is mine to decide."

"What are you talking about?"

Fu Manchu snapped a finger and one of the Egyptians brought forth a ceremonial scabbard. Holding it aloft, he genuflected upon one knee as he handed the blade to his master. Fu Manchu withdrew the sword from its scabbard and held it high admiring it for a moment. He then rested its point upon the ground and, using the sword for a walking stick, he took several paces forward until he stood before Milagro.

"You were stripped of your position for your many abuses of office. You have brought shame upon the Si-Fan like no other who has ever held the title of President of the Council of Seven. You sought to pass yourself off as a reincarnated Pharaoh throughout this Dark Continent in order to violate the Sacred Chamber of the Priests of Thebes. You sought to accumulate esoteric power for your own aggrandizement. You sought to plunder the secrets of the Si-Fan for your own glory and not the betterment of our noble cause. You stole the identity of an honorable friend of the Si-Fan in order to ingratiate yourself with those despicable fascist dictators in Europe, and then, having once sullied the Si-Fan's good name by your association with such vermin, you sought to betray them by conspiring with your fellow Western devils to topple their governments and spread a terrible disease to decimate the young and feeble of their populace."

"You are deranged," Milagro sneered. "Some of what you say is true, yes, but I did not act alone. Your beloved daughter aided me in her guise as Our Lady of the Si-Fan, and yet you have the unmitigated gall to accuse me of irreverence? You lying hypocrite. You know very well that I had nothing to do with the upset in Germany."

Fu Manchu held up a hand to silence him. After a moment's pause, he spoke.

"My daughter was coerced into acting the part you instructed her to play. She acted honorably in coming to me, her father, and explaining all and begging my forgiveness. Her testimony before the Council of Seven was critical to your being removed from office, and my being restored to my rightful position as Council President. She has accepted her punishment graciously, and will shortly be dispatched to Haiti for a period of exile where she may yet redeem herself. After this business with you is concluded, the Council shall have to elect a new member to restore our number."

"You are forgetting our laws, old man," Milagro snapped. "I may no longer hold the Presidency, but my place on the Council is still assured. Do you honestly think that I will be unable to convince them of the truth when I stand before them? The Council shall soon see the error they made in listening to your lies once more. Your day is past, old man. The sands of time have slipped away."

Fu Manchu sighed and lifted the sword aloft, pointing it toward the ceiling of the Temple.

"You forfeited your position on the Council of Seven when you lost your head, my friend."

So saying, he grasped the sword hilt between both hands and swung the blade in a powerful slicing arc that separated the head from Milagro's shoulders and sent it hurling through the air, trailed by a comet of blood, until it came to rest on its side, just a few feet from where I stood. Milagro's face was frozen in a look of shock. That grisly countenance of his was somehow able to convey that particular emotion most clearly.

Fu Manchu turned aside and I saw that Milagro's headless body had collapsed to its knees before the old man. After a moment, the body toppled forward. I fought the urge to retch as I beheld the gore that poured from the severed neck like an overturned pitcher.

Fu Manchu approached me. Stooping down, he grasped Milagro's head by the hair and lifted it high. Turning, he displayed the ghastly trophy for the Egyptians who fell to one knee in reverence. There was a familiar chattering sound and the little marmoset came bounding forward and leaped to the old man's shoulder, perching like a parrot and screeching his fury at the assembled crowd of Egyptians.

"So ends the man who sought to usurp my Destiny," Fu Manchu intoned.

So ends the man who robbed me of my innocence, I thought. Perhaps there was justice yet in this crazy mixed-up world of madmen and murderers.

23. THE GATHERING STORM

I was bound once more and trundled off into the back of one of several trucks that had been assembled outside the Temple. The gate was closed and the flaps tied shut, returning me to darkness. We were on the road for many hours, or so it seemed, and I admit that being emotionally and physically drained, I fell into a deep sleep despite the roughness of the road.

I awoke when the truck lurched to a halt and listened to the opening of doors and the screeching of tires as each of the vehicles in our caravan came to a stop. When the gate was lowered and the flaps untied, I was greeted only by moonlight. Khonsu gazed down balefully as I was bundled out of the truck. I craned my neck to look up at the majestic site of the Great Pyramid.

Giza, we are in Giza, I thought in amazement.

We had traveled several hundred miles since Luxor and I realized that my sleep must have been extended with injections, for I had no recollection of our stopping to refuel, nor had I eaten at all on the road. The feeling of violation in knowing that I had been robbed of whole days of my life overwhelmed me as I was led roughly by my Egyptian captors to what appeared to be nothing more than a section of the massive wall of the pyramid. A hidden door concealed in the wall opened after a complex series of manipulations applied to the brickwork by the Egyptian who led our party.

Passing through the seemingly magical doorway, we entered a well-lit narrow corridor with carpeted floor. This corridor continued on for several feet before opening out into the lower chamber of the Great Pyramid with its eerily glowing limestone walls and queer red granite floor. The Egyptians hustled me toward the far corner where the one who was our de facto leader once more manipulated the brickwork to open another hidden door that revealed a small cell. I was shoved inside as the panel slid silently shut behind me.

The cell was not more than nine or ten feet in length and barely five feet in width. There was no cot or washbasin so I walked over to the corner and slid to the ground. Realizing that the wall was sharp in points, the thought crossed my mind that with a great deal of time and effort, it might be possible to fray the ropes that bound my hands behind my back. I was occupied in this task for some time when the door in the wall slid open and Helga Graumann entered.

She was dressed appropriately for a change in a smart safari outfit and smiled enigmatically at me, leaning against the door that slid shut soundlessly behind her.

"This is goodbye, I fear."

The words sounded awkward considering the nature of our relationship.

"Goodbye then, Helga."

She stepped forward and crouched down in front of me and stroked my brow. I feared for a moment that she would discover that I had set to work on severing my bonds.

"Do not hate me, Michael. We are not so different. We are both survivors who carry scars that none can see. Esteban was different. The damage done to him was all too evident, but for so many others..." she shook her head, "it is not so simple. We...understand one another, don't we?"

I said nothing in response.

She looked into my eyes and, briefly, I feared that she was about to hypnotize me once more. Instead, she leaned forward and kissed me gently on the lips. She pulled away after a few seconds and smiled warmly.

"That was nice," she said. "I don't think I've ever kissed a man that way before."

"People can change, Helga."

She shook her head.

"I cannot change. I am not Helga Graumann. I am the daughter of the greatest man the world has ever known. He is about to take his place in history, and my role is to serve him faithfully until one day...one day..." her eyes blazed with fire as she spoke, "one day, I shall be the one to hold his head aloft as I claim my destiny."

She stood up and strode to the door. The panel slid aside and she stepped through the doorway and then turned back to face me.

"I have arranged for you to have some company. I trust you will be suitably entertained."

She smiled and took a step back as one of the Egyptians roughly shoved a white man into the cell with me. He stumbled toward me in the darkness and slid down next to me. Grey hair streaked white at the temples and a hawk-like nose that resembled the beak of that great bird of prey were offset by eyes as blue as the ocean on a sunny day.

"Nayland Smith!" I cried.

"Hello, Knox."

The door slid shut and we were plunged in darkness once more.

We sat there in silence for a moment as I considered the fact that I had given him good cause to treat me with disdain. I had done everything possible to elude him when we parachuted to safety from the Zeppelin before it crashed. I had repeatedly withheld information and deceived him whenever possible. I was foolish to think that he would welcome my company as much as I did his at this particular moment.

"Are your hands bound with rope?" I hissed.

I could just discern his head nodding in the dark.

"The wall is jagged in places. If you find the right spot, you can work on fraying the rope. It will take some doing, but right about now I can't think of a better way of spending the time."

He sat there silently for a few minutes while I went to work on my bonds. Presently he joined me in the same activity. My wrists were cut by the rope, and my hands were bloodied from the roughness of the wall, as I worked back and forth sawing at the strands.

"We made it to Cairo...Kerrigan and I...we went immediately to where we left Fey...I'm afraid that I have some very bad news."

I froze at his words.

"Anna! What has happened to Anna?"

There was a long pause before he spoke.

"When Kerrigan and I reached the house...it was a shambles. The Si-Fan had been there. Fey, Sir Lionel, your sister...they were gone...taken. There had been quite a struggle from the looks of it. All of the furniture...the doors...the windows...everything was broken...smashed to pieces. I'm sorry, Knox."

I felt numb. I had barely even thought of my sister since we had left for England. I was so sure that she was safe and secure eagerly awaiting our return.

"It had happened quite recently. Weymouth had been round to see them just a couple days before. It is likely that is how they found them...by following Weymouth."

"Damn," was all that I could manage to say.

I felt crippled and helpless. After a lifetime of bottling up my rage, and losing it in one meaningless conquest after another, I had placed all of it in my hatred of a single individual. Milagro was dead now. His severed head had stared at me deaf and dumb...unable to hurt anyone ever again and yet, here I was, hurting anew...grieving over the fate that had befallen the sister that I had abandoned years before. I had squandered everything that had been given to me in this life. Now, all that was left was regret. There was no going back to right old wrongs.

"What of you?" Smith asked.

I shrugged.

"I landed near Luxor and was captured by Milagro. He had slaughtered Hassan and my team that had excavated the secret chamber of the Theban Priests. Whatever secrets he sought there were long since gone."

"Naturally," Smith chuckled. "You yourself saw Fu Manchu and his daughter descend to the chamber from a secret passage."

I nodded my head in agreement.

"It seems that Fu Manchu holds all the cards. He is President of the Si-Fan once more. He executed Milagro for treason."

"You saw this yourself?"

"Yes," I replied. "I saw it with my own eyes. What happened to you? You made it to Cairo. How did you end up getting captured?"

"Looking for you, of course. There was little doubt in my mind that you had fallen into their hands when you failed to turn up. Milagro and Fu Manchu were both on the lookout for us after Fu Manchu crippled the Zeppelin and brought it to ground. I sent Weymouth and Kerrigan to Luxor to look for you while I came here."

"Why here?"

"Elementary, really. Weymouth had located the house where you had been taken by the Si-Fan a few weeks back. The whole event turned into quite a battle for him. Weymouth lost some good men that day, but the casualties on the side of the Si-Fan were far greater. He hadn't found Petrie or Kara there, so we knew there had to be still another base of operation. You had told me that Milagro was masquerading as Khunum-Khufu. What better hideaway for a deranged madman who thinks he's a reincarnated Pharaoh than the Great Pyramid?"

"Yet you came alone?"

"It was a scouting mission only. You see, getting caught was not part of the plan."

"I see. You're brilliant, but inept."

If Smith was about to respond, he was cut short as the door slid open and light flooded into the darkened cell once more. An Egyptian stood in the doorway.

"You will come," he barked at us, hands held at his hips and legs spread wide.

"What do we do now, Smith?" I hissed.

"We come. You heard the man."

The Egyptian led us to the center of the lower chamber to the front wall adjacent to where we had entered from the hidden corridor. A wall panel was manipulated and slid aside to reveal a laboratory where Dr. Fu Manchu stood amidst a collection of beakers and scientific apparatus crowding a table in the center of the room. A device that strongly resembled a photographer's tripod and camera stood in front of the table.

"Leave us," Fu Manchu ordered and, bowing, the Egyptian did as he was bid.

"Sir Denis, you honor me with your presence at this, my moment of triumph."

"Yes, I have heard that you are President of the Council of Seven once more. Congratulations, Doctor."

If Fu Manchu understood the sarcasm in Smith's words, his polite acknowledgement did not convey it.

"That is not the triumph of which I speak, Sir Denis. Within these instruments there exists the weapon that shall bring the arrogant West to its knees, humbled like the whimpering dog that has lost its master and fears to fend for itself."

"*Pox Romana*," Smith breathed the words as if a curse.

Fu Manchu bared two rows of sharp little teeth in a smile of pure malice and nodded his head eagerly.

"Yes, Sir Denis. *Pox Romana*, indeed. There is enough of the culture in this room to bring Europe to the brink of collapse in a fortnight. In three months' time, I shall rule the world, for only I can halt the spread of the plague, and the West, for all its wealth and ingenuity, can never manufacture sufficient quantity of the vaccine, or administer it fast enough, to save the lives of its young and old alike."

"You're a madman as much as Milagro," Smith snapped. "You both deserve death."

"You are wrong, Sir Denis," Fu Manchu hissed. "Esteban Milagro was not responsible for the plague. I was the one who discovered the secret that unleashed the plague centuries ago. It lied buried among the secrets of the Theban priests who first discovered it and spread it throughout the East when Europe was still a land of mindless barbarians. Finding the seeds of the plague made it so simple to combine with Milagro's formula for defying nature and its seasons."

"You couldn't resist, could you, Doctor?" Smith asked. "Like one of the ancients finding Pandora's Box, you had to meddle. You had to see what new atrocity you could create out of the old."

"An atrocity to you perhaps, Sir Denis, to me—it is a thing of beauty. Milagro had unknowingly concocted an elixir that could be used to make any poison a thousand times more potent...any disease a thousand times more deadly. Think of it, Sir Denis, think of the power that I command. None could dare stop me. Not you, not the Si-Fan. I am invincible."

"I suppose that camera is how you projected your face into the airship."

"Correct, Sir Denis, but it is no simple camera. It is an electro-magnetic projector that allows one to transmit one's astral self to any location. It is another modified secret of the Theban priesthood. Its mastery allowed me to not only seek you out and speak with you, but to fill the space in the engines and batteries with my electro-magnetic presence and, by so doing, alter their atomic structure and render them powerless, thus causing the destruction of those blundering Aryan fools."

"This is madness," I cried. "You unleashed that plague at the Munich Conference just to discredit Milagro and reclaim the Presidency of your bloody Council. You won, Doctor. You don't need to continue this Reign of Terror."

"No, Professor, you are mistaken," he said, shaking his head. "Even now, your precious peace conference is collapsing amidst betrayals and pettiness. The storm clouds are gathering in Europe, and the Si-Fan is the world's only hope of staying the deluge that threatens us all. No amount of diplomacy will ever stay the hand of a Hitler or a Mussolini. Fascists do not wish to rule the world, but to destroy it...to decimate its numbers so that those who remain will be easier to herd like sheep. You cry today for the dead you will bury, but tomorrow, you will thank me for saving you from a world led to the brink of catastrophe by the very madmen who seek to split the atom and harness its powers as a weapon of destruction. If the Si-Fan does not intervene now, the world shall not survive another century with such power in the hands of ignorant savages like those that rule Germany and Italy. It is better to let Destiny take its course. Europe is but a child compared to the East, and children are not fit to play with matches."

"No, Fu Manchu, and neither are you!"

Smith sprung forward, freed from his bonds at last, and grabbed the large glass container filled with the smallpox plague. He threw the container directly into Fu Manchu's face.

The old man reached up an arm to protect himself as the glass shattered, cutting him as the contents covered him in a steaming primordial soup.

Fu Manchu let loose a terrible shriek and staggered about the room. I pulled my hands free from my severed bonds and, grasping the table, overturned it in a single heave, sending the beakers and apparatus collapsing against the astral projector. The overturned Bunsen-burner lapped at the contents of the virus and the flames sprung to life all around us, while the astral projector sent forth an unearthly blue light which seemed to transfix Fu Manchu's burning form in an eerie, otherworldly glow.

"Quick, Knox! There's no escape for Fu Manchu this time!" Smith shouted.

Turning, we both began beating on the wall panel, trying to find some means of activating the door before we burned to death with Fu Manchu.

The panel slid aside soundlessly and two Egyptians hurried into the room. Smith and I each grabbed the men and hurled them headlong into the flames before rushing out into the lower chamber as the door slid shut once more.

The lower chamber was in consternation as Egyptians ran toward the room, paying us little heed in their eagerness to rescue their master. Smith and I reached the wall where the panel hid the corridor and battered at it furiously. One of us, in our panic, finally managed to hit the right combination for the door slid open. We ran as fast as we were able down the carpeted corridor and, after a similar frantic exercise at the end of the hallway, gained our entrance outside at last.

We had nearly reached the caravan of trucks when the ground shook beneath us with a mighty rumble, and the sound of a muffled explosion knocked us from our feet. I hit the ground hard and struck my head upon a rock. I didn't realize it at the time, for my only recollection was of diving head first into a pool of inky blackness and knowing Sweet Oblivion at last.

24. NEW MORNING

I awoke in a world of warm, sunny brightness with white walls and the angelic-looking face of my sister smiling down at me as she sat at my bedside.

"Anna, is this Heaven?"

She looked at me in surprise for a moment and then laughed.

"No, silly, you're in hospital...although it might very well seem like Heaven after what you've been through."

"But you died...Weymouth was followed the last time he went to check on you. When Smith and Kerrigan arrived, the house had been destroyed and the three of you were gone...taken or..."

"Gone, yes. Taken, not quite. Lionel had had quite enough of sitting around doing nothing...quite honestly, I'm surprised he put up with it for as long as he did. He determined that we were leaving, so we left shortly after Weymouth...through the window, you see. Fey had just turned in for the night. It seems we missed the Si-Fan by a matter of minutes. Lionel and I knew nothing of it at the time, of course, for we got into quite a row."

"About what?"

"He was determined to go to Luxor to get a look at that site. I wanted desperately to get home to check on Monkey. I won for a change, and it's a good thing I did, or he might have ended up dead with the rest of the team that were excavating the site."

Warm tears streaked my cheeks as I realized that she had safely avoided harm after all.

"What of Fey?"

"He's fine. They found him, along with the Petries, safe and sound in a cell in the Great Pyramid. You nearly brought the ceiling down around their ears. Sir Denis was ecstatic. You've missed quite a bit the week that you were comatose. You had me quite worried, you know. They didn't think you would pull through for awhile there."

"Fu Manchu...tell me they found him..."

She shook her head sadly.

"They found no trace of him when they searched through the debris. Some of the Egyptians claimed that they saw his face...or rather a giant image of his face...amidst the flames, and then it vanished. Sir Denis seems very perturbed, but I expect a corpse will turn up eventually."

I shut my eyes and wondered if the projector that he used to invade the Zeppelin was capable of projecting his physical form from one place to another. Matter transmission seemed like something out of the pulps, but considering his genius, coupled with his knowledge of Egypt's secret past, I was forced to wonder if anything was actually impossible for such a man.

"What now? Are you and Sir Lionel planning to...?" I trailed off, not wishing to finish the sentence.

Anna sighed and crossed her arms.

"Lionel and I have taken things as far as we could. I love him, but I'm not in love with him, if you follow me. Lionel is a man whose only mistress is his work, and a wife could never come between him and his mistress again. He's back home in England for now, until he sets off on his next mad quest. Once you're well enough to be up on your feet, I'll return home to Abyssinia."

"That's home, is it?"

"For me, it is. Did you know that Mr. Kerrigan has written a book on Abyssinia? What an interesting man. A pity I didn't meet him sooner," she smiled, fondly. "Sometimes, I think love is just a question of timing."

"Why should now be too late?"

She laughed and crossed her legs, leaning back in her chair.

"He's besotted with some sweet little Eurasian thing. You know how men are, Michael, you're certainly one of the worst."

"Yes, I've done some thinking about that lately, Anna. I've gone this far in life without ever coming even close to settling down. I think it's time that I start taking life a bit more seriously. The last few weeks, I've done more than just read about world events and studied its past, I've actually lived in the present. Do you know what I've found?"

"That you want to join Sir Denis and Kerrigan in setting the world to right?"

"No! No, quite the opposite, you old cynic. I don't ever want to be a great man or an important man any more than I want to be the Michael Knox I've been for most of my life. I want to be a good man. That's not something I've managed very well up to this point, but I think I understand now. Having seen the world on the brink of war, and worse than war, I realize there is much more to this life than my own pleasure, and there is no way that great men can ever be good men...not with the seduction of power and women to tempt them, or the weight of having to make choices over who lives and who dies. I want a simple, quiet life with a wife and children and pets and...And I still want to go on digs and teach and make a difference in this world by being one of the people that make it worth saving. Does that make any sense?"

"Do you know what I think, my darling brother? I think you've finally decided to grow up. It's about damn time, too."

Shortly after Anna left, the nurse came in and asked whether I felt up to seeing Sir Denis, but I told her that I was rather tired at the moment, perhaps he could call again another time.

I turned on the radio and was relieved to hear that the Prime Minister had returned home safely to Britain. Chancellor Hitler was apparently satisfied with Sir Denis' destruction of the smallpox virus and a successful finish to the Si-Fan's most recent campaign of terror.

The Prime Minister was addressing an ecstatic crowd in London and informing them that the Munich Conference had been a rousing success and that he had achieved "peace in our time" yet again. I switched off the radio and lay back on the bed and sighed.

I thought of Alexandra and the poor displaced people of Czechoslovakia, and how easy it was for great men to sacrifice the lives of others. I could not say that Fu Manchu and Esteban Milagro were any worse than Hitler and Mussolini, or even our own Prime Minister or Nayland Smith in that respect. All of them were men for whom the lives of individuals meant very little. Perhaps that is the mark of all politicians and leaders. Perhaps it is the destiny of all great men. I knew that I wanted no part of their world any longer. I was content to lose myself in appreciating the treasures of the past. If there was a God in Heaven, I did not envy Him in having to pass judgment upon great men who did so much evil whilst seeking only to fulfill their Destiny.

THE END

SF & FANTASY

Henri Allorge. *The Great Cataclysm*
Guy d'Armen. *Doc Ardan: The City of Gold and Lepers*
G.-J. Arnaud. *The Ice Company*
Charles Asselineau. *The Double Life*
Cyprien Bérard. *The Vampire Lord Ruthwen*
Aloysius Bertrand. *Gaspard de la Nuit*
Richard Bessière. *The Gardens of the Apocalypse*
Albert Bleunard. *Ever Smaller*
Félix Bodin. *The Novel of the Future*
Alphonse Brown. *City of Glass*
André Caroff. *The Terror of Madame Atomos; Miss Atomos; The Return of Madame Atomos; The Mistake of Madame Atomos*
Félicien Champsaur. *The Human Arrow*
Didier de Chousy. *Ignis*
Captain Danrit. *Undersea Odyssey*
C. I. Defontenay. *Star (Psi Cassiopeia)*
Charles Derennes. *The People of the Pole*
Georges Dodds (anthologist). *The Missing Link*
Harry Dickson. *The Heir of Dracula*
Jules Dornay. *Lord Ruthven Begins*
Alfred Driou. *The Adventures of a Parisian Aeronaut*
Sâr Dubnotal *vs. Jack the Ripper*
Alexandre Dumas. *The Return of Lord Ruthven*
Renée Dunan. *Baal*
J.-C. Dunyach. *The Night Orchid; The Thieves of Silence*
Henri Duvernois. *The Man Who Found Himself*
Achille Eyraud. *Voyage to Venus*
Henri Falk. *The Age of Lead*
Paul Féval. *Anne of the Isles; Knightshade; Revenants; Vampire City; The Vampire Countess; The Wandering Jew's Daughter*
Paul Féval, *fils. Felifax, the Tiger-Man*
Charles de Fieux. *Lamékis*
Arnould Galopin. *Doctor Omega; Doctor Omega & The Shadowmen*
G.L. Gick. *Harry Dickson and the Werewolf of Rutherford Grange*
Edmond Haraucourt. *Illusions of Immortality*
Nathalie Henneberg. *The Green Gods*
V. Hugo, P. Foucher & P. Meurice. *The Hunchback of Notre-Dame*
Michel Jeury. *Chronolysis*
Gustave Kahn. *The Tale of Gold and Silence*

Gérard Klein. *The Mote in Time's Eye*
Jean de La Hire. *Enter the Nyctalope; The Nyctalope on Mars; The Nyctalope vs. Lucifer; The Nyctalope Steps In*
Etienne-Léon de Lamothe-Langon. *The Virgin Vampire*
André Laurie. *Spiridon*
Gabriel de Lautrec. *The Vengeance of the Oval Portrait*
Georges Le Faure & Henri de Graffigny. *The Extraordinary Adventures of a Russian Scientist Across the Solar System* (2 vols.)
Gustave Le Rouge. *The Vampires of Mars*
Jules Lermina. *Mysteryville; Panic in Paris; To-Ho and the Gold Destroyers; The Secret of Zippelius*
Jean-Marc & Randy Lofficier. *Edgar Allan Poe on Mars; The Katrina Protocol; Pacifica; Robonocchio; Tales of the Shadowmen 1-8*
Xavier Mauméjean. *The League of Heroes*
José Moselli. *Illa's End*
John-Antoine Nau. *Enemy Force*
Marie Nizet. *Captain Vampire*
C. Nodier, A. Beraud & Toussaint-Merle. *Frankenstein*
Henri de Parville. *An Inhabitant of the Planet Mars*
Gaston de Pawlowski. *Journey to the Land of the 4th Dimension*
Georges Pellerin. *The World in 2000 Years*
J. Polidori, C. Nodier, E. Scribe. *Lord Ruthven the Vampire*
P.-A. Ponson du Terrail. *The Vampire and the Devil's Son*
Henri de Régnier. *A Surfeit of Mirrors*
Maurice Renard. *The Blue Peril; Doctor Lerne; The Doctored Man; A Man Among the Microbes; The Master of Light*
Jean Richepin. *The Wing*
Albert Robida. *The Adventures of Saturnin Farandoul; The Clock of the Centuries; Chalet in the Sky*
J.-H. Rosny Aîné. *Helgvor of the Blue River; The Givreuse Enigma; The Mysterious Force; The Navigators of Space; Vamireh; The World of the Variants; The Young Vampire*
Marcel Rouff. *Journey to the Inverted World*
Han Ryner. *The Superhumans*
Brian Stableford. *The New Faust at the Tragicomique; The Empire of the Necromancers (The Shadow of Frankenstein; Frankenstein and the Vampire Countess; Frankenstein in London); Sherlock Holmes & The Vampires of Eternity; The Stones of Camelot; The Wayward Muse.* (anthologist) *The Germans on Venus; News from the Moon; The Supreme Progress; The World Above the World; Nemoville*
Jacques Spitz. *The Eye of Purgatory*

Kurt Steiner. *Ortog*
Eugène Thébault. *Radio-Terror*
C.-F. Tiphaigne de La Roche. *Amilec*
Théo Varlet. *The Xenobiotic Invasion; Timeslip Troopers* (w/André Blandin); *The Martian Epic* (w/Octave Joncquel)
Paul Vibert. *The Mysterious Fluid*
Villiers de l'Isle-Adam. *The Scaffold; The Vampire Soul*
Philippe Ward. *Artahe*
Philippe Ward & Sylvie Miller. *The Song of Montségur*

MYSTERIES & THRILLERS

M. Allain & P. Souvestre. *The Daughter of Fantômas*
A. Anicet-Bourgeois, Lucien Dabril. *Rocambole*
A. Bernède & L. Feuillade. *Judex*
A. Bisson & G. Livet. *Nick Carter vs. Fantômas*
V. Darlay & H. de Gorsse. *Lupin vs. Holmes: The Stage Play*
Paul Féval. *Gentlemen of the Night; John Devil; The Black Coats ('Salem Street; The Invisible Weapon; The Parisian Jungle; The Companions of the Treasure; Heart of Steel; The Cadet Gang; The Sword-Swallower)*
Emile Gaboriau. *Monsieur Lecoq*
Steve Leadley. *Sherlock Holmes: The Circle of Blood*
Maurice Leblanc. *Arsène Lupin vs. Countess Cagliostro; Lupin vs. Holmes (The Blonde Phantom; The Hollow Needle)*
Gaston Leroux. *Chéri-Bibi; The Phantom of the Opera; Rouletabille & the Mystery of the Yellow Room*
Richard Marsh. *The Complete Adventures of Judith Lee*
William Patrick Maynard. *The Terror of Fu Manchu; The Destiny of Fu Manchu*
Frank J. Morlock. *Sherlock Holmes: The Grand Horizontals; Sherlock Holmes vs Jack the Ripper*
P. de Wattyne & Y. Walter. *Sherlock Holmes vs. Fantômas*
David White. *Fantômas in America*

SCREENPLAYS

Mike Baron. *The Iron Triangle*
Emma Bull & Will Shetterly. *Nightspeeder; War for the Oaks*
Gerry Conway & Roy Thomas. *Doc Dynamo*
Steve Englehart. *Majorca*

James Hudnall. *The Devastator*
Jean-Marc & Randy Lofficier. *Royal Flush*
J.-M. & R. Lofficier & Marc Agapit. *Despair*
J.-M. & R. Lofficier & Joël Houssin. *City*
Andrew Paquette. *Peripheral Vision*
R. Thomas, J. Hendler & L. Sprague de Camp. *Rivers of Time*

NON-FICTION
Stephen R. Bissette. *Blur 1-5. Green Mountain Cinema 1*
Win Scott Eckert. *Crossovers* (2 vols.)
Jean-Marc & Randy Lofficier. *Shadowmen* (2 vols.)
Randy Lofficier. *Over Here*

HEXAGON COMICS
Franco Frescura & Luciano Bernasconi. *Wampus*
Franco Frescura & Giorgio Trevisan. *CLASH*
L. Bernasconi, J.-M. Lofficier & Juan Roncagliolo Berger. *Phenix*
Claude Legrand, J.-M. Lofficier & L. Bernasconi. *Kabur*
Franco Oneta. *Zembla*
L. Buffolente, Lofficier & J.-J. Dzialowski. *Strangers: Homicron*
Danilo Grossi. *Strangers: Jaydee*
Claude Legrand & Luciano Bernasconi. *Strangers: Starlock*

ART BOOKS
Jean-Pierre Normand. *Science Fiction Illustrations*
Raven Okeefe. *Raven's L'il Critters*
Randy Lofficier & Raven OKeefe. *If Your Possum Go Daylight...*
Daniele Serra. *Illusions*

CPSIA information can be obtained at www.ICGtesting.com
Printed in the USA
LVOW091112120812

293983LV00001B/30/P